MW01243011

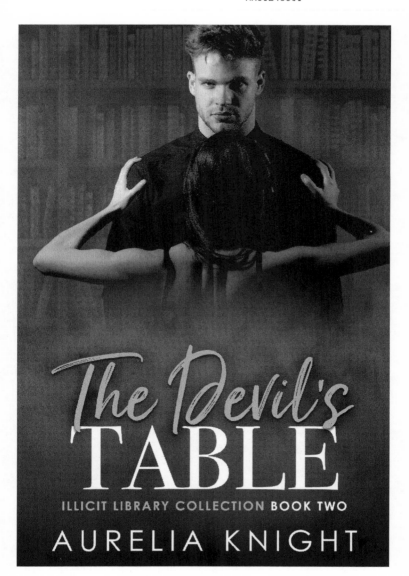

The Devil's
TABLE

ILLICIT LIBRARY COLLECTION BOOK TWO

AURELIA KNIGHT

The Devil's
TABLE

Copyright © 2022 by Aurelia Knight

All rights reserved.

No portion of this book may be reproduced in any form without written permission from the publisher or author, except as permitted by U.S. copyright law.

All characters and other entities appearing in this work are fictitious. Any resemblance to real persons, *dead or alive,* or other real-life entities, *past or present,* is purely coincidental.

CONTENTS

This book is dedicated to every person who read and enjoyed Maybe Hiring even a little. Thank you for taking a chance on Mason and Claire.

WARNING

This book contains explicit sexual content and graphic violence that may be upsetting to some readers.

The Devil's Table is a darker story than Maybe Hiring. Mason and Claire are both recovering from trauma, and that is rarely pretty.

Some of the bigger triggers include: discussions of suicide, suicidal ideation, gun violence, child abuse and abduction, and mentions of sexual abuse.

If you need a more comprehensive list, please don't hesitate to reach out on AureliaKnight.com

I promise that Claire and Mason have a happy ending in their future.

ONE

Claire

Six Days After the Events of Maybe Hiring

This is shit. I thought to myself as I rubbed the sides of my hands against my eyes. The back of both my hands were all stuffed with needles and wrapped in a sticky tape that made my skin sore. I flinched at the way the movement tugged my skin. The ache in my stomach protested as I moved my arms, and I dropped them to my sides, unable to hold them up for another moment.

The painkillers pumping through my veins were strong enough for me to manage the pain with only a few pathetic groans and grunts, but they made my head foggy and I couldn't keep track of the time. The IV machine standing beside me beeped as it filled me with saltwater and morphine.

I shifted slightly, trying to bring some blood back into my numb butt cheeks. Sharp, stabbing pain twisted through my gut, and I whimpered. Mason reacted instantly, waking up from his nap and scooting closer. His chair squeaked against the tiled floor—the noise registered like an explosion in my head.

"Do you need anything, baby? Should I call the doctor?" he softly crooned as he brushed his fingers against my face in an achingly sweet gesture. His lips hovered so near to mine, and in any other circumstances, I would close that distance.

I gulped, my dry throat sticking to itself as I tried to swallow. "No, please don't." I grabbed the hand tracing my face and stared into his spring-green eyes, trying silently to convince him I was okay.

During the time I was unconscious, Mason had appointed himself as the head of my medical care as well as my surgeon's number one tormentor. The fact I could fill that role for myself was inconsequential. He claimed his attitude stemmed from an incident between them where the doctor tried to kick him out before I woke up. But I suspected the *event* had very little to do with his overprotective behavior.

He would be like this no matter who my doctor was and the way Mason cared for me did things to my ravaged insides.

"If you need anything, I'll get him. I don't give a fuck if he's sleeping. I'll pull him out of bed." He drew a quick breath in through his full lips.

I sighed, wishing he was joking. "If I need another surgery, I'll need him to be well-rested, as will the rest of his patients. I'm *okay*; please don't bother him."

We stared at each other in loaded silence until the hard determination in his eyes softened. "Of course, Claire, but I worry about you." His hands moved to the column of my throat, smoothing the tangled hair clinging to my sweaty skin.

"I know. I love you too, Mason." He smiled genuinely at that.

"I love you." He took my hand in his, paying special attention not to disturb the needles and tubes. He kissed each of my fingertips before nipping each pad. Heat swirled through my belly, but before it could sink lower, the painkillers dulled it away.

"Everything is okay, Claire," his voice was rough from lack of sleep, stress, and god knows what else he carried on his shoulders. He'd been sleeping in the armchair in the corner for days, but he would easily fall asleep in the crappy visitor chair he now sat in just as often.

Everything was *not* okay and part of me wanted to say so. A man stalked and shot me, attacked me in my home, and attempted to end my life. Mason called in god only knew what favors when he believed my stalker was affiliated with his criminal past. Despite my hopes, he would *have* to answer for those calls.

I wanted to tell him I wasn't stupid and those meaningless platitudes were aptly named. I didn't want to be told things were okay when they weren't. Looking around the room, I remembered the smell of gunpowder, and the sickening knowledge of how deeply Tyler—no, *Charles*—invaded my life. How could anyone claim things were okay?

But I couldn't find it in me to argue with him. We were both so tired, and the breath to give voice to those thoughts evaded me.

"What now?" I got those words out, but I could barely keep my eyes open. They stuck shut each time they closed, popping apart unevenly as I tried to stay conscious. I kept fighting the exhaustion, fighting the pain that dragged me toward sleep rather than keeping me up. I needed to know what was waiting for us, or rather *coming* for us.

"Now, we get you better." The nonchalance in his tone roused me. My eyes darted his way in time to catch him shrug his broad shoulders and see his lips twitch with the approximation of a smile.

"Mason," I glanced back and forth, making sure there was no one walking past the door. "I know he's dead, I *saw*." I saw him kill the man who stalked me. He came in like an avenging god, and he saved me. He also learned the man who stalked me did so because of an old grudge and a shared girlfriend.

Charles would have killed me much sooner, but playing with and then breaking Mason's new toy? That was irresistible. "What *now*?" I insisted. "Do I have to speak to the police? Will they charge you? Thank god you're a lawyer..."

"Nothing, none of that. I took *care* of it. We need to take care of you," he insisted.

"Mason, that is not... What about my apartment? It must be a... mess," the words came out like sticky mush.

"It's all details, baby. Don't worry about it. I promise I'm taking care of everything." There was a flicker in his eyes resembling guilt.

"Mason, what's happening with my apartment? Where I live is not detail..."

"We'll talk about everything when you're feeling better." He laid my hand back down and stroked my fingers.

Those "details" were monumental problems. Even as tired and messed up as I was, I understood that all of this had to have consequences. The cops had to be involved, and if they weren't, that meant someone much scarier was.

There was something about my apartment he didn't want to tell me, and I wondered how they cleaned up so much blood. What kind of deal had he made to take care of *things*?

"You wouldn't lie to me, would you, Mason?"

"No," his green eyes filled with desperate determination.

"But you also won't tell me everything, will you?"

Guilt shone in his eyes. "I'll keep you safe."

"That's not..." my words slurred. The machine connected to me beeped, signaling another dose. *That is not an answer. Fucking pain killers...*

Two

Mason

10 Days Later

I sat at my desk, anxiously kicking the brushed African black wood. My designer would have a fucking *heart attack* after the lengths she'd gone to buy this thing. I rarely twitched or fidgeted, but extenuating circumstances had me practically vibrating in my seat and ready to pummel expensive furniture I actually liked.

With my office sitting on the twentieth floor of an expensive high-rise, the city lay at my feet like Claire once told me she expected of me. Floor-to-ceiling windows showcased the surrounding buildings. The mix of old and new gave the city a superficial charm. Naked trees stuck up from the sidewalk and their leaves blew across the ground, swept away by the breeze.

The decor was posh and modern, everything you'd expect from a young high-end lawyer's office. The same designer decorated the house. Which was also beautiful, and I paid a small fortune for her work, but I was starting to wonder if that was worth Claire *hating* it. I would demolish the house and build her a new one if it would make her happy, but I suspected it was less about the structure than it was the discovery that her apartment had been cleaned out and re-rented while she was in the hospital.

I understood why she was angry. No one liked having their choices made for them. And angry was exactly how I felt when her landlord called her phone a mere four days after the shooting to tell her she had sixty days to vacate before he filed for eviction. I could have told her, but that would have allowed her to pick another place to live, and sometimes I couldn't help myself. I don't think she fully understood what being mine entailed. If there was anything I learned from thinking she was dead, it was that my soul couldn't exist without hers.

I needed her safe and with me. More than that, there was no reason *my girl* should go back to a rundown shoebox apartment. Not when I had the means to provide for her and give her the type of life she deserves. I tried to set her up with the best doctors, a therapist, and any other support she may need, but she vehemently refused.

In short, she wasn't taking it well. Nor was she taking well the vague answers I was giving her for where I was going. She didn't seem outright suspicious yet, but it wasn't hard to see her frustration growing with each passing day. Ways to lessen her stress and alleviate her suffering were constantly popping to the forefront of my mind.

Maybe if I let her redecorate, she would consider the house her home too and start to forgive me. Or maybe there was no simple answer and no couch or settee that would make all the shit we'd gone through simple.

Everything inside me rebelled against sitting at this desk instead of going to her. Making things right was a lot more complicated when I wasn't *with* her. There were a dozen men stationed around the house. I hired them and flew them in from overseas, ensuring my father had no influence. Legitimate mercenaries might seem like overkill to some, but it didn't feel like enough. My fingers tapped against the desk in time with my foot, and I had to stop myself.

I pushed through some paperwork, checked my correspondence, and did everything I normally would, but I couldn't wrap my head around being Mason Dubois any longer. This life seemed so easy a few weeks ago. Most days, I could convince myself it was all I ever wanted. *Things are so different now.*

I needed the cover story, power, and influence my career afforded me, but going back to this existence was like trying to squeeze into an old suit. The seams tightened around me as I worked, and I swore I felt the buttons popping as the pressure inside me built.

Just as I decided I couldn't wait another minute, that I needed to see Claire, someone banged their fist against my door like a cop breaking up a rowdy party. I worked to bite back my violent impulses. *Who the fuck is that?*

I picked up my phone, casually placed it against my ear, and dialed my secretary. "Why didn't you announce I had a visitor?" a bit of venom leaked into my professional tone.

"He asked me not to. I'm sorry, sir. He's a cop." Katie's mousy voice broke around the word cop.

"Okay." I hung up the phone and made a mental note to find a secretary who understood the gravity of my situation. "Come in."

The door opened, and the ugly mug of Officer Grant greeted me. His grin revealed smoke-yellowed teeth as his feet ate up the distance between the door and my desk. Grant was in his early forties, with blunt features and beady eyes. He started working for my father when he was barely over thirteen. I'd known him my whole life, a fact I wholeheartedly wished I could deny.

"Long time no see, Rick," the tone of my voice clearly conveyed that I would have preferred it to be longer. I kept a small sitting area to receive clients in the middle of the space with the best view of the city. He plopped his ass down into one of the plush white chairs. I smiled through the urge to kick the shit out of him.

"Hello, *Mason*," he struggled to use my given name, preferring the nickname given to me years earlier by him and a few others. "Mr. Sharp asked me to have a word with you," his voice was like gravel and broken things grinding together—fucking grating.

"Oh, did he? The king descended from his throne to speak to the likes of you? I'm surprised." I stared him down, watching his face redden. Jealous prick always wished he could take my place as his son. I sighed at the thought of anyone *wanting* David as a father.

"You're not really in the position to make smart-ass remarks, Baby Sharp." A smile cut across my face as he broke and used the nickname. His hand twitched toward his gun, but I wasn't worried. If this was about that, I would have been dead before I arrived this morning.

"From where I'm standing, it seems like a prime position, so how about you tell me why not?" I leaned back in my seat, putting my hands behind my head, I kicked my feet up on the desk—the picture of ease and not giving a fuck. His glare ran up and down my body with blatant disgust. "What is it, Grant? Like what you see?" I winked.

Grant stared me down as he walked over to my desk and picked up my name plaque. He ran his finger over the engraving, tapping hard on the name *Dubois*. "It's simple, Mr. *Dubois*. We cleaned up quite a mess for you. Your girl's apartment, that old friend of yours, but we kept a few notable pieces to tie you back to the crime if need be. I put a few limbs on ice, somewhere nice and safe.

8

"There's nothing for you to worry about, really. Your problems are being swept away and all you have to do is play ball. Do as he says when he says, and eventually, you'll have worked off your debt."

He waved his hands around my office. "You're a talented lawyer with an excellent reputation. He can use that. Even though you're a sissy mama's boy who hasn't gotten his hands dirty in years besides throwing a tantrum over a hot ass and a tight cunt."

I kept my expression smooth, not revealing my violent imaginings. Grant didn't deserve to think of my mother, let alone speak of her. And Claire? It took everything in me not to cut out his tongue. Officer Grant's death wasn't part of the plan, but now it was inevitable.

I swallowed, working through the knotted tension in my throat. "Tell my father he can contact me himself if he wants to talk terms. I have a few things I've been meaning to tell him. Now, you can see yourself out."

"Or what?" he challenged.

"I'll show you how much it stings to get your skull pounded in by a sissy mama's boy who hasn't gotten his hands dirty in years." I shrugged back. The stress relief of pounding the shit out of this fuck was something I could use.

"He thought you might be less than pleasant. Take this." He stood, handing me a letter. "Read it and think your options over. I'll see you and that sweet bitch of yours soon." He walked out, slamming my door shut behind him.

I considered going after him, but I had made enough rash decisions out of anger to last a lifetime. Grant would die soon enough, but I was done killing without a plan.

The letter burned white-hot in my hands as I looked over my name written in a small script. Flipping it over, I raised my eyebrows at the theatrics of the wax seal affixed to the envelope. "God, you're a pretentious fuck," I told the paper.

9

I popped it open, holding my breath as I saw the tiny birds adorning the paper. I unfolded the letter, disgusted to read the words he wrote on *my* mother's stationery.

Mason,

I warned you not to owe me, and now I'll warn you not to defy me.

I have enough evidence to put your little whore in prison for the rest of her life. Did you think I would come for you first?

She will probably be fine. She can find a lesbian to eat her pussy and forget all about you. But you will never recover.

If you're not motivated enough, she can die like your whore of a mother. A car accident is so commonplace. People die that way every day.

-DKS

My fists shook, crumpling his letter into a ball before I shoved everything off my desk. The sweeping crash of things had Katie running into the office to see if I was okay. I couldn't hear her words as she stood there looking terrified. He admitted it, finally. I always knew that he killed her, but the confirmation shredded me beyond my wildest imaginings.

He was no stupid man. He never sent this letter expecting me to play along peacefully. My father wanted a war, and I would give it to him.

THREE

Mason

Two Months Later

S *hit, I really hate snow*, I thought to myself as I navigated the crumbling sidewalk. The warehouse district was a dilapidated section of downtown, often forgotten as the factories lining the streets all closed down about fifty years earlier.

The street lamps stuck up irregularly, smashed or blown out, and with no push from the city to fix them, they remained broken. The snow cut the visibility further until navigating the road was nearly impossible.

The icy fractals clung to every available surface, turning black the moment they met the filthy pavement. I brushed a hand over my hair, knocking loose the forming icicles.

The only two guys I truly trusted, Vick and James, walked on either side of me. The former vibrated with tension, and the latter was incredibly at ease; I had to laugh. Vick wore the protective older brother burden like a badge of honor. He wouldn't let up despite James turning thirty this year.

We found the right alley through a mix of muscle memory and sheer luck. The buildings resembled one another, and with the snow creating a white wall, you could barely see a few feet ahead.

Together, the three of us spent an inordinate amount of time in the warehouse district in our youth. More specifically, this warehouse. The familiarity settled over me like itching powder.

Before their mother's abduction and sale into the skin trade, she was a syndicate indebted prostitute. The proprietor, Francis, turned her out and acted as her pimp for years. She dragged James and Vick with her wherever she went, often leaving them sitting together in the warehouse while entertaining men upstairs.

My father thought I had a lot to learn from Francis. Through an unfortunate twist of fate, their mom was the first person to suck my dick, on her knees beneath the table while I learned to hustle cards. "You gotta keep a better poker face than that, boy," Francis barked from beside me as I watched her mouth in fascination.

I suppose my father was right; back then, Francis *had* a lot to teach me.

I pressed my back against the wall of the alley, pulling out my gun and training my aim on the door. The snow was milder here due to the shelter of the brick walls.

A small series of windows glowed from the very top of the building. Francis preferred the warehouse dimly lit when he sat alone in the early hours of the morning to weigh his money.

I gestured in warning to James and Vick before I shot the lock. You might need to worry about someone calling the cops in other places, but not here. The people living here would never willingly bring law enforcement into their world.

Vick stepped up beside me, unwilling to wait until I pushed the door open. His foot blasted the panel back and into the wall with a bang, pulling the hinges out and leaving the whole thing dangling.

"Getting impatient, Vicky?" James piped up from behind us as I surveyed the damage with a disbelieving look.

"If you want to stay here all night, that's your business. Can we get on with this, boss?" He hovered in the entrance, waiting for my say-so.

"Patience, Vick. This may take a while." I stepped into the warehouse ahead of him, glancing around. He and his brother followed closely. The first floor stood empty except for the tables and chairs folded against the wall, just visible from the light of the loft.

Francis sat at his desk like he was the foreman overseeing operations, and this was still a machining plant. "Mason, why the fuck did you shoot my door?" his voice sounded just as I remembered: gruff and smoke-beaten.

"Didn't feel like knocking." I shrugged as I made my way to the center of the room. "The years haven't been too kind to you, have they?"

"Can't say they have," he agreed as he finished slipping a stack of cash into a bag. He straightened another set of bills and placed them inside the scale as he surreptitiously reached for his gun.

"I wouldn't." I aimed mine at his head.

He glanced up, his watery blue eyes stared straight through me. "Come on, Mason. I don't want any trouble. I'm too old to be caught up in your young men's bullshit."

"Our issues run a little deeper than that." I tilted my head from side to side, sizing him up.

"You turned thirty-two last month, didn't you? You're a young man. Jimmy and Vick are young men, and this," he waved a hand toward the broken door, "is bullshit."

13

"I'm so flattered you remembered my birthday." I wasn't. He had a gift for remembering the little stuff. "Why don't you come on down, nice and slow, and we can talk about why I'm here."

Francis was damn smart for a grimy bastard. His skill with numbers and his attention to even the smallest detail were how he became one of my father's most trusted allies. That, and their mutual affection for piles of money and beating up prostitutes.

He pushed off the desk as he stood, grunting like an old man. At about sixty-five, he looked more like eighty. "You'll have to be patient. The knees aren't what they used to be."

"Vick, James, go ahead and help him down."

He held up his hands, "No need for any of that, boys." He picked up the pace, abandoning his plan to stall us. Without the act, he descended the stairs much more quickly.

James pulled out one of the folding chairs lined up against the wall with the card tables and opened it for him. "Have a seat, Franky."

"James, Vick, you boys are looking well." Francis sat down, facing us with resignation. They stared back silently, refusing to give him the satisfaction of a response.

The differences between the "boys" and his memories would undoubtedly be night and day. They were both tall men now, though Vick resembled a brick wall while James was leaner. They both had black hair. Vick's eyes matched his hair in intensity—black fucking pits. James' eyes were just as creepy. His light brown eyes glowed red when the light hit them the right way. A girlfriend once called them "cognac" eyes, and he never shut the fuck up about it.

Francis stared at the two of them in an open challenge. If I didn't cut things off soon, Victor would lose his patience and kill the man with his teeth.

"I need some information from you, Francis, and I'm going to get it." I kicked the chair, claiming his attention. "Usually,

14

I'd say something to the effect of this can be as easy or as hard as you make it, but why be cliché when everyone here knows you like it rough?" I didn't mean the words to be a dig at my guys, but they both tensed up at the reminder of how many ways Francis fucked and beat their mother.

"Fair enough. What do you want to know, Mason?" he laughed to himself, utterly confident that I couldn't break him.

"Fear and money can garner a lot of power, but it's flimsy, isn't it? I need to know exactly who's loyalty my father doubts, every one of them."

He laughed harder this time, "What use would that be to you? You can't possibly believe you can beat him. Do you think you're half the man he is? You're a joke, a laughingstock!" He bent in half, laughing so hard tears gathered in his eyes. "Go back to your office and practice law like a good boy. You have no place here."

"I didn't ask your opinion on what I do with the information, but you're going to give it all the same." I nodded toward Vick. "Tie him up."

Vick pulled a length of rope out of his pocket and moved behind Francis. Francis tried to fight him off but was nowhere near quick or strong enough. In a matter of moments, Vick had his hands tied together and to the back of the chair. His feet followed, secured to the legs.

Francis thrashed wildly and Vick cocked his fist before connecting hard with Francis' face. "The rope is a natural filament. Shit burns, doesn't it? That was what you preferred to use when tying my mother up for you and your friends to rape, wasn't it?" Vick's face hovered an inch from Francis', close enough to see the flicker of doubt in the pimp's eyes as he worried Vick might treat him the same way he would the girls he extorted.

"Can't rape a whore, Victor." The words barely left his mouth before Vick punched him again. His head snapped back from the force, and blood poured from his now broken nose. The broken nose wasn't adequate for Victor, and I watched him prepare to strike Francis again.

"Enough, Vick." He turned to me with a vicious glint in his eyes, like he would attack anyone who might try to stop him. I glared until he calmed down enough to remember our purpose. Francis tortured his mother, but my father sold her. We had a bigger enemy ahead of us.

"Names, Francis," James reminded him.

"Fuck you!" the old man spat.

I stepped in front of Francis and patted him on the knee. "This might sting." In one swift move, I pulled a pocket knife from the pocket beneath my lapel, flipped it open, and drove the blade into his leg as deeply as it would go.

"Fuck you!" he growled through the pain.

"No thanks, Franky. I've seen what you do with your dick and if that's any sign of how you maintain your asshole, I'm not interested. James, Vick, would either of you want to take a turn with Franky's asshole? I bet it's virgin, but I also bet he doesn't wash it."

Francis glanced between the two of them, *fear* flickered across his face. "What? Scared to be raped, Franky?" James quirked an eyebrow at him. "Not so much fun when you're the one tied up?"

When Francis didn't respond, James slapped the knife sticking out of his leg. He groaned miserably and bit out a curse, but didn't shout or cry. As I told Vick, this was going to take a while.

"May I?" James gestured toward the knife. The sadistic gleam in his eyes didn't instill confidence in his ability to control himself until Francis talked.

"As long as you remember why we're here."

"How could I forget?" James smiled at Francis with a terrifying carnal pleasure. His need for pain and death etched itself across his face as clearly and easily as a carefree smile.

I understood his motivations all too well, and in some ways, I was even more bloodthirsty than James. Maybe I had more to prove than pure revenge. "Now, Franky, tell my friend here who is on David Sharp's shortlist of potential defectors?"

Francis snarled, revealing blood-stained teeth. "You look like your mama, James. Pretty eyes, soft mouth. I could turn you out just like I did with her. Shame she's dead."

"You're lying. You don't know that." James gritted out. *If* Francis was telling the truth, it would be the first word they had heard of their mom since the syndicate took her.

"Oh, but I do." Francis smiled, a grim twist of his lips. "I killed her myself."

"For your sake, I hope that's true." James smiled as he dragged the knife across Francis' cheek, cutting through his flesh and exposing the bone beneath. He slapped him hard, splashing blood against his suit.

"Fuck!" Francis screamed, finally giving in to the pain. And that was nothing compared to what was in store for him.

Four

Mason

A while later, I stood above the mess formerly known as Francis. My stomach turned as I considered his remains splattered across the concrete floor like gruesome confetti. This *was* a celebration after all.

So many twisted avenues of my life started right here with the guidance of this man. There was a time I feared him almost as much as I feared my father. Now, he was nothing more than a broken pinata whose secrets had tumbled out like penny candy. In his final tormented moments, Francis broke, just like I knew he would.

Among the list of random slip-shod criminals was one that settled in my chest like a brick: Daniel Moore, a name I hadn't heard in years. We were best friends at Rutherford Prep and he always had my back, whether or not I deserved it. Getting him involved with the syndicate was one of the greatest regrets of my life.

Speaking of my regrets, Vick took a page out of my book and stomped Francis' skull into bits when we finished questioning him. It was an incredibly brutal death and a salute to another one of the worst mistakes I'd ever made. I didn't think Vick knew he was being a cunt, but he was.

The mist of gray matter brought me back to Claire's apartment, to the moment I knew for certain she was gone. I didn't feel human, not at that moment or any time I remembered it. I battled for some semblance of control, every part of me tensing, but the only thing that would calm me was her.

Slipping into bed beside her and losing myself in the scent and feel of her wasn't a viable option. It was too late to catch her sleepy and unaware; she would wake up soon, alone and angry as hell. I hated to think of her face when she realized that once again I didn't come home, and I wouldn't tell her where I had been.

Lying to her was wrong, I believed truly that I was objectively wrong. I knew the same thing when I killed people, even those I considered deserving. Being the bad guy wasn't new to me, and I needed to protect her more than she needed to know what fucked up shit I had to do.

My gaze flicked over to James sitting in the chair Francis previously occupied, leaning back and gawking at the ceiling like he was drunk off his ass. His rust-stained fists twisted up in his black hair. Vick rested on the ground with his hands at his sides, coated in as much blood as his brother. He stared at the remains, particularly the gun sticking out of Francis, with bitter acceptance. This revenge was long in the making, but it didn't undo the past

"Get your shit together. We've got work to do," I said.

They both glanced at me, too stunned and sated to move. Vick stood first, making a piss poor effort to wipe his hands off on his blood-soaked suit. "Should we call the guys to clean this up?"

"No. Let's send a message." I thought of the letter my father sent me, and what I wanted to say in return—*You're next.*

19

"Some message, Mason." James laughed as he rose from the chair to join us.

"Talk to your brother about that," I rolled my eyes indulgently at them. This was definitely overkill, but they waited a long time for this and they deserved their retribution.

"Did you *need* to shove your gun up his ass, Vicky?" James elbowed him playfully.

"Damn right, I did."

Sixteen years earlier

Rutherford Prep, what a joke. The entire student body was nothing but self-obsessed jerks; the teachers were pompous assholes who talked down to everyone. Even the hot cheerleader, Rebecca, who kept flirting with me, seemed nice enough and I still couldn't stand her. I hated them all, everyone in the world for that matter.

Why did *my* mother get hit by a drunk driver? How could she leave me alone with my father? She knew exactly what type of man he was. I couldn't focus on the aching sense of loss, not if I wanted to keep moving one foot in front of the other.

I ignored the voice in the back of my mind that reminded me how comforting it must be to simply not exist.

Another less defeated voice whispered, *What if your father set her up? What if he killed her?*

I desperately wanted to disregard that thought as crazy, but each time I tried to convince myself, the lie fell flat. I watched him beat her for years, was it really so much worse to kill someone? How many tears and broken bones added up to a life? And how many lives had he taken from her?

He enjoyed beating me too, and I wondered if he was some sort of vampire sapping the life out of those around him. Was that part of me to? David Sharp was capable of anything. He made me do *horrible* things, but would I become just like him eventually?

All the thoughts in my head were pooling together, swirling into something dangerous. I couldn't stay in class listening to Mr. Banks talk about history for another second. I asked for the bathroom pass to prevent myself from kicking the shit out of Ben Burns. Pretty boy asshole kept chewing his pencil like a beaver.

Instead of feeding it to him, I went to the bathroom and climbed out the window. The pane didn't open wide enough for a graceful exit, and I caught myself on the track, ripping my obnoxious wool suit and throwing off my balance. I landed on an absurdly manicured bush that was a perfect sphere prior to the impact.

I beat a path down the sidewalk, not sure where to go—definitely not home. My gaze flicked up in time to see two boys standing almost shoulder to shoulder, blocking my route. The big one looked like an overgrown meathead. The younger of the two was a foot shorter and not nearly so muscled. I recognized them from Francis' warehouse, Vick and his little brother, Jimmy. Despite seeing them more than once a week for the last few years, I'd never spoken to them.

"Look at this asshole, Vicky." Jimmy had a nasal voice. He still sounded like a kid, even though he more closely resembled a teen.

I kept moving, not sparing them a glance. I didn't have time for this shit, and I did not want to take my anger out on a couple of kids whose lives were shittier than mine. No, I wanted to feed Ben Burns his pencil.

"You Mason Sharp?" Vick asked as I stepped off the sidewalk to get around him. He already knew the answer.

"Who's asking?" I bit back. "If we're going to play stupid, then let's play stupid." Vick cocked his fist and punched me in the face without hesitation. I didn't see it coming, and I didn't even flinch before the strike fully connected with my jaw.

The fucker hit hard. I fell sideways, slamming my hip and elbow on the pavement before landing on my back with my backpack beneath me. They both burned like hell, but as pissed as I was, the physical release of pain felt good.

I tried to stand, but the little one, Jimmy, stomped on my bag, dragging me back to the ground. I was going to choke the fucker.

I hastily pulled my arms out of the straps and stood. "Go back to the warehouse, assholes." I didn't give a fuck about the books or fighting them. *Keep it. Kill me. I don't fucking care.*

Vick reached out and grabbed me by the hair, pulling me back. He swung hard, punching me in the ear. The ringing sound practically pierced my brain, and strands of my hair tore as I ripped myself free from his hold. I would cut that shit off the minute I got home.

I turned quickly, ducking another blow. I lunged, punching him hard on the nose.

He swung wide, and his fist connected with my rib. "Fuck," he cursed as he lost his footing. I swung again and again, hitting him twice before he regained his balance.

"What the *fuck* is this about?"

"Our mom, you piece of shit," he grunted as he spat blood on the pavement and charged at me again.

"I've never met your mom!" I shouted as I landed a blow to his cheek.

"She sucked you off, dirtbag!" Jimmy shouted from the sidelines.

"Jimmy, this isn't about that. Shut the fuck up." It was hard to tell beneath the red spots and bruises forming on his face, but I thought Vick was blushing.

"How the fuck is it my fault your mom gets paid to suck dick?" I rarely felt so genuinely baffled.

"Our mom is gone because of your dad. He said she's used up! They sold her!" Tears gathered in Jimmy's eyes as he shouted.

His mom was pushing forty, and while she was still hot, she was a low earner compared to the younger girls Francis brought in. I hated how he prostituted girls who were barely older than me, but there was no way for me to help them. There was always another girl, always another pervert.

"I'm sorry about your mom, kid, but it was probably Francis. He's her pimp." I didn't want any trouble with these two. I felt bad for them. They—along with everyone else—needed to leave me alone.

"We heard him say it! He fucked her and then told Francis to sell her!" Jimmy cried actual tears, and I couldn't even look at him. After being smacked and told "men don't cry" enough times, witnessing it made me vaguely nauseous.

"We figured we'd take what your daddy loves, so he would understand what it's like." Vick flashed me a nasty grin as he picked up his fists.

I flopped forward, laughing so hard my stomach hurt. It had been weeks since I laughed. "You guys are fucking idiots," I tried to breathe through it. "My father hates my guts, and I'm pretty sure he killed my mom." My face throbbed and ached from my bruises, but the laughter wouldn't stop.

"Stop fucking laughing, asshole." Vick shoved me.

"Dude, just stop. If you want revenge, this is the wrong place to get it. I might even be willing to help you if you stop being a dickhead." I stood to my full height, wiping the tears out of my eyes.

They stared at one another, having some kind of silent conversation. I'd seen them do it at the warehouse, but I figured they had some repressed taboo shit going on that they needed to work out.

"Why would we trust you?" Vick finally asked as he tore his gaze away from his brother.

"My mom is dead, and I've got no one left." *One friend.* I mentally corrected myself. Daniel deserved much better than me, but I couldn't question his loyalty. "I don't give a fuck if you trust me."

I turned and walked down the sidewalk, heading toward my original path. Follow me or not, what they did next was their business.

"Is your mom really dead?" Jimmy shouted from far closer behind me than I thought he would be.

"Yeah." I picked up my pace, but they were on either side of me now.

"We're not sure if ours is alive." I pitied both of them. My mom's life sucked, but their mom's life was on another level. "How can you help us?"

"I don't know how yet, but he's going to pay. My problems with my dad have nothing to do with the two of you."

"Wait, do you really think you have a chance against him?" Vick grabbed my arm, pulling me nearly to a stop.

I yanked out of his grip but stopped walking. "No, but I'll die trying."

He considered me for a moment. "My name is Vick, and this is my little brother, Jimmy." He nodded toward the prick.

I rolled my eyes, "Obviously."

He cracked the tiniest smile at the insult. "Francis from the warehouse; we want him too."

I met his stare, surprised to see how black his eyes were. The kid resembled a demon and if I was headed to hell anyway, he would fit perfectly. "Deal. You fucks already know I'm Mason. Have you eaten anything today?"

24

"Fuck you! That's none of your business," Anyone who hung around the warehouse knew Jimmy had a big mouth and it got him into a lot of trouble.

I just stared at Vick, waiting for him to answer. He glanced between me and his little brother, his face smoothing out in resignation, "No."

"Vicky, don't tell him that," Jimmy argued, but I cut him off.

"Shut the fuck up and follow me, both of you."

"Where are we going?" Vick's voice came softer now, unsure.

"To the diner."

***

I looked at the brothers standing at my sides the same way they did that day. A lot had happened between us since then, but at least I made good on half of my promise.

"Shut the fuck up and follow me, both of you." James laughed and Vick sighed. We walked toward the door. The two of them were going to be miserable in the cold, sopping wet and covered in blood. But before we tested that theory, a thud sounded from the loft.

Our heads cocked in that direction. There was a deep moment of silence before Vick's voice boomed, "Come down, or we come up, and if we come up, we're shooting."

A few moments later, a gangly kid of about seventeen came to the top of the stairs with his hands up. "Don't shoot, please. I-oh fuck, oh my god." He got a look at Francis and puked over the catwalk instead of the railing. *Thank God for small favors,* I thought as it dripped down the metal slats and to the concrete flooring below.

"Fucking Christ," I slapped my palm against my forehead, knowing for a fact I wouldn't be killing this kid.

"Come on down. No one is going to shoot." The blatant irritation in my voice failed to soothe him.

"Okay, okay, in a-" The kid puked again while James and Vick both turned their backs on him, reasonably sure he didn't plan to shoot us.

"God, that fucking stinks," Vick made a retching sound.

"I'm guessing he needs a minute," James piped in. He changed very little since we met and I took them to the diner. Ever a loudmouth and a prick, but he and his brother were genuine friends.

The kid dry-heaved for a few moments before he approached the stairs on shaking legs.

"Take your time, not as if I have anywhere else to be," I called up the stairs, getting antsier by the minute about going home to Claire. I had a lot of blood to wash off, which would be easier if she was still asleep.

He hurried down, stopping on the bottom step and eyeing the blood like it would reach out and grab him.

"Who are you?" I barked at him, out of patience with the entire night.

"My name is Casey, I am, I work for Francis. Well, worked for him, seeing as he's dead now, extremely dead. See—"

"You're babbling," I interrupted his shaking and muttering.

"Are you Mason Sharp?" He met my eye, which was more than I would have expected. There was something so familiar in his stare. It took me a moment to recognize the desperation.

"I am."

"Sir, I want to work for you." He twisted his fingers together, looking like he wanted to puke again, but he kept his eyes on mine.

"Why would *I* want that?"

His cheeks turned bright red. "I know a lot of shit, sir. I'll tell you everything, including that there are more people on that list than he told you. Francis has me watching their accounts."

I didn't sense any deception in him, just a violent need for something and the belief that I was the person who could get it for him. "Why would he trust you enough to do that? You're pretty wet behind the ears, kid."

"My mom was one of his girls. I knew him my whole life. I'm good with computers, and I can do a lot of things I'm not supposed to do with them."

"She *was* one of his girls?"

"She-she went missing. I don't know where she is. At first, I thought she ran. I wouldn't blame her if she had, but she didn't take any of her stuff and I just... Something is wrong," he choked around the word wrong, likely imagining scenarios that weren't half as bad as reality. "Francis promised me he would help me find her. He trusted me completely because I'd do anything he asked to get her back."

"I'll tell you the truth. Your mom is probably dead, and if she's not, she's wishing she was. I don't have the time or the resources to find her, and Francis there was the one who sold her."

His hands clenched and opened repeatedly. His face turned a deeper red, this time from rage instead of embarrassment.

"If I found her myself, would you help us?"

My eyes ran over this broken kid. *Fuck, what am I? A magnet for the motherless? Does this shit have a specific pheromone?* "If you found her, I would help."

"Then please, sir, let me work for you. The information is worth it, I swear."

I didn't trust him, but I saw his potential. I believed he was telling the truth, or at least enough of it to consider taking a risk on him. If I could be careful with what he gave me, it could prove valuable.

"You'll talk terms with Victor here. I have somewhere to be." I nodded to Vick and turned on my heel to head out the door with James behind me.

Five

Mason

The cold air swallowed James and me as we left the warehouse and Francis behind. Vick took off with the kid, Casey, to have a proper chat about the services he was offering and what he wanted from us. Victor would let me know if he thought the kid was worth the risk, and I trusted his judgment implicitly.

The black SUV sat on the curb, running. The snow had lightened significantly and billows of exhaust formed white clouds behind the car. I climbed in first adjusting myself so the blood wouldn't fuck up the leather. The stretch Cadillac was fully decked out with perpendicular bench seating similar to a limousine. I shot James a disgusted look. "Put your hands in your lap, you fucking savage."

"We're both covered in blood, your seats are fucked either way." He smiled as he tipped his head back. "The detailer *loves* you."

"I'll make you the detailer and see if you wouldn't prefer less blood."

"You pay him enough to retire to the Maldives; I'll take that position if you're offering."

"Back to the house, please," I told the driver, as I shook my head at James. I settled into the smooth seat, trying to think of a game plan for how to deal with Claire.

"What are you telling Claire?" James asked.

"Reading my mind, Jimmy?" I smiled wryly.

"Nah, you just got that look on your face like you're doing calculus. You're shit at math *and* lying to her, so it makes sense they look the same."

My jaw ticked, "I'm telling her nothing, now fuck off." My tone clearly closed the subject, but James never was one to take a hint. The sappy bastard thought of her as a friend and he hated that I kept so much from her. How did he think I felt about it? Did he think bringing it up every night was going to change the situation?

He was stomping on my last nerve. I had half a mind to punch him in the jaw and remind him who he worked for, but I couldn't, not where it concerned her. I liked him caring for her. It made him do a better job of protecting her, even if it drove me insane.

"Your girl can take more than you think. I saw her that night at her apartment. She wasn't sobbing or screaming. She's been level-headed about the whole thing. Even handled getting shot pretty well; she's better suited to your lifestyle than you realize." He tapped his fingers against his leg, more keyed up than I expected after how zoned out he was in the warehouse.

"What lifestyle is that, do you think?" my sardonic tone didn't distract him from his point.

"Which one do you *think*?"

"I understand you like her, and this makes things harder with you and Emma, but you don't know her as I do. Claire is *not* okay, and she does *not* need to know we killed a man, shoved a gun up his ass, and bashed his brains in. Now, shut the fuck up about her."

"Vick did most of those things."

I closed my eyes as I took a deep breath. He meant well, but he was poking too close to an injured part of me, and like an animal, I wanted to lash out.

He put up his hands in surrender and leaned back in his seat with an agreeable expression, but I knew all too well how quickly he slid that mask into place. "I wasn't suggesting you tell her every detail..." His voice was light as if he wasn't dancing along the edge of my patience.

I would never seriously hurt James, but I would kick his ass if he didn't shut up. I would enjoy kicking his ass if he didn't shut up.

He did though, and the ride dragged after. I couldn't drift off, or stare at my phone, or lose myself in a book like Claire. I simply stared out the window and thought too hard.

The driver dropped me at the keystone of the tiled, arch-shaped driveway and drove James back around to the gatehouse he and Vick shared on the property. When Gains shot Claire, we came up with the arrangement, and the setup worked out rather well. They were nice digs, and free rent was a definite pay bump. With things so up in the air concerning my father and the syndicate, I needed someone to be with Claire constantly. Lawrence, Victor, and James were the only people I entrusted her safety to.

She had a lot of opinions about that too.

I crept into the house, cursing myself for all the marble. No wonder Claire felt like this was a museum rather than a home. I didn't choose it, but I also never saw a reason to remove it.

Slipping into the butler's pantry, I rummaged around until I found a garbage bag. I stripped my clothes and shoes, tied them off, and then stuffed them into the back of one of the seldom-used cabinets. I would dispose of them before anyone noticed.

I scrubbed my hands in the closest bathroom, but they still had a red tinge. I pleaded with the universe for Claire to be asleep as I crept up the stairs on silent feet.

She sat on the couch with her profile facing me. Her gaze flicked over briefly, catching my stare before dropping into her lap. The tangles in her hair told me she must have gotten some sleep even if a nightmare woke her. Her gaunt, exhausted eyes gave merit to my theory.

The sun wouldn't be up for another hour, but the news played on the TV. Her obsession with it made her miserable, but her misery didn't stop her from watching. From the corner of my eye, I caught Charles Gains staring back at me. I cursed fate that we both appeared at the same time.

"Why are you watching this shit again, baby?" I tried to speak softly, but there was an undeniable edge of frustration in my tone.

"They raised the reward to four million now." Those stress lines I loved to watch disappear were harsh now. She picked up the remote, clicking the TV louder. I took a breath, trying to control the emotions raging through me as I listened to the newscaster. The pain and anger were so intense I couldn't understand them beyond a desire to crush and tear.

Fucking prick couldn't leave us alone even in death. I wanted to raise him from the dead and kill him again. I wanted to make it hurt this time. Killing Francis left me more conflicted than I wanted to admit. Killing more frequently was making me edgy. I didn't enjoy taking people's lives—most of the time—but the violence was addictive.

I worked through the urge to blow up. My stomach churned as I tried to make sense of everything. *Fuck me*. I wished none of this was necessary.

Claire didn't notice my reaction, wrapped up in the lies and memories as she was. Nothing was going right, nothing happened as I planned. The part of me craving control stood on the edge, waiting for an opportunity to regain some normalcy. I walked over to her and grabbed the remote from her hand. Her lips popped open in shock, and I ignored how soft and pretty her wet mouth was.

Still fueled by the controlling thing inside of me, I turned the TV off, pulled off the back cover, and slapped the batteries out of the remote into my hand. I went to the French doors leading to the balcony and threw the batteries as far as possible. They bounced off the driveway with a satisfying crack, and the act filled me with a childish sense of satisfaction.

The room dropped into freezing silence. She glared at me in disbelief. "Your stupid, fancy TV doesn't work without a remote!" she huffed out a breath.

"Yeah. That is the point."

She widened her eyes and turned away from me.

"You shouldn't keep watching this shit. This obsession is not healthy." I walked back toward her, closing the door and regretting letting the freezing air in as she shivered.

"Are you an expert on healthy behavior or obsessions?" *That* was sarcastic as fuck.

"One yes and one no. I'll leave you to figure out which is which." I smiled despite the wholly serious situation. We both knew my expertise didn't extend to what was healthy but I could live off her pussy juices, and I was sure that crossed the line into obsession.

The pinch in her lips told me she wanted to say something but held back. I continued, "But none of this is your fault. Baby, please stop torturing yourself." I needed to touch her, but I stayed back, hoping the dim light from the bathroom wouldn't be enough for her to see my face and hair. Her refusal to look at me was beneficial for once.

She waited so long to speak that I didn't think she would answer. "Tell that to his victims..." she muttered under her breath as she pulled her long legs up and leaned on her knees.

"If I could, I would," I assured her. "But I don't think I would have to. If those poor souls have any idea what's going on now—and I don't think they do—you are the last person they would blame."

The sour look she gave me told me the words did not impress her. "This is not a joke, Mason."

"I didn't think it was."

She wrung her hands as agony surfaced across her perfect features. Justice for his victims had become her obsession. Claire was tenacious and the lengths she might go to make things right made sleeping difficult.

Her eyes flashed and narrowed like she just remembered something that pissed her off, and her back straightened. I secretly loved it when she got mad at me. I loved the way her graceful body poised to strike. Her chin would raise and the awkward girl would transform into a woman who handled her own. She didn't recognize that about herself.

I didn't get that satisfaction this time. I liked to rile her up, goad a reaction out of her, not hurt her. She was too tired and too... *Fuck;* she looked empty.

"What was her name, Mase? Did you take her to an early breakfast?" The sun peeked over the mountains to the east. Even if I did cheat on her, who the fuck eats breakfast this early?

I worked to control my temper, but my voice came out hard and commanding. "I don't need to explain what we are to you, Claire. You and I both know what we are. And, I'm fucking *starving.*" I shot back, staring deeply into her stunning brown eyes. They were wide in shock. Her lips slightly parted, and it took everything in me not to sink my teeth into her plump bottom lip.

How could she believe there was an inch of space in my heart for anyone but her? The idea infuriated me. She shivered delicately under the intensity of my stare.

The urge to claim her, to prove to her she belonged to me, was fucking primal. The only things keeping my hands and tongue off her were the tears rolling down her cheeks and the blood on my skin.

"Oh, really? Is that why you're walking toward the shower? You're just going to stay out all night, come home, wash the pussy off you and act like everything is normal?" Her full bottom lip quivered, and I stepped toward her, pulling her off the couch by her hands.

I didn't have any fetish for the blood I spilled, and I certainly didn't want to stay coated in Francis for any longer than necessity demanded, but I couldn't leave her feeling that way. "That's not what's happening here." Her red-rimmed eyes finally rested on me.

Those eyes scrunched, trying to adjust to the low lighting. "Holy fucking shit, Mason. You're covered in blood!" she gasped as she pulled her hands out of mine and took a step back. "What the fuck are you doing? Why aren't you coming home, and why won't you just tell me the goddamn truth about it?!" Her hands slapped against my bare chest, emphasizing each question.

I lifted my hands and fisted them in her hair, pulling her forward until her face hovered an inch from mine. She slapped me once more before her hands dropped to her sides. Trembling, her lips parted, and the breathy gasps she let out tasted like pain mixed with the sweetness of her arousal.

These were cosmic entities between us, far more than emotions. She was fucking gravity, anchoring me.

"Don't you get it, Claire? You don't want to know where I've been. You don't want to know what I've been doing. But one thing is for sure, I am not cheating on you." I wanted to kiss her, but I couldn't risk infecting her with any part of Francis.

She fought against my hold on her hair, expecting my kiss. She gasped wildly as her hips ground against me, pressing my erection into her soft stomach. Her hands clawed at my chest, no longer slapping.

I waited for her to flinch away in pain. This was a lot, but her wound seemed to ache less lately. With my grip on her hair, I tilted her head back, and she responded easily to the command.

My free hand trailed along her perfect cheek, down her neck, and across her clavicle. I slid my fingers around her throat, not squeezing, just holding her. An image of me stuffing my face in her tits while she squirted all over me was strong in my mind.

"Take a nap." I bit off both of our fantasies, trying to infuse as much command in my tone as possible. "I'm going to shower, and we're going to spend the day together." Her lips trembled, and it took all my self-control not to yank her to my mouth and taste every divine inch of her. "I miss spending lazy time with you, baby. We're going to lie around and I'm going to make you come until you cry."

I wiped a stray tear off her cheek, hating that she was crying for the wrong reasons. "You want that, Claire?" I crooned as I stroked her cheek with one hand and held her neck with the other. "Do you want to be my perfect little slut and come so hard that you'll cry? It'll hurt, baby, but I think you'll love it."

"I'm not sure..." but the breathy whisper in her voice gave her away.

My cock ached, desperately urging me to stick it somewhere tight and hot, like Claire's perfect pussy or her virgin ass. I couldn't stand the thought of adding to her pain or her ass would have been mine many times over by now.

Her hungry eyes ran over the bulge pressing against my boxer briefs, reading my thoughts. Well, not the ass bit.

Fucking take it. I taunted her with my eyes, willing her to reach out and grip my cock in her hands.

Her gaze skittered away, breaking the intensity. "You don't have anywhere to run off to?" Her eyes found their way back to mine, but her tongue and teeth toyed with her bottom lip.

She sounded so young for a moment, and her big brown eyes were full of pain and fear.

"Not for today, baby. Go lay down and sleep." I released her neck and ran my hands through her hair, tucking the wild strands behind her ears.

She gave me a small, tired smile. "This isn't the first time I've seen you covered in blood, and I'm still right here. It's time you start trusting me." She squeezed my hand as she headed back to the bed. Her words played on repeat as I watched her climb in and snuggle into the down. All I could think about was how much I wanted them to be true. Except I didn't believe they were.

Six

Mason

Claire was snoring into her fluffy pillow by the time I finished in the shower. I ran a hand over her hair and stroked the side of her face lightly without disturbing her. She didn't sleep enough, and my contributions to her stress killed me.

I wanted to spread her thighs, lick and suck every drop of cum out of her. That would relieve both of our tension, but she needed to rest more than she needed to orgasm repeatedly.

She spent too many nights awake, wracked by guilt or wondering where *I* was. Part of me demanded we be honest with her about everything, like she and James both wanted, but neither one of them saw what I did. She was spiraling, clinging on by her fucking fingernails, and I couldn't make things worse on her.

I went to my dresser and pulled out some lounge clothes. I would be happier naked, but they were a symbol, telling Claire I would not put my suit back on to leave when I was done with her.

I sat on the couch, content to observe her while she slept. The swells of her breasts rose and fell in a delicate rhythm. Her pink nipples puckered against the nearly sheer fabric of her shirt, and I hoped she was dreaming filthy dreams instead of nightmares.

Her legs twisted in the blankets. Her shorts stuck in the dip between her ass cheeks, exposing the perfect globes I loved to smack, bite, and slide my cock between. I ached at the sight of every glorious inch of her.

The slight swell of her belly, the jiggle in her ass and thighs, the parts she considered undesirable, turned me on. Her curves were the roadmap to my destruction or my salvation. I wasn't sure which way the scales would tip.

I took my hard shaft in my hand and wrapped my fist tightly around it, preparing to edge myself until she woke.

Pre-cum bubbled on my dick as I thought of all the ways for me to worship and defile her. Her healing delayed so many of the things I wanted to do with her. We had little time to explore the darker side of what we both liked before that waste of space shot her.

Claire was my open book, my good girl, and my pretty little slut, and I would never love anyone but her. My balls tingled, and my cock hardened as she untangled her legs and spread her thighs. The thin strips of fabric from her shorts and panties rested to the side, exposing her pussy. Memories of her taste exploded on my tongue as I imagined sliding in there and waking her with an orgasm.

The sight of her was too much. I didn't have the will to fight the building sensation tingling in my spine. My whole body tensed as I choked my dick hard enough to shoot streams of cum over my stomach and chest. I groaned as I spilled. *Fuck, what a mess.*

She rustled in the bed, her eyes opened in alarm for a moment before they settled on me. They widened in obvious interest and her lips formed into a perfect "o" I would love to fuck. Her expression lacked all hints of shame, and the tense little lines between her brows eased.

"Is that your cum?" her voice came out raspy and full of sleep. My balls tightened in response, my dick already getting hard again.

"It is, but it could be yours if you'd like."

"Oh, really?" her tone dripped sarcasm, but her interested gaze touched my skin like a brand.

"Come here and lick the cum off me." Her body jerked slightly, and I would have loved to feel the way her pussy tensed.

"Why would I do that?"

"Because we both know how badly you want to." I'd bet my trust fund she was sitting in a puddle of her juices, and there was no reason for either of us not to get what we wanted out of the situation.

She smiled at me as she stood from the bed and walked toward me with a sensual sway to her hips. Claire had a habit of saying no to the things she wanted, not only with sex but everything. Nothing gratified me more than watching her let go and enjoy herself.

"On your knees," I instructed, while her brown eyes widened with a mix of arousal and irritation. She obeyed, falling to them with the effortless grace that avoided her in daily life—further proof we were made for each other.

"Look at me." Her eyes met mine. The sun was rising and the faint rays made the brown molten. "You're so sexy that even when you're sleeping, I spill loads for you. Are you going to be a good girl and help me?" I gestured to my cock, which was already hard again with the excitement of this new game. Cum still dribbled from the tip and I wanted to feed it to her before she went to work on the rest.

She looked up at me, weighing her options for a moment. She leaned forward, spreading her thighs. The move drove me wild, even if it was only to get comfortable. Her soft tongue ran from my balls to the tip of my cock. She placed her hands on my knees, pushing up to reach my abs, and her hot tongue licked up every drop I spilled for her.

"You taste delicious," she hummed as she finished her work and slipped a few cum covered fingers into her mouth.

"Fuck," I grunted, "I will never get enough of you."

Her soft giggles sounded like music.

I patted my lap, "Come here so I can fuck what's mine, and then you can suck the mess we made off me and I'll eat it out of you."

"I belong to myself, actually." Her pretend haughty voice would have made me laugh if she hadn't just taken the head of my cock into her mouth.

"You're mine, Claire. Now, come here and sit on my lap." I pulled my cock free and angled it in my hand at the perfect position for her to impale herself.

"What makes you think I'm yours?" Her thighs readily parted as she straddled me, resting her ass and pussy against my bare cock with her shorts and panties between us; the damp fabric pressed against the back of my hand.

I wound my fingers through her curls, pulling until she gasped. My girl liked when I made things hurt. I leaned forward, licking and sucking bruises onto the cleavage exposed by her tank top.

She rolled her hips, mindlessly grinding against my cock. My lips ran up her throat, my tongue trailing the smooth expanse before biting the fine skin of her jaw.

"What makes me think you're mine?" I trailed my fingers along her spine and into the cleft of her ass. "Maybe the goosebumps all over your skin, or the little twitch in your hips when you instinctively want to get closer to my cock. Possibly the way you lick up my cum or run to me to spread your legs."

My teeth bit into the soft skin at her collarbone and she let out a moan that was all mine, just like the rest of her. "Or you know as well as I do exactly who you belong to."

"I could stand up," she tried to sound stern, but the breathy cadence in her voice spoiled the act.

I slid my fingers beneath her shorts and tugged her panties aside. "By all means, boss lady." She'd earned the nickname when she got the librarian position, but I loved to tease her with it.

She didn't move a centimeter. Her eyes silently begged me to give her what she needed. I lined myself up with her entrance and pulled her down hard.

Her sharp cries of pleasure filled the room.

"Mason," she whined as I forced her to take every thick inch of me.

Her walls gripped me so tightly, I fought to keep my entire cock inside of her. "You're so fucking tight, baby. I swear I could cum from you twitching around me." Right on cue, her muscles pulsed, quivering over my length. "Fuck yes, good girl."

"Am I really your good girl?"

I pulled her nipple into my mouth, lavishing the skin with hot, wet kisses. "My best girl."

"I feel like a dirty slut," her words came out garbled as I held her hips and pounded into her. "Fuck me like I'm a dirty slut."

"You're both, baby. You're my good girl and my dirty slut. But no matter what, you're *mine*." Her legs tensed up as her orgasm tore through her. She leaned into the crook of my neck, screaming her release. As if her pleasure commanded my own, I came with her, reveling in filling her tight pussy with my cum.

SEVEN

Claire

S pending the day with Mason was more wonderful than I expected. We ate great food, laughed, and joked. It was perfect in its effortlessness. When we were together that way, it was so easy to remember why I loved him.

My need for him screamed from every part of me. We fucked repeatedly, and each time he fretted over my injury, kissing the areas around the scars. I was getting stronger, enough to take his dick, and as I got swept up in the magic of him, of us, the tension drained away, and for those few hours, I felt okay again. I forgot it was only for a day, which broke me all the more when he left again.

I didn't want to think Mason was cheating on me, and when we were together it was simple to believe he wasn't. What was I supposed to assume when he came home at dawn regularly and went straight to the shower?

A voice whispered in the back of my mind; *he's not a cheater, he's a killer.*

I pulled my knees up to my chin and rested my head on them. I spent an incredible amount of time in Mason's bedroom since being shot; lying on the couch specifically, just like I did with the scratchy old piece of crap I had in my apartment. The furniture was a lot nicer here, but the uselessness felt the same.

The apartment, couch, and almost everything I owned were all gone now. None of it was valuable, but it left me hollow to have nothing truly my own. Mason offered to let me redecorate. He *wanted* me to influence the space and make it ours instead of his. The man would give me the moon if I asked for it, but I didn't want to settle in. Getting comfortable sounded a lot like tempting fate; Charles Gains left no part of my life untouched.

The television played softly. I flipped between the major news stations until I found what I was looking for: Priscilla Gains sobbing over the whereabouts of her son. Though this was a replay, I had seen it live—plus a hundred times since—I let her voice fill the room.

I doubted I would ever forget the first time I saw her on the news begging for help to find her son. I had only been back from the hospital about a week and my head was still foggy, but even so, I could see how much I resembled her.

We shared the same brown eyes, brown hair, and light olive skin. But it was more than that. The way her cheeks sloped, the m-shape of her top lip, even the shape of her brows. The knowledge of why Charles chose me didn't give me closure, it filled me with potent existential dread.

I couldn't comprehend why I was torturing myself like this. I could only listen to the guilt inside me demanding my suffering, and this was an effective way to get it. Charles Gains was a murderer, a monster who tried to take my life. He deserved what he got. His mother was a pedophile who made her child watch while she cheated on her husband.

These were terrible people. I believed that to my core. But what about Charles' victims? Did the women he stalked and killed for fun deserve to remain unknown and without justice? Who was I to take that chance away from their families? If it wasn't for Mason and me, Charles Gains might still be out there killing, but he also may have gotten caught.

I thought of the father I'd never met, the mother who wouldn't take my calls and still didn't know I had a stalker or that he shot me. People say not knowing is the hardest part, but the sentiment left me conflicted. Priscilla Gains kept repeating that line, time and time again, across a myriad of networks: "Please, if you have any information, come forward. Not knowing is the worst part... I just need to know what happened to my son." Would knowing help? The jury was out.

Every time I heard her shrill voice or saw the curls in her brown hair, I wanted to choke her with one of the elaborate diamond necklaces around her throat. *Her fault,* I told myself time and time again, but I knew the truth. We were all responsible for how things turned out.

She abused Charles. Charles killed those girls. His death had to stay a secret because of me. There was a logical line of responsibility, with Mason's name tied up inextricably with mine.

Still, I couldn't keep going like this. My hands shook, and tears blurred my vision. I had to do something, anything, that might ease this. If I could stop watching the fucking news, I'd take the improvement.

My phone rang loud and demanding, interrupting my thoughts. I choked back the tears, sounding somewhat normal, "Hello?" I didn't spare the screen a glance as I answered.

"Hi, Claire. This is Gavin Wolfe. How are you doing?" I nearly dropped the phone as my heart spasmed.

No one other than Mason ever called me, allowing a rare exception for James or Vick. Emma texted me a few times, but she never called, and other than that, it had been radio silence for months. I took a deep breath, trying to remember how to speak and interact like an ordinary person. "Oh hi, Gavin. I'm well and you?" I didn't quite manage it.

"I'm doing fine, thank you. Exceptionally busy, of course. Not to make a pest of myself, but have you confirmed with your doctor your official return date?" he sounded so normal I wanted to scream. Like nothing ever happened, like he didn't hire me because a crime boss asked him to.

"Uh, no, no bother at all. Can you hold on one second?"

"Sure." I barely caught the word as I put the phone down, placed my head between my knees, and tried to see through the panic.

I wasn't ready to go back to work. Physically, I could handle it if I took things easy. I still couldn't do any heavy lifting, but someone could help me. The real problem was that too much happened there, and too much happened to me.

Curl up, hide, run. The urges were so strong that I nearly gave in and hung up the phone. I'd been close to giving up a lot of times lately, but I kept going. This job was my dream, and while that didn't feel like it meant much right now, I knew when I was more of my normal self, I would hate that I let the opportunity go.

I would need to go back, or they would replace me. As frightening as the first option was, the idea of the second devastated me. Mason promised me he would ensure my safety when I was ready to return. Did I trust that? I did. He was so protective of me that I couldn't breathe sometimes, but I trusted him to keep me safe.

A stroke of inspiration hit me. The library had always been a place of discovery for me. Since I was a little girl, books temporarily solved many of my problems. Alone, bored, needing to escape your world? The library had a million solutions. My biggest problem—outside of my relationship with Mason—was my guilt.

I needed to meet my problems head-on. That is what this obsession with Priscilla Gains was trying to tell me all along. I would go back, and I would find Charles' victims myself. I wasn't foolish enough to think about telling the police, but if I discovered who they were, I could find a way to help their families.

I picked up the phone, hoping I hadn't kept him waiting too long. It could have been ten seconds or an hour. "Gavin, I'll be back next Monday."

"The seventeenth?" his tone lifted in surprise.

"No, the twelfth." I didn't need time to second guess myself. I needed to get out of this house and do *something*.

"Of December? That's six days from now,"

"Yes, it is," I agreed.

"Are you certain?"

I hated him questioning me when I honestly wasn't. "All cleared with my doctor and ready to go." I tapped my fingers against my knee and rolled my eyes.

"Well, wonderful. Emma and Kiana will be so happy to have you back. The two of them have been struggling to keep up with your duties, even with the work you've done from home." About a month ago, I started doing some of my normal tasks remotely. It was a simple matter compared to this.

"Thanks, Gavin. I can't wait." I didn't even need to lie; I would be a ball of nerves until then.

"See you then."

"See you." I hit the lock button, ending the call. The idea of going back terrified me, but this was the only way forward for me: going back to the places that scared me, turning over stones until I found something to hold on to.

I turned up the volume on the TV, knowing I would have a lot less time for Priscilla soon enough. "Please, he is my only son. I need to know my baby is safe." Delicate tears trickled over her cheeks. "I'm raising the reward to six millio-"

I clicked off the TV. "He's dead."

46

EIGHT

Claire

A few hours later, I stood in the "hers" closet surrounded by tons of clothes, bags, and shoes I hadn't picked for myself. Mason didn't choose them either, and I wondered what the person who selected this wardrobe for me looked like. Did she resemble me and Priscilla Gains?

A lot of the pieces were normal and functional, if not entirely too expensive. Others made me wonder if they thought I'd be attending many red carpet events. Mason was absurdly rich, but he was no socialite.

My fingers and my gaze drifted over a silk nightgown. When the doctor finally released me from the hospital, I came home to all of this and nothing else. My apartment was gone, along with all of my things. When I saw some of the price tags, I had a small meltdown.

Mason removed all the tags after that and while I didn't panic entering the closet anymore, I did eye everything dubiously. Not that I wasn't grateful. I was—incredibly so—for all of his generosity and his desire to take care of me, but his entire lifestyle scared me. There was just too much damn space. I knew how nuts that sounded, but I was used to smaller places.

The news trickled in from the bedroom while I flipped through the polished wooden racks. I eyed the couch toward the back of the closet, "I'm surprised he didn't put a TV in here."

Thinking about what to wear for my first day back at work reminded me how nervous the whole ordeal made me. What message did I want to send? Could the right outfit take care of my lack of confidence? And what would I tell Mason when he inevitably found out?

A loud bang came from the first floor and I jumped, letting out a startled gasp I wished I had swallowed. The universe was reminding me that time was fleeting and my problems wouldn't wait until I was ready for them.

My heart pounded painfully as Mason's voice carried up the stairs. "Claire, where are you?" he sounded pissed. He already knew. *Damn it.* I sighed before yelling back, "Bedroom!"

He walked in a few moments later. The news cut off, and he was through the door and behind me in no time. The anger emanating from him stood like a third person in the room. Luckily, the closet was bigger than my old bedroom and there was plenty of room for all of us. I rifled through the clothes, even though I already decided on an outfit, just to avoid his furious glower.

"Do you want to explain what I just heard?" his tone sent goosebumps skittering across my skin. I smelled his cologne mixed with his natural scent as he closed the distance between us. He hovered behind me, and my pussy responded to his heat at my back.

"Are you being intentionally vague? How would I know what you heard, Mason?" I leaned back surreptitiously, brushing my ass against his cock. He stilled, and when he didn't respond, I flipped a sweater aside twisting my hips and repeating the move.

His incredibly powerful hands gripped me, effectively stopping my attempt at diversion, and pulled me harshly against him. "You told Gavin you're going back to work." The barely controlled rage in his voice made me shiver. "In. Six. Fucking. Days." he continued, his voice going deadly soft.

I stumbled, but his hands held me steady. "No need to get so upset." Instead of the haughtiness I aimed for, I managed a breathy whisper. "You won't tell me about your work. I won't tell you about mine." I pulled a dress out of the closet, examining it for a moment before putting it back.

His fingers dug into my flesh, and I moaned at the bite of pain coupled with the strength of his hands. "I have six clients, currently, down from—"

"That's not the work I'm talking about, but you knew that." A hanger slammed on the rail as I put another piece back a bit too hard.

"Why would you tell him you're ready to go back? You're not." His lips skated along my jaw, his stubble tickled my skin. His anger was a frightening undertone to the seduction.

"How would you know? You're never here!" His grip loosened, and I pushed his hands off of me, turning to face him. The outfit I chose was a winner, powerful, the very opposite of how he saw me. "You're *not* here. You *don't* talk to me, and you *don't* trust me."

"I do trust you!" the conviction behind his words made me laugh out loud.

"Whatever this is," I gestured between us and the palpable heat that actually burned and ached with all the shit left unsaid, "this is not trust."

"Claire..." the huskiness in his voice mimicked longing and if I gave in to the soft way he said my name, I would stay home as he wanted. I would give in, give up my career, and everything else because I was weak where he was concerned. Nothing that should matter did when he said my name that way.

"My going back to work is my business." I needed distance to break this spell between us that felt like lightning in my veins and tasted like lies and heartache. "I am curious... Which one of our phones did you bug? Or did you bug both of us?" He had to. It was the only way he would have known what I agreed to so quickly.

He had the good grace to look apologetic, "Just his. I promise."

I splayed my hands on his chest, destroying the distance between us. I didn't know if I wanted to fuck him or fight him. Why not both? A bit of the rage boiling inside of me calmed. "If you've bugged his phone, I can assume you have a close watch on the Gavin situation,"

"I told you I did." He pressed his lips softly to mine before sweeping my tongue with his own in a hot, wet kiss. The ache in my heart moved to my pussy and some primal part of me insisted that all the issues between us were easily solvable with a thorough fucking.

I pulled back, needing to settle things before I let him and my libido both fuck me out of going back to work. "Mason, I made my decision. I'm going back in six days and that's the end of it. It's not like I'm going on an extended expedition. I am only going to the library."

The hardening in his eyes frightened me, not because I thought he would hurt me, but because that determination promised action. "This is so far from the end of it, you have no idea," he fisted his hands at his side, looking so damned stressed my heart ached for him.

"You have the power to stop me, Mason. I don't know anyone with more sway over me than you. But I'll never forgive you if you use that power over me and this city to manipulate me to your whims. The only way I'm not going back is if you think Gavin will hurt me. Look me in my eyes and tell me he's going to hurt me." It was a redundant statement as he stared into my eyes.

"Keeping you safe, even from yourself, is not a whim. It's a fundamental need."

Heat rolled through me, but I ignored the utterly distracting statement. My self-destructive tendencies were not his business. "Will Gavin hurt me?"

"He wouldn't dare." His face twisted in disgust, and I wasn't sure if it was thoughts of Gavin or that he sensed his argument weakening.

"Then, I'm going back."

"Not yet. You need more time." He placed his hands gently on the sides of my neck, keeping my eyes on his. "You are still healing, still getting through everything that happened. It's a lot, Claire. You are not a machine and it's okay to need help. Let me take care of things for you." I wanted to. I wanted things to be normal and easy, but they weren't.

"I need to go back to work. I need to face things head-on. You will not change my mind on this."

"We'll see," he grunted as he let go of me. He turned toward the door and stormed off without another word. The front door banged and a moment later, I heard the tires on the gravel driveway.

I hated fighting with him, but I needed to do this. It would be all too easy to let him fuck me into compliance and keep me in this behemoth house. The inactivity would kill me. I needed action.

Nine

Mason

I climbed into the car where James waited for me. He blinked in surprise when the door opened. "Took care of things already? Jesus, Mason, you're losing your edge in your old age." He raised one brow at me, but I had no energy for innuendo.

"Not exactly." I wasn't in the mood to discuss Claire or our disagreement.

"Why doesn't that surprise me?" he sounded tired more than anything else. He didn't want her to go back either. As much as he thought she was capable of handling my life, he knew she was still hurt.

A man I didn't recognize sat behind the wheel and I eyed him hard. "What happened to... what was his name? Carlos, was it?" My argument with Claire must be knocking me off my game because a stranger in the car is something that would usually catch my immediate attention.

"Didn't work out, had to let him go."

My brow raised. "Permanently?"

"Nope, he just had a weak stomach is all." I nodded my head considering, and when I inclined it toward the new guy he answered my unspoken question.

"Outside hire," James assured me, but his gaze ran over the man with just as much suspicion.

"Did you call the doctor?" I murmured low enough that the driver would have trouble hearing.

"I did," James answered. "He said that physically Claire is fine to go back with restrictions. He's still suggesting she seek therapy, but he's happy to say whatever you like if compensated."

I stared at my hands as I considered what Claire said about not forgiving me for excessive meddling.

"Are you actually going to do it?" James' shock was apparent.

"No." I ran my hands through my hair, trying to grapple down the urge to do exactly that. "No, I was hoping he had a different opinion, that's all." His dubious look told me he was unconvinced, but he nodded.

"Is Gavin still at the library?"

James picked up his laptop off the seat beside him and started typing, "Yes. The software that Casey designed is amazing."

"City Library in midtown," I told the driver. "Has he spoken to anyone since he called Claire?"

"His wife and his boss, both of whom are currently overseas. Not that I could tell where." *My father, wonderful.*

My jaw clenched, "Did they discuss anything worth mentioning?"

"G asked him about the shipment coming in later this month; he followed the script to the letter. His boss didn't sound suspicious, though you won't know for sure if the call went sideways unless someone winds up dead." Normally, I would put up the privacy divider for this type of conversation, but I wanted to watch the driver's reactions.

"You think the girls are going to be up to snuff this time?" My words came out hungry and predatory, and they made me sick. James' top lip pulled back from his teeth, but he kept his eyes on the driver as I did. The backs of his ears turned bright red. Embarrassment, excitement? Either way, it was too strong a response to the relatively benign statement. I could be talking about a strip club, maids, or anything really.

My father dabbled in a lot of things, but his most lucrative endeavor was human trafficking. He bought and sold young women, and helped smuggle them into the country, acting as the middleman between the abductors and the rapists.

I knew in my gut that he offered the man driving the car one of those girls in exchange for information on me. I smelled the fear on him, the tension in his shoulders as he stared at the road a bit too hard. A brief flicker of conscience told me I didn't know enough to make that decision, but I trusted my gut.

We pulled up outside the library and wasted no time getting out of the vehicle. I kept pace with James, making sure no one was around to hear us. "Kill him."

"Now?"

"As soon as we get back."

"Yes, sir," he agreed as I opened the door to the library. I tried to ignore the way he fidgeted. The man was as cold as they come unless there was a certain blue-eyed strawberry blonde around. I didn't know if Emma was working today, but James sure did.

She didn't notice us as she stood at the circulation desk, concentrating on her task. James killed men without blinking, but one word from Emma could break him.

"Good morning, Emma." She jumped at the sound of my voice.

"M-Mason! What can I do for you?" Her eyes flicked to James and her posture stiffened further.

"Is Mr. Wolfe in?"

"He's in Claire's office." She looked back toward said office, hoping he might walk out on his own. "Should I tell him you're heading his way?" She picked up the phone, ready to enter his extension.

"No, Emma. I think I'll surprise him." I winked as I pressed the lever down, ending the call. "Oh, and while I have you, Claire may be coming back to work in a few days," I hoped to delay her return, but in the event I failed, Emma needed reminding. She gawped at me in apparent shock, "remember what we talked about? Loose lips, yeah?"

She nodded her head without hesitation. "Yeah, I won't say anything, but is she okay? Is she ready to come back? I texted her but..."

"She's fine, Emma. You don't need to worry too much." I smiled at her encouragingly while guilt twisted in my stomach. It was shitty enough I was lying to Claire, but making her friend do it too made me especially low.

"Do you need me, boss?" James asked. His eyes were trained on Emma and had been since we came in. She tried to ignore him but utterly failed.

"No, Gavin and I will be just fine without you." I turned and headed down the hallway leading to Claire's office. This place was fucking huge; there had to be another spot for him to work other than in her space.

"No, James. It's not enough!" Emma's voice echoed down the hall and I laughed to myself, thinking of the people reading and studying in the immediate vicinity.

I pushed the door to the office open without knocking. Gavin glanced up from behind Claire's desk, his surprise well-concealed. Take-out boxes and other nonsense littered the space. Claire's personal items were shoved into a box and resting on a stool in the corner. "Mason, what can I do for you today?" he asked as he pushed his glasses up.

"We need to talk." I slammed the door shut behind me.

"I suppose we do," he agreed as I pulled out the chair opposite him and took a seat. "Your father is getting suspicious of the repeated mix-ups. You're going to need to figure something else out if you don't want to blow my cover."

Gavin had been interfering with the scheduling of pickups and other petty inconveniences to slow down the movement of the girls. It was only mildly effective, but it was the best move I had for the time being.

I knew from the conversation I had with James in the car on the way here that my father had not said as much, but Gavin was shrewd enough to pick up on the subtler clues of mistrust or lie about them to suit his needs.

I nodded slowly, deciding to play along for now, "Fair enough. When is the next exchange? Are there any auctions coming up?"

"Two weeks for the exchange. No auctions until after the holidays."

"I'll figure something out by then." I typed out a quick message to James, telling him to take a second look at the conversations between Gavin and my father, and shoved the phone back in my pocket. "But there are more pressing matters for us to discuss."

"Enlighten me then." The slight condescension in his tone had me itching to remind him how he'd gotten that scar on the side of his face or why all of his teeth were veneered. Perhaps he just liked me shoving my gun down his throat.

I cocked an eyebrow at him. "Cut the shit."

"No shit to cut, I assure you." He held up his palms in a placating gesture that didn't reach his eyes.

"You asked her to come back to work without my permission. You would do well to remember, Gavin, not only am I happy to hurt you, but I also have the means to ruin you." When I started surveilling him a few months back, he quickly tucked away the messier aspects of his life. Before he noticed us trailing him, we'd caught footage of a young teenage boy living in his apartment, and sleeping in his bed, all while his wife slept in their lovely colonial in the suburbs.

Two ways I differed from my father were his incredibly bigoted hatred of gay people and his tolerance of pedophilia. He would kill any of his men for liking other men, but if they liked to abuse children, that was a nonissue. Under normal circumstances, I would *never* use a person's sexuality as leverage against them. But Gavin was a pedophile, and as far as I was concerned, those who commit sex crimes against children don't deserve the standard considerations of decency.

Gavin, the grade-A creep, got a look at the kid when he was supervising a shipment. He told David the boy was dead, killed while trying to fight back. In reality, Gavin took him home to his secret fuck pad and he had been servicing all of his sick needs ever since.

Vick and I went to the apartment and got him out before Gavin got home that same day. That kid didn't owe me shit for helping him, but he sure felt like he did. He told me emphatically that he wasn't afraid to tell the truth about him, including something about feeding him to dogs, but I don't speak a lot of Spanish.

It wouldn't come to that, though. Gavin's professional reputation meant too much to him and I wouldn't put the kid into that situation. But the promise—along with the constant surveillance—was enough to keep Gavin in line.

"But you won't ruin me," he argued in a soft, assured voice. "You have no reason to since I did not ask Ms. Green to come back. I simply asked her when her doctor cleared her to return. It shocked me to hear she was coming back so soon, but what can I say? The library needs her."

I wished he was lying. I would have loved the excuse to beat the fuck out of him. "Claire is to remain safe and happy at all costs and if you or this position infringe upon that, I will prove less forgiving than my father would be of your sexuality."

"I understand that." He swallowed hard but remained otherwise unphased. I didn't know which part of the threat bothered him more, the promise of violence or the reminder of what my father would do to him when he learned the truth. Of course Gavin didn't realize I was counting the days until he no longer served a purpose, and *I* could end him.

"Remember your place with me." I picked up the name placard off the desk that read *Claire Green*.

"And where is that? So, I might remember..."

"First, it's not in this office. This place is massive. Is your name *Claire Green*? Do you deserve to breathe the same fucking air as her, let alone share her space and shove her belongings into a box?"

"I don't think it's so serious as all of that. I am her boss, Mason, and using her office is within normal."

"You're a bottom feeder, Gavin. You have a perfect opportunity to spin this situation so that no matter who comes out on top, you look like a proper soldier playing your role. But neither of those outcomes will be an option for you if you don't mind yourself with Miss Green. Do you understand that?"

"I do."

"If anything happens to her—"

"I'm dead. I'm quite aware." He pulled his phone from his jacket pocket and checked the time. "Believe it or not, I have no interest in seeing Ms. Green harmed. She's good for the library, and keeping her safe is desirable for me, considering all that you know, *Mr. Sharp.*"

The move was so dismissive, so disrespectful that I lost a touch of my control. If he had only been flippant about me and my authority, I wouldn't have allowed his words to bother me, but he was checking his phone while discussing Claire's safety.

I stood in front of Gavin, and he looked up at me with obvious confusion. Pulling my pocket knife from my breast pocket, I opened it and tested the weight in my hand. I wouldn't shoot him in the library and there was no use leveling a threat I wouldn't follow through on, but I would cut him.

"Do you want to know a secret about me? Something I don't like people to know..."

He gulped as I pressed the blade against the side of his loose-skinned neck, "Okay"

"I prefer a blade over a gun because it's so much more personal. And personally, I would enjoy slicing you apart."

"You've made your point." From the sweat gathering on his brow, I supposed I had, but instead of relenting, I pressed the knife into his skin until a drop of blood seeped out.

I relieved the pressure and sat back in the chair. "On to more pleasant business then,"

"Like what became of Francis Santini?" His eyes narrowed.

I smiled outright as I thought of it. "And? What became of him?"

"Someone killed him, stomped him to a bloody pulp. Fucking gruesome. Some thugs were reaching over their pay grade. David is out for blood." His lips twitched in amusement. "You know they were good friends, don't you?"

"Huh, that's a shame. Francis was such a nice guy, a lot like you, don't you think? Maybe I should send pops a condolence card."

"You'd have to know his address for that,"

"Have you found where he's hanging out, Gavin, or are you just teasing me?" my bored tone was false, and he knew it.

"No, he hasn't told me." My surveillance backed that up.

"Huh, well, I had a question about loyalty, questionable loyalty, really. Something you're exceptionally skilled at sussing out. Which of his men are on the shortlist of defectors?"

"Why might you want to know something like that?" He leaned back in his chair, considering me. The light sheen of sweat still present on his brow foiled the attempt at nonchalance. The devious wheels spinning in his head would only be more obvious with a fat rat using them for exercise.

"Paulo is looking forward to the day he gets to tell people what kind of shit you did to him. He wants them to kill you." His mouth dropped open before quickly closing. "Did you think I killed him or sold him? Or otherwise got rid of him? I didn't."

He scratched his beard. The idea of David Sharp finding out he was gay, and a thief, was a truly terrifying prospect. "There are a few names I can give you, but I wouldn't know them all."

"Make me a list, Gavin. Quick but thorough." I waited impatiently while he wrote out the list by hand and passed it over to me. "Pleasure doing business with you."

"Pleasure is all mine." The door slammed shut behind me.

I unfolded the paper as I walked back to the atrium. This was a shorter list than the one Francis gave me. Francis wanted to die so badly by the time we were done with him that I doubted some of what he told us.

There's a point with torture that the answers you're getting are nonsense. They'll tell you fucking anything to make it stop. It's a skill to hold back from that point, an art to knowing when you're causing enough pain to get the truth before you topple over the edge into senseless lie-soaked agony. Gavin was a different story. While some of those names were certainly valid, some were likely traps. But either way, there *Daniel Moore* was once again.

James stood two inches behind Emma, who was bent in half over a broad return bin filled with books. His hands hovered over her hips, ready to grab her at the first sign of a misstep. "You know you want it, shortcake. Don't pretend you're ignoring me when we both know you're trying to tease me with what I'm missing."

"Fuck off," she shot back, and he laughed.

"James," I said, interrupting the tension between the two.

"Thank Christ!" Emma muttered as she lifted her head out of the bin with a handful of books. "The ones on the bottom are a bitch when you're short, and your associate is lacking boundaries." She put the books down on the counter and reached back in for more.

"This isn't over," James warned, slapping her on the ass before coming to stand at my side.

Her pale, freckled cheeks were bright red in her embarrassment as she lifted herself out of the bin. "Fuck you, James!"

"Anytime you like, shortcake. I'll be seeing you shortly." He winked at her, and her mouth dropped open in outrage.

"Have a good day, Emma." I contained my laughter as we left the library. She was embarrassed enough without my help.

The day was uncomfortably cold. The bright sun and the nearly transparent skies taunted me with thoughts of warmer days and closer stars. Our steps quickly ate up the sidewalk.

"Why do you call her shortcake, James?" I asked, preparing myself for the likelihood I didn't want to know.

"Because she's got pretty strawberry blonde hair, and her pussy is sweet as cake." He got this slightly glazed-over look in his eye at the thought of her.

I shook my head at him, "Stop thinking about her pussy. We have recruiting to do."

"Oh, yeah?" He liked the idea of new blood a lot more than Vick did.

"Yep." I pulled the list out of my pocket. "Some of them even match what old Franky told us."

"So, they're both telling the truth, or they're both lying? Which are you betting on?"

"Both, always both."

Ten

Mason

Five very tense days later, James stayed behind with Claire while Vick and I took a ride into the high-end district where all the expensive shops were. The icy trees flew past, giving way to the squat historical buildings that gave our city its distinctive charm.

Three days earlier, I gave up my attempts to delay Claire's return to work petulantly, but those efforts were pointless other than to drive the wedge between us further. She had decided, and fuck, that woman was stubborn.

I understood why she was angry with me for trying to forcefully intervene; Mason Dubois was never a controlling man, not with anyone. It stunned me to think I was capable of such base fucking urges. I was no better than a caveman, and I wanted to come in her, and on her, and make sure everyone understood who owned her, provided for her, and kept her safe.

I wanted other men to smell my cum on her. The brain that lived in my head rather than my cock understood how fucking ridiculous that was and that I sounded insane. When you love someone inside and out, like their breaths and heartbeats are your own, things are bound to feel different.

I recognized that while my worries were valid, my methods made me an asshole. I tried to make things right with her in several ways: words, apologies that didn't work because they sounded false, gentle touches, fucking—lots of fucking.

Sex was the one thing completely right between us, though more intense and emotionally fraught than before. I fucked her more often than not when we were alone, ate her pussy every chance I got, and figured out the right angles and pressure to make her cum like a geyser or a much more moderate puddle.

But heavy silences loaded the quiet moments I wanted to spend talking and holding her, and I missed her smile like fucking homesickness. There wasn't much downtime either between pursuing the leads Casey found and the names on both lists. I wasn't home as often as I should have been.

In a late-night internet search born of sadness and desperation, I found a particular antique store with truly beautiful and unique jewelry. Maybe if I found something special for her, she would see how much she meant to me. My hope may have been a temporary fix, but it was real.

I wanted to bring Claire with me and let her buy anything and everything she wanted. Buying her all the things she never had would fill me with pure satisfaction. Claiming and caring for her were primal needs I found harder to ignore by the day.

I didn't suggest taking her out with me today because she wouldn't like the amount I planned to spend on her. I would get her to relax in time. The thought of lavishing her with things and worshiping her silk-wrapped, jewel-coated body made my cock achingly hard. A fantasy I was unwilling to let go of.

Claire liked presents, even if she was too stubborn to admit how being cared for soothed something ragged inside her, but visible price tags were a major issue. Money was no issue for me, I donated to charity regularly, and I had every intention of spending exorbitant sums on her. So, I removed the damn tags and would continue to remove them from everything I bought for her.

As we stepped inside the shop, we were immediately hit with the soothing, musty scent of old clothes and books, and I relaxed an inch. Gleaming wooden furniture, globes, elaborate feathers, and clocks lined the path to the counter, where rows of jewelry nestled in silken pillows lay beneath the glass.

"How can I help you today?" a professionally dressed middle-aged woman asked from behind the counter.

There were a lot of things here Claire would enjoy. Her love of old and forgotten things was part of what endeared me to her. She cared about the stuff other people forgot about entirely. I pointed to one of the antiquated globes in the corner. Even from this distance, I saw how startlingly wrong the borders were. "I'll take that."

"Of course, sir." She stepped out from behind the counter, but I waved her off.

"My friend and I will take care of it." I nodded to Vick, "I'm also looking for something unique, though I'm not sure what yet." I looked down at the case

"*That* is the best place to start when looking for antique jewelry. Can you tell me anything about the recipient?"

I smiled to myself at her deft handling. I didn't actually say I was looking for jewelry, but she scented an easy kill. "She's a little quirky and sensitive, but she's fierce too. She makes me laugh. She's smart and deeply compassionate." The saleswoman had a dreamy look in her eyes, and I cleared my throat. "She's a librarian, so naturally she loves books."

"I think I have something perfect." She moved to the end of the case and pulled out a stand with a necklace dangling from it. She placed the golden book in front of me. A delicate floral design with emeralds and diamonds decorated the cover. "It's a locket. One hundred and twenty years old, give or take a few years, twenty-two karat gold, the diamonds are each..."

Her voice transformed into a bland buzzing as I picked up the little book, surprised by how little it weighed. I imagined the piece hanging around Claire's neck, resting over her heart, in the valley between her breasts. "You're right. It *is* perfect. I'll take it."

"Oh, excellent!" I laid the necklace back down and then handed her my credit card. I walked away as she rang everything up.

Finding a shelf of old books, my breath caught when I noticed the selection of field references. I picked each up, checking the covers for the one my mom used to read to me. One of them came from the same publisher but was a few years off. *So close.* I groaned to myself, wondering if I would ever find another copy of that book.

When she finished settling everything up, I took the tiny package and stepped outside. Vick had already brought the globe to the car and waited inside. The air was dry and cold as hell, weather that chaps your cheeks and leaves you red and miserable. I watched the people milling down the street. No one paid any particular attention to one another despite how thick the foot traffic was.

I tucked down the alley to the right of the shop. The space between the buildings stood clean, lined with stylish bricks and overflowing flower pots. A few neatly rowed trash cans and recycling bins stood in a line. A gangly figure pushed away from a doorway.

Casey, the kid we picked up at Francis' warehouse, stepped out in front of me. He had proven himself useful in the short time he worked for me, and as good with computers as he claimed. My weariness remained as that skill could be more dangerous than useful in the wrong hands.

"Hey, Mr. Sharp," he kept his voice low, his hands in his pockets, and his head tucked down into his hood. That look may blend in the warehouse district, but he stuck out like a sore thumb here.

"You need to stand up straight. You look like you're casing the place for an old lady to mug."

"Maybe I am," he teased as he pulled a cigarette out of his pocket and lit it.

I smacked it out of his hand just because of his smug expression. "That shit won't fly with me, Casey. Act as if you belong or people will notice you. Do me a favor and prove you're not more trouble than you're worth."

His hands raised in a placating gesture. "Kidding, I swear." Pulling his hood down and straightening to his full height, he leaned in a little closer to me. "None of the lower-level guys know anything about problems with Moore, but a few of the mid-level men suspect something is up. There is a rumor that he and Hector were getting up to some extracurriculars together, and your pops didn't like that. I don't know what's true or what they're mixed up in, but that's the word."

"Did you get anything of value to me other than pointless conjecture?"

"Just this," he pulled a thick envelope out of his pocket and handed it to me. "I found a few accounts. You should be able to track them pretty far. I would have given them to Vick, but you wanted to meet me so..." He shrugged a little and stuffed his hands back into his pockets.

I wanted to meet with him today, so I could look him in the eye and decide if he was trying to fuck me over. "When you find something, contact Vick or James immediately. This better have been worth my time today, Casey." I took the envelope from him, surprised by the weight of the paper.

"It will be," he insisted.

"Remember what I said, Casey. If you don't fit in, you stand out. And you don't make it long in this city when you stand out."

"Yes, sir."

I nodded, dismissing him. He slunk through the alley and into the back door of a business. I waited for a moment before turning my back. Casey likely wouldn't kill me, but no one knew who could be waiting inside those buildings to take a shot. I turned, holding my breath until I reached the car on the curb.

"Where to now, boss?" Vick asked as I stepped back inside the car, and Lawrence pulled smoothly away. I cranked the control for the heater, turned up the fan, and unbuttoned the top of my coat.

"I've got to get a picture of my cock printed, and I need James to research a few wire transfers. A lot of transfers," I amended as I opened the envelope and flipped through the pages.

He nodded his head like this was a typical request. "Sounds fair, you fucking pervert."

I laughed as I settled into the leather.

What Casey told me rolled around in my head. If Daniel was on the shortlist, I couldn't afford to lose that opening with him. Outside of our history, he held a position of significant influence.

As the top architect in our city, he had built everything of note in the last six years. His influence was exactly what my reputation needed. What *I* needed might be another story. There was a lot of shit surrounding Daniel I would rather forget.

Eighteen Years Earlier

The blistering sun beat down on my neck and I wondered how businessmen wore full suits in ninety-degree weather—unfeeling robots. My gaze flicked around, landing on a multitude of the machines. They surrounded me, pretending to give a fuck that my mom died. *Social obligation.* The bitter words ran through my mind.

Blonde hair fanned around her face. She used to tell me she was a towhead, whatever the fuck that meant. Her soft hair was the only part of her that appeared normal. Her once beautiful face was pasty and painted on. Like they copied her likeness from a funhouse mirror. Her nose tipped down slightly instead of up. Such a simple change made her into a different person. She didn't look this bad earlier, but the sun was intense, and whatever they used to repair her face after the accident was melting.

"You deserved better," I whispered to the empty shell that used to be my mom. I couldn't sense her in that body anymore. We weren't religious, but undoubtedly there had to be a soul for her to feel so fucking empty now. Her coffin rested on a riser beside the grave they dug to bury her. My father stood off to the side, speaking with a never-ending line of sympathizers.

He smiled a sad tight smile for each of them, and at first, I thought the expression seemed genuine, but how many times can you repeat the same gesture and have it be real? It was as fake as the people parading before him, people my mother couldn't stand, people who didn't care about her.

Eventually, the crowd died down, and most of the people left. My father performed his grieving widower role until a hot girl in her twenties walked up to him and took his hand in hers. His lips kicked up in a very different smile than the ones he offered the others.

She was extremely blonde, like my mom had been, though, unlike my mom, she had fake tanned skin. I watched as he murmured a few words to her. She blushed furiously as she sunk her teeth into her bottom lip and smiled up at him like he was *incredible*. My father slowly traced something into her wrist and she walked off, looking over her shoulder to check if he watched her ass as she went.

Rage filled me as I turned away from the man I was ashamed to resemble so closely. A few stragglers stood at the curb or dithered near their cars. My eyes stung from crying all night. They were dry now and would stay that way if I wanted to make it home without a black eye or busted lip. In my father's book, it was fine to invite your mistress to your wife's funeral, but crying for your dead mom was an unforgivable offense.

I wished *he* had died.

I flexed my fists, pulling out the small field reference mom always used to read to me. I tucked the book beneath her stiffened hand as the sounds of her whistling bird songs played in my head.

Who knew what happened when you died, but I hoped pretty birds surrounded her and sang her songs. And that David Sharp could never hurt her again. "I love you," I told my mom one last time.

They lowered the coffin into the ground, and I threw in a handful of dirt. My father walked up beside me and repeated the gesture. He turned to leave, expecting me to follow him into the limousine waiting on the curb.

Wiggling into the leather seat, I got as close to comfortable as possible; I needed all my strength to ignore whatever shit he wanted to say. I bit the inside of my cheek until the skin broke and bled to remind myself that getting punched in the jaw hurt worse than keeping the tears inside.

"I'll miss her too," his voice sounded unnaturally soft, a convincing act. That grieving widower shit might have worked on the guests at her funeral, his associates, and his mistress, but not on me.

"Yeah," I agreed lamely, distrusting everything about this interaction.

"But that's no excuse not to act like a man. My life isn't ending because hers did." He shrugged, and I hated the fact I looked like him more than I did before. Why would his life end when it was so full? I thought of the young blonde bold enough to come to my mother's funeral. "You're fourteen now. You are a man, and it's time you learned what's expected of you." I practically heard the words he didn't say: *Now your mother is gone.*

I flicked my gaze up to meet his. "Yes, sir." There were no words or actions to get me out of whatever he planned.

"Warehouse thirty-two," he snapped at the driver who unwaveringly pulled away. We rode in silence for a few minutes while the fear slithered deeper. "You remember when Francis taught you how to shoot a gun?" my father's voice sounded smooth and comforting, which made me all the sicker.

"Yes, sir," my voice grew deeper by the day but chose that moment to crack.

His big hand came up and smacked me hard across the face. I held perfectly still after the initial impact, knowing if I flinched or made a noise of pain, he would hit me again and again until I stopped making sounds and took his beating "like a man". He smiled for a moment, enjoying my suffering, enjoying what a "man" I was.

The warehouse he took us to sat a few blocks from where Francis taught me how to shoot a gun. The lesson involved a man-shaped target and verbal coaching about shooting to kill vs. shooting to maim.

Someone inside opened the door for my father and me, shutting the panel behind us. Ancient machinery filled the giant room, and the dust and metal in the air were suffocatingly thick.

Six men surrounded a man tied to a chair in the center of the open space. I glanced away from his blubbering face. Nothing made me as uncomfortable as a man crying. Didn't he know what happened to weak men? What the man next to me did to the weak men and boys he was meant to protect?

My father made no introductions and gave no explanations, but the weight of all of their gazes crushed me. Time stood still as all six of them appraised me with expressions ranging from pity to excitement. I still wore the damn suit, but I wasn't hot anymore. Ice shot through my veins, leaving a hollow ache behind. *Dad* pulled his gun out of his pocket and handed it to me.

"Kill him, Mason."

That explained the way they all watched me. "I-I don't think—" I stared at the gun as I mumbled, trying to remember how to speak and act the way he wanted. *What about what I want?* I wanted to scream the words at him. *I don't want to be a murderer!*

"You kill him, or I kill you. What's it going to be?" He flicked his wrist and the gun impatiently toward me. I took the weapon from his hand and stared at the metal. My mind raced, and my pulse beat so loudly in my ears that I thought my head would explode.

I looked at the man set to die, wondering if he had a family. Did he have a son who would cry over his grave? A son who would leave behind his most prized treasures to keep him happy in the afterlife, though he wanted nothing more than to keep those treasures for mementos.

I hesitated for only a moment. My thoughts came quicker than they ever had fueled by adrenaline. Seconds passed as I thought through all of this. That was enough time for my father to pull another gun from his waist and press the barrel against my temple. "Now, son."

As I lifted the gun and took aim at a man for the first time, I swallowed hard and tried not to shake. I nearly pissed myself, but I managed not to cry as I pulled the trigger. I shot three times, twice in the chest and once in the head, just as Francis taught me. My father didn't lower his gun immediately. He smiled like a madman and I wished the look was pride, but it was something so much darker. For a moment, I hoped he would end it all for me.

He didn't. He put the gun away and barked, "Clean this up," to the men watching. David Sharp turned and left the warehouse, and like the dutiful heir I was, I followed him.

My father said nothing on our ride back, not a word of praise or explanation. He didn't hit me, and he let me keep the gun.

Our manor had always been an over-the-top display of wealth and power, but with my mother here, there was love. The place was nothing but empty and doomed now, and I couldn't wait until each board burned. I wanted to burn with them.

I ran to the top of the spiral staircase, stumbling into my bathroom in time to grip the sink and puke into it. The toilet was only a few more feet, but I wouldn't make it. I retched for a while before trying to clean out the fucking sink. Goddamn, disgusting.

I couldn't look at my face in the mirror as I cleaned, and the few times I caught myself, I turned away. A nearly carbon copy of my father looked back at me, younger, but a killer all the same with *his* green eyes and dirty blonde hair. I never wanted to see either of us again. After I finished cleaning the sink, I climbed into the shower and scrubbed my skin until I burned all over.

I didn't want this life anymore, any part of it. Running away was impossible. I would never go far enough to avoid the person in the mirror, a murderer, a disappointment. Nothing at all would be so much better than this. Nothingness didn't hurt. This was agony.

I got dressed in something that probably didn't match, but who cared? I pulled my flip phone out from under my pillow. My father didn't know about the burner phone I kept in the hopes my mother would leave him. I pulled up my contacts and dialed my best friend: Dan.

"Mason, are you okay? I tried to say hi to you at the funeral, but I understand..." he was off on a rant before I said hello. Daniel was a nerdy kid, sweet, and my mom loved him. His mom died a few years ago, and with a father as nasty as my own, we were very close.

I couldn't go through with this without saying goodbye to him. "No, I'm not. This is the end for me, man. I just wanted to let you know you're a good friend. You deserve better than me." A moment of tense silence passed as I picked the gun up off the bathroom counter and turned it over in my hand.

The same gun I had just used to kill a man for no reason, or a reason I would never know—and what was the difference between the two things, really? Staring at the mirror, I no longer saw myself but the man who crafted me in his image. I looked like him. I dressed like him. I killed like him.

"She will never forgive you." Daniel interrupted the storm of my thoughts. His voice sounded calmer than I expected.

"She's dead. What does it matter?" I lifted a pack of cigarettes out of the crumpled jeans lying on the floor. Pulling one to my lips, I flicked my lighter and took a deep drag. I loved my mother, but I wasn't sure I *forgave* her.

We could have avoided so much of our suffering if we had left. She could have left. Her family had tons of money. *She* had tons of money my father couldn't touch no matter what, and he hated her for it. *We should* have left, but we stayed for God only knew what reason.

My dad would beat the fuck out of me if he caught me smoking in the house. "He can't hurt her anymore, and I can't disappoint her. It has nothing to do with her."

"Does it really feel like she's gone, Mason? After my mom died, she told me bodies fail but love never dies. Do you think she fucking lied to me?" he tried his hardest not to yell. If he woke his father up, there would be consequences.

"I'm not calling her a liar," I answered hesitantly. "Her love belonged to someone else. I'm not the same person anymore. He ruined me. I can't feel anything. I'm nothing. Even if it still exists, I don't deserve her love.

"Mason, please, just give it tonight. Think things over and we can talk in the morning. Do you promise not to do anything tonight? I can't lose you too, man!"

For a minute or two I thought, leaving him in frozen silence. "I won't do anything tonight, I promise." Although I wouldn't agree to talk things over with him tomorrow, I could at least do that for him. If he understood what I was now, he would regret having talked me out of ending my life, if only temporarily. I hid the gun under the pillow I didn't sleep on. "Don't worry, I mean it, I promise. Good night, Dan."

"Night, Mason," but he didn't end the call.

I hung up the phone and stubbed out the cigarette. Hopefully, an open window and a few sprays of cologne would be enough to hide the smell and avoid a beating—it wasn't.

And that wasn't the only time Daniel convinced me it was better to live.

Eleven

Mason

I breathed a sigh of relief as I left the upper crust of the city. The shops and cafés with their pretty primped people and tiny yappy fucking dogs grated on me. I printed the picture and went back to the house, expecting to sneak past Claire and fight about that too.

I hated fighting with her, but I was morbidly eager for the inevitable subtext layered fuck after. My heart sank when I realized Claire was not home at all. My sinking heart stood back up and raced off as I called Victor. He said she just wanted to drive around. She had wanted to do that a lot lately.

I sat in my office, reading over the accounts Casey found. I grudgingly smiled as I flipped through them. There was a lot of useful information here, which James verified when he made Casey show him step by step how he found it. I had to admit that the kid did a good job.

At about five o'clock, I called the offices of Mr. Daniel Moore, the most prestigious architect in our city. His secretary was more than unhelpful. Moreover, she was nasty as she told me

Mr. Moore's schedule was full for the next three years. "If you're not a current client, you have no business with him, and if you have no business with him, he has no time for you."

She was right as much as it irritated me. I didn't have any architectural business for him and fuck if I didn't envy that firm-handedness. That's what I needed in a secretary and I spent some time thinking about poaching her to avoid the inevitable: dealing with someone who used to be so important to me.

I thought about how to handle things for a while before deciding to call Casey. He earned a little trust, and it was a job I needed done quickly. Casey gave me Dan's home address after a few minutes of muttered curses and ferocious clicking.

"Why the fuck is a home address locked up this tightly? Even the damn tax records are sealed, and that's not legal. Even if a shell corporation held the property, I should have access to the tax records."

"If the address was locked up so tight, how did you get it?"

"I'm good, Mr. Sharp," his tone lacked all boastfulness; it held just honest confidence in his abilities.

"You're okay," I jokingly corrected him.

I drove by the apartment building the next day where two guards stood out front dressed in black suits with little headsets. Surely there were more of them inside. That didn't bode well for the simplicity of getting to him at home. The prick was going to force me to do something creative, and that pissed me off, considering how many other things I needed to be doing.

Claire and I were still fighting, but we fucked the moment I came home from scoping out the building. I called Casey again while Claire slept off the orgasmic haze.

"You want to be upgraded from okay to good?" I murmured into the phone as I watched Claire sleep.

"Absolutely," Casey chuckled.

"Find me an in with Daniel Moore. I can't access him at his office or at home. I need a public place where I can surprise him."

"Are you going to kill him?" his voice squeaked. "Sorry, not my business."

I sighed audibly. "No, it's not your fucking business, Casey, but if it makes you feel better, I am not planning to kill him."

"I'm sorry, sir," he sounded properly chastised until he mumbled, "he has guards,"

"I do too." I reminded him, "Are you nervous for me, Casey?"

"No, of course not. I'll find you an in," he assured me. I hung up the phone and climbed back into bed beside Claire.

Later that night, Casey called and told me he found Dan's lunch reservations for the following day. The restaurant was booked out for months, but a pile of cash can take you far in life.

Claire overheard part of my conversation with James about our plans for the following day. We fought about it for a while. Then we had another angry, practically feral go at each other.

She demanded I explain the context of what she overheard. I responded by making her come twice while I buried my cock in her pussy and sunk my teeth into the back of her neck, holding her in place like a fucking animal while I pounded into her.

The plan for her to return to work the next day was still in place, and the tension between us was palpable as she kissed me goodbye. Victor stayed with Claire while James and I drove over to the restaurant in the middle of the financial district. When we arrived at the restaurant, the hostess blew us off, but her eyes widened when I flashed her a thousand dollars cash, and sure enough, we had a table beside Mr. Moore's.

"You sure about this?" James glanced around the room nervously. Fine linen wrapped the tables and walls painted in a dull salmon surrounded us. I paid him a lot of fucking money, but he still was not entirely comfortable in places such as this. Hell, I wasn't either. Spending a few grand on lunch seemed silly, no matter how much money you had.

James' gaze narrowed on the suited and armed men mixed up among the waitstaff. They were employed by the restaurant, and surveyed the room with an intensity that went beyond the standard security guard. A necessary precaution in a place that served politicians and royalty.

"Of course I'm sure. We're going to eat an absurdly expensive lunch, and if I run into an old friend, who's to think anything nefarious? I'm certainly not." I picked up a piece of bread and started buttering it.

"Your track record for convincing people of your bullshit *is* astounding," he rolled his eyes, "but Dan won't buy that."

"No, he won't, but that is not the—" I stopped mid-sentence, noticing Daniel and two enormous suited men entering the restaurant. The two of them had to be brothers. Their appearances were so alike: dark hair, pale skin, dark eyes, and piles of overgrown muscle. "We won't need to wait long to see how this works out," I told James as I inclined my head toward the door.

James' eyes flicked to the entrance and back quickly. "Officially too late to change your mind." He breathed out a sigh as he ran his hands down his lapels.

"Was that ever a real possibility?"

"No, I guess not."

The server came over at that moment and took our drink orders. She gave James a series of long flirty glances he didn't seem to notice with his head stuffed with Emma. We never mentioned it, but both of our relationships being on the rocks gave us an added sense of camaraderie. I was certain both situations would work out eventually.

By the time the server left the table, Daniel and his men had settled in at two separate tables. His men sat near enough to him to intervene if someone approached, yet far enough for

Dan to ignore them while he ate. His security looked over the room, gazing at us for a hair longer than everyone else.

"How do you want to play this, Mason?" James' voice ticked up an octave.

"Innocently, of course." He narrowed his eyes at me, and I rolled mine at him. "Just talk like a normal fucking person, James, and when he notices us, he notices us."

"You think he remembers me?" James' cheeks turned pink, and I cracked a smile at the question and the corresponding memory.

"Yes, I am sure he remembers you stealing his wallet and punching him out. He may or may not still be angry about that."

One of Dan's men had been eyeing me since they sat down, though I doubted he recognized me. It was likely the fact he *didn't*, coupled with how near to Mr. Moore I sat, that had him on edge. I met his stare and when I didn't drop my eyes in submission he murmured something to the moose beside him.

Both of their heads tilted slightly toward us now, and rather than break eye contact, I stared back. One of them pulled away from the table and leaned in to murmur something in Daniel's ear. He turned toward us with an amused expression on his face but stopped cold when I caught his eye.

"Mason," the word popped out of his stunned mouth with no thought.

"Daniel," I answered, trying to infuse my voice with some of the genuine surprise he felt.

"And Jimmy," he continued, sliding his eyes over to the man seated across from me. "What a pleasant surprise."

"That it is," I answered before James had to come up with something. Catching him without a comeback was a rare occasion. "Care to join us?"

"I wouldn't want to intrude, but it's been wonderful to see you again." Which meant no, but politely.

"It wouldn't be an intrusion at all, and you are eating alone, aren't you?" His head tipped toward his guards, but we both knew they weren't companions of his. "You know what?" I continued, "I'll be the one to intrude, old friend." I stood up and dragged my chair to Daniel's table. "Come on, Jimmy."

"Shouldn't Jimmy sit with Gerhart and Dimitri?" He gestured toward the staff table.

"We don't stand on formality, do we, James?"

"Not that I've seen," James chuckled.

"Gerhart, Dimitri, join us." I smiled at the two men, who eyed me like they were looking forward to peeling off my skin.

Daniel gave them a slight nod. There really wasn't enough room at the table for three, let alone five, but the two brutes pushed their table together with ours.

"What brings you here this afternoon, Mason?" Daniel asked as soon as everyone settled. He picked up a piece of bread and buttered it. Thick silver shocks streaked through his jet-black hair. He was graying at thirteen, so it shouldn't surprise me, but it was intense to see his youthful face beneath the contrasting shades.

"A pleasant lunch and the reservation I made six months ago," I smiled easily as a runner placed my drink on the table, and I took a sip.

"I'm surprised you didn't bring your girlfriend, seeing as you waited so long to eat here."

My drink caught in my throat at the mention of Claire, but I choked it down before anyone noticed. "The reservation was for two, and I had already invited Jimmy. Wouldn't want him getting jealous."

"No, you wouldn't want that," his dry tone made me laugh, and even Dan cracked a small reluctant smile.

"How have you been, Dan? What's it been? A decade?"

"About that long. Things are going well for me, though, I can't say I've heard the same for you."

James' eyebrow lifted in surprise at Dan coming right out with that.

"Funny, the things people say..." I drifted off as I took another sip.

The two black-haired fucks with him smiled at one another, thinking I was denying those rumors.

"Francis Santini, Charles Gains; you've been a busy boy," Daniel commented as I read through my menu.

"Do you know what you want already?" I asked him.

"The chef prepares something especially for me when I come in. I can tell them we'll be two more if you like," there was a taunting edge to his smooth tone. "Four I suppose," his eyes flicked toward his own men.

"Oh no, I wouldn't dream of interrupting your meal more than I have. You know what you want, Jimmy?"

"Steak."

"Figures," I answered him. "Oh, Daniel, I wasn't talking about the rumors about me. As you know, most of those are true; the ones about you, I'm not so sure."

The three of them glanced back and forth between us for a moment. "What rumors?" one of his men spoke, surprising me with his thick eastern European accent.

Daniel waved him off, and he dutifully shut his mouth and sat back.

"Don't worry, Daniel. I'm not the type to share meaningless conjecture."

"Of course you're not," he agreed.

The server returned and took our orders. There were several minutes of strained conversation where James and I pretended to be completely at ease.

"How's the architecture business, Dan? I visited two of your buildings, and they're inspired."

"Seeing my designs come to fruition has been extraordinarily fulfilling," he agreed with a charismatic smile,

"How's practicing *law*?" he tested the word like it didn't quite fit.

"Not bad, but probably much less fulfilling." I winked at him, and our meals arrived together. We dug into the food, which was incredible, and James and I kept chatting away about nothing and everything, making little jabs at Daniel about the rumors.

"It was brave of you to come here today," Daniel told me as he finished up his meal and patted his lips with a cloth. "Brave, but fucking stupid. You are a single misstep away from a bullet in your head, courtesy of your own father. If I were you, I'd run away quietly, and not poke the bear." The men at his sides smiled, pleased with this turn of events. "Lunch is on me, by the way. I'll be letting your father know we spoke. He dropped a fat stack of cash on the table and the three of them stood.

"Thanks for lunch, Danny. It was nice seeing you." I smiled up at him.

"Sorry about punching you in the face," Jimmy snarked.

"Are you sorry about stealing my wallet too?" Dan cocked his head to the side.

James mimicked the movement. "Not particularly, but I didn't need to punch you. It was easy enough to rob you without that too."

"Things change, Jimmy. Best you remember that. You too, Mason."

He fixed the lapels of his jacket, and the three of them left the restaurant. I stacked the bills, straightening them out and counting to make sure it was enough. At the bottom of the pile was a small handwritten note, barely legible, scribbled as it was.

Your office, tomorrow at noon.

Twelve

Claire

T he outfit wasn't the same, but the black dress and red sweater were damn close to the skirt and blouse I wore the day after Mason and I started talking, and then again when I quit the office and told "Tyler" off. I'd been imagining how it would feel to wear them for days, and spent a lot of time speculating about that office and all the ways things could have gone differently.

The original version of the ensemble cost me only twenty dollars and came from a clearance rack at a close-out store. I felt like Cinderella. Magic had elevated my entire paltry life into something grand, though I couldn't shake the feeling that, like the fairytale, it came with an expiration date attached. I loved that Mason wanted to take care of me, but part of me rebelled against his efforts. *Trusting someone else to take care of you isn't safe.*

I stood in "my" gargantuan walk-in closet; the outfit lay over the incredibly chic champagne-colored settee. I sat beside the clothing, fingering the buttons of the cashmere sweater. I opened them carefully, almost reverentially.

The true red flattered my complexion perfectly. The black dress hugged the swell of my hips and clung to my thighs in a way that was professional but sexy. I pulled my hair up into a neat bun and applied a touch of makeup.

I gazed at myself in the mirror when I was done, trying to make sense of how I could appear so healthy while still aching and raw. I looked good, possibly even great. That couldn't be right. Something clawing and deadly had settled into my soul. Its poison needed to have a visible effect.

I left the bedroom with my head held high, despite the nearly constant urge to collapse on myself and wither away to nothing. Lawrence had the car warmed up and humming. I was uncomfortable with people waiting on me all the time, but in this one instance, I didn't mind. Who wanted to be cold first thing in the morning?

"Morning Lawrence, morning Vick," I said amiably as I climbed in. Lawrence said good morning, but Vick ignored me. I assumed his surly mood had something to do with the added stress my and Mason's fighting caused him. I felt bad about making his life harder, but it wasn't my fault he worked for a control freak. If he didn't like his boss' attitude, he could try a career that didn't involve crime.

"What are your plans for the day, Vick?" I tried to force some pleasantries out of him to keep him from spoiling my mood.

"Same as always." His tone wasn't necessarily rude, but cool and dismissive.

A single eyebrow inched up my forehead as I asked, "Which is?"

"Whatever Mason says." He stared me in the eyes without blinking as he spoke. "He *is* the boss and a pretty smart guy who's only looking out for your safety. Try listening to the man some time."

I rolled my eyes and turned my back on him to stare out the window. I had more than enough of trying to be friendly. "Go ahead and hold your breath on that one, Victor."

"You dislike having me around enough to want me dead?" his deadpan tone made the joke all the funnier.

I giggled, shooting him a smile, despite how irritated I was with his attitude. "If I wanted you dead, you would be." I made a finger gun motion at him and a little sound effect.

He huffed out a nervous laugh. "God, you have no idea how true that is." I smiled nervously, afraid to ask for and hear the confirmation of what I feared. I knew Mason would kill for me, he *had* killed for me, but he wouldn't kill according to my whims, would he?

As soon as we pulled up in front of the library, I jumped out of the SUV. If Mason wanted to keep me out of work for my safety, I would have stayed gladly. If he thought his father would make his move while I was there, or Gavin was going to use my position against me, I wouldn't argue. I would have stayed home if it was the right thing to do, but I wouldn't put my life on hold because he didn't believe in me.

Finding the front door open surprised me despite making sense; the place had been opening without me for months now. That's what I repeated to myself as an uncomfortable sensation flipped in my stomach. I pushed the thick wood back. A wicked cocktail of excitement and foreboding made me lightheaded.

The smell of the books leaked out, creeping across my face like a lover's caress and a phantom's touch. The paradoxical moment nearly overwhelmed me and sent me running home. I focused through the panic and pushed myself forward. My heels clicked on the tile as I walked under the skylight and a swell of memories crashed into me. Both good and bad, from meeting Mason to Charles following me in the early hours of the morning, and a hundred more.

It took me longer than normal to reach the library's central space. We weren't open yet, so the place was empty except for Emma, who stood behind the circulation desk. She hadn't looked up yet, but even from this distance, I could see the dark circles under her eyes. More than circles. They were bags, puffy and hot looking. Had she been up all night crying? She had pulled her light red hair into a tight ponytail, unlike any of her usual styles. Even her outfit was drab. Her hair was longer than the last time I'd seen her and impeccably straightened. The little lines of stress around her eyes gave credence to the assumption that she was up late crying.

"Hey, Emma," I walked up to the circulation desk, hoping not to sneak up on her.

I startled her anyway. She flinched the tiniest bit before smiling at me. "Hey, Claire. I'm so glad to see you. How are you?" her normally sultry voice sounded raspier than I remembered, but the words felt genuine.

"I'm alright, happy to be back." I imagined a daytime TV host stepping forward to announce *that was a lie*.

"We're happy to have you. Any big plans for your first day back?"

"I'll probably spend most of it at my desk." I shrugged, not very excited. "There's a lot for me to catch up on, and I can't lift anything heavy for a while." The prospect of not being useful enough terrified me, and for a moment, I forgot I was in the position of authority in this scenario.

"No one will mind helping with the heavy lifting. I am so happy to have you back." She placed her hand briefly on my arm but looked back down at the pile of books she was checking in. Her attempt to close the conversation was sudden and obvious.

"Me too," I agreed, waiting a moment for her to say something else or even look at me. "Is something wrong?" The two of us didn't talk much while I was out, but I wasn't in a sociable mood. She texted me a few times, and I thought

I texted her back at least twice. Was she put out I didn't encourage a conversation?

"Just guy stuff," she assured me with a wave of her hand.

I didn't quite believe her, but I let it go. "Okay, I'll see you in a little while. Tell me if you need anything."

"Mhm," she hummed, keeping her eyes trained on her work.

I left her to it and went to see my office for the first time since I ran from the room, believing Mason was my stalker. I rolled my eyes at myself, but cold, stark fear quickly replaced the exasperation. I kept my eyes pointedly away from the hall that led to that locked basement door. That mystery didn't haunt my dreams any longer, but I still yearned for the truth. However, forcing my way down there was not going to help anyone today. My footsteps grew louder, quicker, echoing the pace of my heart as I tried to reach the sanctuary of my own space. I needed to slow down, calm down.

I was a hair away from running, which was not only against library rules but highly unusual. I forced myself to walk the rest of the way calmly, even though I couldn't catch my breath. My numb hands shook as I pulled the key out of my pocket and worked it into the lock. The door gave easily. Whoever had been in here last didn't bother to lock up.

I closed it behind me as gently as I could manage before leaning against the door and sinking to my butt.

Deprived of air, my lungs burned for oxygen. A separate living entity was trying to tear its way free from my stomach, and I couldn't tell what hurt worse, the bullet wound or that thing inside of me. I looked around the office, trying to ground myself. Panic attack, I reminded myself. There's nothing inside of me.

So much was the same, but little things were in different places and it smelled wrong, like leftover cologne and food. My box of stuff sat on the desk, packed up and waiting for me. The comforting words took on another meaning. *There's nothing inside of you; you are hollow. If it weren't for you and Mason, the police could have solved those girls' murders. You're in love with a killer. You're empty. You should have died too.*

The last thought was enough to startle me out of the tumble of crashing thoughts. Dying was one thing I didn't want. As awful as everything was right now, I didn't want to die. I had to be full of something, much like the trash overflowing against my desk.

Finally, it occurred to me that someone worked here regularly. You didn't accumulate that in a day. I took in the little details all around me as I forced myself to breathe. A brief knock on the door startled me to my feet. "Yes," my voice squeaked and ripped through several octaves.

"Claire, I need your signature on a few things." Emma's voice set me further on edge. The slight calm I managed evaporated while secrets and lies buzzed around me like pressure in my ears.

"Just a second," I kept my voice low, hoping she wouldn't figure out I was right on the other side. I tiptoed over to my desk, grimacing at all the little bits of someone else left in my space—*nothing in this world is truly mine.*

I sighed aloud, knowing that the thought was dramatic and unfair. Someone had to do my job, but couldn't they have worked somewhere else?

"Come in," I told Emma, well past what might have been a normal amount of time, but I got settled into my desk and plastered a calm enough expression on my face.

She walked in, looking more stressed and exhausted than before. "This should only take a second." She passed me the papers with a tight smile.

I took them from her and flipped through the pages, pretending not to care much about my next words. "Emma, who's been working here?"

"Oh, uh, Gavin mostly." A hint of her perfume remained in here as well. I made the connection now that she stood next to me, a gingery spice that lingered on my things.

"Mostly?"

"Yeah, I've done a little work here when I needed to, but Gavin has been here almost every day." She shifted from foot to foot.

"Oh," I flipped through the paperwork. "Thanks, Emma. I've got these from here."

"Sure," she turned to leave.

"Emma, do you mind taking the trash out? The bag is too heavy for me to lift right now." I glanced at the bottles and food wrappers, wondering how many of them were hers and how many were Gavin's. There was no reason for her to use my office. I could understand Gavin using it as my boss, but not her. A kernel of resentment popped inside of me.

"Of course." She pulled the bag out and fastened the ties off, leaving without another word. Taking out the trash didn't upset her, and she didn't even seem upset I was back. If I had to guess, I'd say *Emma was scared*.

I had another panic attack right before lunch when I opened the drawer I kept the creepy notes in. A scream threatened to strangle me when I saw them sitting exactly where I left them. I was certain someone would have gotten rid of them. I put the papers in my purse, determined to burn them as soon as possible.

The ordeal soured my stomach and made me completely unwilling to eat. Despite that, a delivery man showed up with a slice of pizza and a salad. I wondered which of the overbearing men responsible for my protection ordered it. Mason was too angry to take the credit if he did, but Vick was just as likely a candidate.

Since Charles shot me, I spent an incredible amount of time with James and Vick. I liked them both, but something about Vick's quiet, grumpy demeanor endeared him to me. I didn't mind that he was quiet, but when he was angry, it was disconcerting.

I ate a few bites of the pizza and a few of the salad only because of my guilt. My doctor was very clear that my body needed substantive meals to heal properly. The pain from the injury had been enough that it was hard to keep an appetite. I no longer needed the painkillers my doctor prescribed, but they compounded the problem when I did.

I ate as much as possible before I left the rest on my desk, hoping I would get hungry enough to eat some more. I didn't.

At about three o'clock, I unburied myself from the mountain of administrative tasks I still had to finish. I hadn't seen Gavin all day, for which I was grateful. Coming back here was enough of a task without having to face him immediately. He and I exchanged a few emails that were all professional and library-focused. The normalcy made me twitchy, but the nicety was preferable to the alternatives.

A lot of things were falling apart in my absence; the most upsetting of which was the community programs. The children's section featured a weekly story time, which Gavin indefinitely postponed prior to my return. I reinstated the program and secured a popular local children's entertainer for the week before Christmas. The kids would love it, and I planned a full event with treats, games, and prizes. I'd made real headway on the organizing when I realized Gavin had been telling the truth; they needed me here.

Doing a good job on something that mattered filled me with satisfaction. I felt buoyant, lighter than I had in months. Something I did was going to make kids happy and bring them joy. I hadn't thought of murder victims in hours, and for a bit, I felt like the old me. I left my office, determined to tell Emma I was leaving for the day, prepared to chase that high as far as possible.

If I called Mason before he got too deeply involved in bullshit, he would come home and fuck me. As mad as he was about my returning to work, he had a hard time denying me when I begged, a weakness I planned to exploit fully. It'd been so long since we flirted like we used to. I missed the intimacy of the dirty messages we used to send one another. I considered snapping a picture of my pussy and sending it to him.

A devilish smile spread across my face as I thought, *what the fuck,* and ran to the bathroom to show him the goods. I snapped the picture and sent it off, hoping that the silly gesture might act as an olive branch. *Trust me, I showed you my pussy. Wonderful logic, Claire.*

I washed my hands and left the bathroom. I peeked around the atrium quickly, surprised when I didn't see anyone other than a few patrons perusing the racks and looking over the bulletin board. Memories of finding the note filled my mind, stealing my breath and making my hands shake. *Not now. Ride the high while you can.* I turned away, taking a deep breath.

I walked down the corridors, peaking between the shelves until I finally heard Emma's voice. She tucked herself into the area where Gavin told me the teens like to have sex.

"James, please stop doing this." Tears hung in her voice, and once again, my heart stopped. I paused a row back from where she stood and slid behind the shelves so she wouldn't notice me.

For the last few weeks, I had been having more vivid memories of the things that happened in the days leading up to the shooting. At first, everything was a blur of color and pain, most of it indecipherable. The details pulled themselves together eventually, and I remembered the night at the club I saw Emma dancing with a man. There was tension between them, intense and heated. I didn't recognize him then, but in hindsight, the picture fit.

"I don't care if you love me." The lie fell harshly from her lips, and if I recognized it, so would he.

"I can't. This shit is too fucked up. It was all fun and games when you were just mysterious and possibly dangerous." I faintly made out the sound of an angry voice buzzing from the other end. Perhaps he was calling her a hypocrite or telling her there was no way to choose who you love.

"I can't be in love with a killer. Your whole lifestyle. I can't do this. You shouldn't try to make me just because you think you love me, you selfish fuck." She listened for a moment, "You're ruining my life." She ended the call, and I waited a few moments while she quietly sobbed.

I couldn't turn around the way I came and run despite how much I wanted to. I tabulated how much time it would take to seem like I wasn't eavesdropping before saying *fuck it* and stepping out from my hiding spot. "Hey, Emma? Are you okay?"

She jumped a little and sniffed, quickly wiping the tears with the backs of her hands. "Oh, Claire, hi, I'm sorry. Yeah, I'm fine."

I opened my mouth to tell her I was leaving early, but my suspicions choked the words off. "I need you to do something for me up front."

"Of course."

I walked straight back to my office, assuming she would follow me. I closed the door behind the two of us. "Emma, what's going on here?"

"What do you mean? It's your first day back and you have a lot to catch up on but—"

I turned to face her, giving her the icy glare I'd been staring at in the mirror for months now. I knew better than anyone how unnerving it was. "Who's James, Emma?"

Her fair skin went impossibly whiter. "He's uh, well, he's nobody." She picked at an invisible lint on her skirt, refusing to meet my gaze.

"Is he the guy you were with that night at the club?" I did not know James was one of the men in my apartment after Charles broke in, but he confirmed that when I asked him weeks later. I wondered what he told Emma that night when he left her on the dancefloor.

She stared at me, her eyes and mouth round in shock. "He's, well, I..."

"Attractive guy, black hair, whiskey-colored eyes, and a brother named Vick?" Her eyes went wide with what looked like love, heartache, and desperation, and I truly pitied her if she thought she could escape him. Not when her every denial sounded like she was begging for him too.

"Yeah, that sounds a lot like him," she confessed so quietly. "Do you, do you know?" her whispered words were barely audible.

"Do I know what, Emma?" I was only giving her half my attention, using the rest to run over every interaction of ours that I remembered, to discover where the lies and manipulations hid.

"Who Mason is..." her voice trailed off with a leading lilt, wanting me to show my hand before she decided how much of her own to reveal.

"The better question is, did you know who he was all this time?" I tried to keep calm, but the anger in my voice shone through.

She shifted from foot to foot as tears gathered in the corners of her eyes. "Yes, but it's not what you think." She held up her hands in a pleading gesture.

"So, you stood over my shoulder while I tried to figure out who he was, encouraging me and chatting with me, knowing the truth the whole time."

"No, I didn't. I promise, not until that night we went to the club together. That's when I made the connection between the face and the name."

"Do you know what's going on here?" I gestured around the room, indicating the library and all the nefariously tangled webs winding through the place, webs I was still scarcely aware of. "Did you know when I first started?"

She bit her lip. "I'm really sorry, Claire. So sorry, but I can't—"

"Are you working for him, for-for Gavin?" I was about to ask about someone else but changed my mind at the last moment.

Her eyes darkened like she knew exactly what I was thinking. "Of course not. I would never work for *them*. I'm trying not to get killed. Please, Claire. Let me explain, but not here."

"No, you can go." I turned away from her and sat at my desk, pointedly waiting for her to leave.

"He told me I can't. James. Mason. Mason and James both told me I couldn't say a word to you. I'm so sorry." Tears streamed down her cheeks as she spoke, and the exhaustion she carried all day felt crushing. She turned around and left the room, her soft sniffles faded as the door slammed. I dropped my face into my hands, exhausted in ways I'd never imagined possible.

A text came in at that moment, and I remember the impulsive picture I sent to Mason earlier.

I'm going to suck your clit until you cry.

Thirteen

Mason

James sat in one chair with his feet up on the other as he flipped through a magazine. My fingers flew across the keys as I worked through the issues I had with my remaining clients. James didn't need to be in my office for this meeting, but he insisted, and I knew he was nervous about leaving me alone with Daniel.

"You *can* actually be useful for something other than taking up space. Look out the window and you'll see an entire city full of criminals needing a shaking down." I told him pointedly, hoping to spur his ass out of my chair. He rolled his eyes and kept flipping. If anyone was going to sit around and do fuck all here, it should be me.

He waved toward the laptop set up in the corner, "Casey did the hard work setting up the program. That thing is scanning records faster than I ever could. We just wait for it to beep."

"Which gives you an opportunity to do other things besides hovering like a mother bird. Dan isn't planning on killing me today."

"I'm not a mother bird, hardly even matronly, and you *hope* Dan is not planning to kill you today." James not being matronly was an understatement. Not only was he a killer, but he was also a fucking asshole.

"What use are you to me then? I can listen for a bell."

"Yes, but I also hover like a mother bird. You're much too important to hover and listen for a bell yourself, Mason." The asshole flipped the page. "Do you ever buy new magazines? This shit is three years old."

"I'll hop right on that." I continued reading through the deposition for my oldest client. They would prove complicated to shuffle off to someone else.

The intercom ringtone played on the desk phone. "Yes,"

"Daniel Moore and two associates are here to see you." My new receptionist, Stephanie, said.

"Tell them to wait, please," I answered before ending the call. I snickered to myself as I set aside the paperwork and pulled up a game on my phone.

"Are you playing one of those Quest of Whatever apps?" James laughed.

"Important business," I assured him as I shot at the invading forces of an orc army. After I finished my orc massacre, I picked up the phone, immediately reaching Stephanie. "Tell Daniel to come on through but leave his associates behind."

I heard a smile in her voice, "Of course, sir."

"James, act like you're not an asshole for a few minutes, yeah?" I kicked my head toward him and his bullshit.

He closed the magazine and moved to a more appropriate chair for a meeting, sitting up and appearing surprisingly professional considering how relaxed he'd been a moment before.

My office door opened and Stephanie walked through with a cup of coffee in her hand. Daniel followed behind her, looking over the room with his suspicious blue eyes. Stephanie placed the mug on the desk. "Mr. Moore, please let me know if you change your mind about some refreshments, and James, anything you might—"

"James can get his own drinks, Stephanie." I interrupted her.

She blushed ever so slightly. "Of course, sir." Daniel nodded at Stephanie before his eyes drifted over to James, and his expression hardened. Stephanie smiled at us, accepted my thanks, and left the room. She had a similar position in a securities company and understood the demands of the job. She would be more likely to knock you on your ass than let you in without my say-so and had otherwise worked out wonderfully.

It was a shame to let Katie go. She was mostly a great secretary, which is why I gave her an excellent reference and a whopping severance. She wasn't even angry with me when she saw the check, and I knew for a fact she had found a comparable job.

"Why are my men outside if Jimmy is sitting right there?" Daniel asked with an unmistakable air of irritation.

I wondered if he worried about me making a move against him or if he just didn't like to be separated from his bodyguards. "I don't trust your men," I told him truthfully.

"I don't trust Jimmy." he retorted.

"He won't punch or rob you, Daniel. No need to fret."

"You're fucking hilarious, Mason." He rolled his eyes as he stomped across the office and plopped into a seat opposite James, staring him down for a moment. "What the fuck was that yesterday?"

He glanced around the room, looking for cameras, most likely. "There are cameras, no mics," I told him as I flipped through some papers on my desk. "You're being paranoid."

"You should be more fucking paranoid."

"So what I'm hearing is true then?" I pushed up out of my chair and sauntered over to the one opposite them. I couldn't help the self-satisfied energy I exuded. "Things are a little tense for you lately?"

"Hearing, what a funny way to say tortured out of Francis Santini," he grumbled the words like a petulant child, trying his best to dampen my mood.

"Had the two of you become good friends in my absence? Perhaps I should have sent you some flowers or offered my condolences?"

"Good to know you're as much of a prick as ever," he made an annoyed sound in the back of his throat. "You should understand me well enough to realize I don't fuck with his side of the business. Anything Francis touched was grimy. I wouldn't care about the old piece of shit except he gave you my name, and now you're following me."

"You're definitely paranoid if you think running into each other at lunch means I'm following you."

"What would you call it?"

"Absurdly expensive salmon and an opportunity to catch up with an old friend? But, I'm curious where you heard that nonsense about Francis and myself?" My skin prickled. There were five people in the warehouse that night: Francis, James, Vick, Casey, and me. Francis didn't tell anyone anything after James cut out his tongue and he was dead soon after.

"They're both assumptions, Mason. You killed him and showed up beside my table at a restaurant you *did not* have a reservation for when I haven't seen you in over a decade." His posture was tense.

"Maybe I wanted to talk to you about architecture. Your secretary told me you wouldn't speak to new clients. How impressive of you." James rolled his eyes at me, but Daniel didn't see it.

"Looking to build a skyscraper, are you? Maybe a fucking bridge?" He threw his arms up in the air. "Always an ego trip with you, man, but naming a bridge after yourself is a step too far."

"You don't have the faintest clue how far my ego extends. You'd be quite lucky if the commissioning of a bridge satisfied me."

"And what name would hang on the sign, Mason? Dubois or Sharp?"

"Elizabeth Dubois is the name I'll choose for my ego trip. Do you remember her?" I barked back at him.

"Are you really asking me if I remember your mother? We're starting whatever this is off with bullshit, perfect." A sincere look of grief quickly entered and left his gaze.

"My father admitted he killed her. I don't know if you had any part in his confession, but Officer Grant showed up at my office a few months back and brought me a handwritten letter from dear old *dad*." I tried to keep my voice even, but the memory filled me with rage.

"Officer Grant washed up on the banks of the river three counties over."

I shrugged my shoulders, unsurprised they found him. I didn't weigh him down or anything. "What of it?"

"Just seems like a lot of people around you are winding up dead, not comforting for someone sitting so close." He turned toward James with a nasty smile. "Might want to crawl out of his asshole before you end up dead, Jimmy."

"Fuck you too, Dan," he answered with an easy smile.

"Are you avoiding the question, Dan? Did you know he confessed to killing my mother?"

"*No*, I didn't," he sounded uncertain, like he didn't quite believe what I was telling him.

"I would have shown you the letter, but I tossed it in the river along with the messenger." I flashed him a grin.

Dan shook his head in disbelief while James snickered. "You're a fucking curse, man. Showing up in public next to me was not okay. You're going to get me killed."

"You were going to wind up dead anyway." I brushed off his concerns. "Besides, why would you come here with your guards if you were so worried about being seen with me?"

He shrugged. "I was planning to be unpleasant."

"I *told* you!" James exclaimed.

"Unpleasant doesn't mean murderous, James."

Dan's face scrunched up in disbelief. "Come on, Jimmy, I wouldn't come *here* to kill him."

James gave him an appraising look that told me he was losing his patience with this game.

"That is what I heard from Francis Santini and why I came to find you." I interrupted their bickering, hoping to prevent an escalation between them. Despite my positive attitude about everything, this could easily turn into bloodshed, and Stephanie was an entirely innocent bystander.

"Oh, really?" he mocked, "What did I do to earn a bullet?"

"I was hoping you would tell me because while Francis gave you up, he didn't say why. But there are others who've heard about your loss of favor, and they also simply don't know why." He hid his mild look of surprise. "Did you think he was the only one? You're high up in his organization. People are interested in such a long fall. They're talking about it."

He let out a deep breath, his fingers tapped on his knee, and his eyes darted around the room again.

"Cameras, but no mics," I repeated.

"You need to stay away from me, stop talking about me, and shut the fuck up about what you hear." His hands were in his salt and pepper hair, and with it sticking up, he looked like a mad scientist.

"Why would I do that?"

"I'm hoping because you're smart, though I'm doubting my memories of you at this point because, clearly, you're a fucking moron."

I put my hand to my heart and opened my mouth as if his words wounded me. "Come on, Dan, you must have done something big if you're this testy about it."

"This is a waste of my time," he muttered.

"Out with it, Dan. Not like telling me will hurt you. I won't know more than my father already does."

"Will it convince you to fuck off and leave me alone? To give me a *chance* of surviving?"

"It might."

He sighed, utterly frustrated with me and his situation. "Delano Agrest."

"The man who engineered my father's imprisonment, and cost him his entire laundering system?"

"The same," he mumbled.

"What about him?" There were a lot of things I considered options for his crimes against my father, but Delano Agrest was not on the list.

"We had a brief conversation. He contacted me. I took the call, not realizing he was the chair of the city council over there. I got off the phone real quick when I realized who I was speaking to, but it circled back to David, and now..."

"It doesn't matter if you said anything. He doesn't trust you." I finished for him.

"You know how he is when he doesn't trust you."

"I do," I agreed grimly. "It's shocking you're not dead already."

"I don't have an explanation for that." He swallowed like he was afraid that meant something especially awful for him.

"You carry a lot of pull amongst his men, don't you?"

"Some, of course. What are you getting at? It's not as if people liking me will prevent my death."

"No, *they* couldn't do anything to prevent your death." I took a sip of the now room-temperature coffee Stephanie brought for me. "Now, back to the reason I was looking for you."

"You said it was to warn me your father was considering my end," he interrupted. That reminded me of the old Daniel, he always assumed he knew everything. And he was right most of the time—smart fucking bastard—but not always.

"I didn't. I was looking for you because I want you to work with me." His eyebrows shot up in surprise but immediately settled. "It's no secret I want my father dead."

"He knows, you know, guys on the streets in neighboring cities know," his input was already helpful. I wasn't aware word had spread *that* far.

"You may not want him dead, but you need him dead if you enjoy living."

"Living's okay," he shrugged. "What's your plan, Mason? I'll call your pops and put in my two weeks' notice, switch everything over lickity-split. There's a new boss in town." Half his mouth kicked up in a smile.

"That's a ridiculous plan." I deadpanned. "I think a better one would be for you to give me your loyalty and your influence, and I kill my father. Once he's dead, you can have part of his territory, *and* you'll live to a ripe old age. You could even go back to school and become an engineer."

He smiled at me, and while it was tired, it felt genuine. "I like architecture."

"But do you love it?"

"No, I don't." The wistfulness in his gaze kindled the hope my old friend may remain inside this syndicate entrenched stranger.

"You can have a secure life, Daniel. One you love, not one you were told was for you. You may act like you believe the rumors about me, but you understand better than anyone what I'm capable of. I will do this, and you would be better off being on my side when I do it. But forget that for now. Let's keep things casual. All I need is your assurance. If I can trust you not to repeat our conversations, I'll give you mine; I'll keep you alive."

"You can trust me not to repeat this, Mason, but I sincerely doubt your ability to keep me alive."

"I'll just have to prove you wrong."

"Let's hope I live long enough for that. I'll see you around, but not by surprise." He stood, and we shook hands before he left the office without a word or glance in James' direction.

"How do you think that went, boss?"

"Not sure, James. Better than bad, if I had to guess." I sat there for a while wondering if I could trust my judgment where Daniel was concerned or if my desire to have my old friend back clouded my opinion of things. I was all too familiar with that desire.

Now that Dan and his men had left, James did too; he had to take care of the business I teased him for ignoring. He and his brother were more than just soldiers, and I counted myself lucky to call them my friends. Especially considering they had every right to side against me.

Several Months Earlier

I hovered outside the coffee shop I'd taken Claire to earlier that day. Guilt swamped me over how I left things with her and how angry she must be. I couldn't help it. When I heard what the barista said about a man watching Claire, I lost it.

I chose this place for the meeting I arranged because of that. I told her if she saw him, to point him out to me. While my intensity scared her, she nodded in agreement. Her expression betrayed how afraid for Claire she was; hopefully, because of the person following her and not me.

What I didn't know was whether this man was one of my father's men or someone whose relative I'd killed. Either option was fully plausible, and neither boded well for Claire or me. There were other offshoot options. Sometimes people thought they could use me as a bargaining chip against my father. It never worked out well for them. I wasn't an easy target, and my father couldn't give a fuck.

I needed help from people with connections in the syndicate who could both call in favors and maneuver the system. That was the only way I had to keep her safe: find out who posed the threat and then eliminate the risk, whether that was through force or negotiation. Sadly, I was in no position to do that on my own.

There were only two people involved with the syndicate I had any shot at all with, James and Victor. I tried an old number, and by some odd stroke of luck, Vick answered. He was as shocked to hear from me as I was that he still had the number.

We hadn't left things on good terms. I made him and James a lot of promises I didn't deliver on, and they thought very little of me after I walked away to try and have a normal life. I abandoned them, and there was a good chance they wouldn't help me now.

I took a deep breath and stepped inside, finding James sitting at a table with a muffin and a coffee and Victor leaned up against the counter flirting with the girl I spoke to earlier. Victor's face was turned away from me, but his size gave him away.

I cocked my head to the side in question. That didn't fit with my memory of Victor. He usually got his girls by sitting there looking handsome and scary; they approached him.

James smirked at my response, "Guess she's special."

I walked over to his table and sat down. "It's nice to see you, James." Last I'd seen him, he'd been a scrawny sixteen-year-old, but he'd grown into himself. All hints of childishness had disappeared from his face, and even his suit showed how *James*—not Jimmy—liked people to see him.

"Why don't you get yourself a coffee and something to eat before we chat?" he offered, but the suggestion was a test of the power dynamic.

"I'm good."

He smiled, but it wasn't a cheerful expression. "How have you been?"

"Which would make you happier, that everything has been wonderful or that my life is shit?"

"Haven't decided yet."

"Let's wait for Victor," I told him, and he leaned back in his seat. His gaze roamed over me. I met his eyes and held them for a moment.

"Okay," he broke our eye contact and ate some of his food.

Victor finished flirting with the girl and came to sit at the table. "What are we doing here, Mason?" Vick asked the moment his ass touched the chair.

"We're having a chat." He hated when I played dumb, or played any games, really. Vick was naturally so direct.

"About what? It's been a real long time for this to be a friendly visit." He wasn't wrong.

"This is a friendly visit in most regards. Well, it is on my part. The two of you are free to decide how you feel about it, but it's also business."

"Business how?" James asked, and Victor shot him a dirty look. Clearly, they agreed Vick should take the lead, and as per usual, Jimmy couldn't stick to that. I smiled at the two of them.

"There's reason for me to believe the woman I'm seeing is being followed." I glanced around the coffee shop, grabbing the eye of the barista, who gently shook her head *no*. "She likes to come here, and he's followed her here before."

"There's a reason to believe it's because of you." Vick finished.

"I need help. The two of you are well connected, trusted even."

Vick looked back and forth to make sure no one watched us. "You know exactly why."

I did. After I bailed on them, they were broke, and already in over their heads, out of options for finding their mom other than continuing to work for the syndicate while doing their own digging. "I do, and that's a big part of why I'm here. I need to make a lot of things right."

"Get to the offer, Mason, we're not in the mood for a reunion," James quipped, and I couldn't help but smile. I really missed the two of them.

"I need help with my girlfriend. I need to know who's watching her and why. If my suspicions are correct, I need people behind me. Loyal people that care about you aren't exactly in abundant supply. I am truly sorry for bailing on you guys. I saw a chance for a simpler life and I took it."

"What makes you think we could be that for you? I understand why you want access to our connections, but it's been too many years for you to think you can trust us or that we give a shit." Victor said.

"I know the two of you well. I have for a long time and I don't think the time has changed how much you love your mom." They both exchanged a loaded look, but neither of them spoke. "I will pay the two of you incredibly well, and I will do my best to make good on the promises I made you when we were kids."

"All of that is a bit of an extreme response to someone watching your girl." Victor scoffed. "Maybe he's just a garden variety creepy fuck."

"I don't believe that, and I don't think you do either. The two of you know how bad this is if this person answers to my father, which, I'm certain he does. If not to him, then indirectly through the multitude of enemies he's given me. There's no shortage of people who want me dead.

"I want to keep my syndicate involvement as minimal as possible, but I want my girlfriend safe, and I want my father dead as much as I always have."

They looked back and forth between each other, having another silent conversation. "How much money?" James asked

I threw out a number, and their eyes widened in surprise. "Okay, we're in," James answered, and Vick shot him a glare.

A moment of tense silence passed. "We never blamed you, Mason. If we could have gotten out, we would have too. It's good to see you again." Vick added, and I wasn't sure if it was the cash inspiring his words or how he sincerely felt.

I swallowed hard anyway. "You too, my friend."

There was more conversation after that. A lot of catching up and exchanging of details. They started working for me immediately and things quickly escalated, but at the very least, I was certain of their loyalties. They would never side with the man or the organization that stole their mother. Our friendship was nice, but their devotion to her, and to each other, was something I could count on.

FOURTEEN

Claire

I arrived early enough the next day to be sure I'd be the one to open the library. The desire was petty and presumably meant nothing to anyone else but me. Opening that door was comparable to holding the key to a magical realm full of possibility. I couldn't let this simple joy become another lost and broken thing I once loved.

I believed in magic, not because I'd ever seen proof, but because of books. Mountains of them filled with indefinite worlds and possibilities. Even when life was shitty, I trusted in that magic, that transformative ability.

I never gave all that much attention to the villains, stalkers and killers lurking in dark corners. They made for points of interest and battles to fight. Perhaps I should have considered them more. Weren't some of my favorite books the ones with the deepest shadows?

I disarmed the security system and flipped on some working lights. The enormous overheads stayed off until opening. I reflected on my relationships with Mason and morality as I moved through my morning tasks. He tried his best to tell me the type of man he'd been before we were "official".

The gesture was silly, as we were both far too involved for that to matter. Nothing would have made me walk the other way, but I started believing what he said about himself. If he was as awful as he swore he was, what did that make me? Complicit, or worse? Not that the moral ramifications mattered, because I would still choose him.

Emma arrived about twenty minutes later. I was so consumed in my thoughts that I jumped when she opened the door. "Good morning," she said as she walked in and took off her coat. Bits of snow clung to her hat and shoulders.

"Good morning," I agreed. "It started snowing?"

"Yeah, we might have a white Christmas."

"Maybe," I muttered before briefly discussing the day's tasks, then running away as quickly as I could manage.

Waiting for the opportunity to question Mason or James about what she said was proving difficult, primarily because I hadn't seen either of them. I wanted to give him the benefit of the doubt, but as of recently, I could so easily imagine Mason telling her to lie to me. I could see the exact angle of his lips and the set of his jaw, domineering and irresistible.

I wondered what day Emma went from being a standoffish stranger to someone more knowledgeable about my situation than I was. Confronting Mason wasn't about getting answers so much as him knowing all his efforts to keep shit from me were pointless. Just like his early efforts to warn me off.

He didn't come home the night before, arriving in the early hours of the morning to sleep beside me for an hour before leaving. I, for one, slept like the dead, but my body was still aware of his presence. By the time I woke up again, he was gone.

Seeing Emma added insult to injury, but I had a long list of problems with Mason that didn't involve her, and far higher on my list was the tension between us. The effects of our strained relationship tipped from anger and pain to feral lust without notice. Everything about him made me lightheaded. Swearing Emma to secrecy was comparatively low on the list when I held it up against things such as murder.

Kiana proved much easier to deal with, but I wasn't under the delusion that she might become a friend. She was an excellent employee and a kind person, and that is where I should have left things with Emma. I made this relationship personal, and that was my fault.

Kiana came in about an hour later and asked me if I needed help with anything. I did. There was a lot of catching up to do. She wound up assisting me for the entire morning as we dug through the piles.

"I'm sorry, Claire. We should have done better." Kianna shook her head as she reread the plans for the kids' holiday party.

"Nonsense. You guys did great," I disagreed.

Gavin should have done better as the library is ultimately his responsibility.

I wondered if he'd called Eileen, the old librarian, in my absence. The manner in which they parted ways led me to think not. How much did she know about this place? She warned me about Gavin, but did she understand the full necessity of the warning?

"I'm not sure about that, but I'm glad you're back." She sighed. "This is going to be so much fun. I wish I was a kid."

"Do you want your face painted?" I teased gently.

"Why not?"

I had no suitable answer for that. "We can probably make an exception for you. Actually, I'm planning some games that need adult instruction. Might you want to be that adult?"

"Oh, that would be so much fun!" She clapped her hands, and I couldn't help but smile. At least someone was happy.

"I'm glad I'm back too," I said to myself as I dug into my paperwork. She brought me a sandwich at lunchtime and then went back to her regular tasks. I was much better off with her assistance and glad for her company. She was a nice enough person, and seeing as I hired her, I doubted she was in on the bullshit around here, but who knew?

Shortly after lunch, Gavin came to visit me. I jumped in surprise when I caught him standing in my open doorway. He was as well-groomed as I remembered, only more tired. Perhaps all his fucking scheming was wearing on him.

He smiled at me as he stepped through the door. His suit was a dark gray and well-fitted enough to make him look almost handsome. "Ms. Green, it is so good to see you back. Are you getting on alright?"

The normality stunned me. He had been that way on the phone too. I assumed he wouldn't be able to hold that perfect calm in person. Yet he did. His expression was open and utterly calm. He looked so much like the man who took a chance on me and gave me a shot at my dream, but all that was a lie. That person never existed. David Sharp made the call to hire me.

His level shoulders and relaxed smile lacked all hints of tension. My thoughts spun in circles. "Very much so, thank you, Gavin. What can I do for you?"

He stepped into the room, closing the door behind him. "Nothing really. With you being gone, stopping by every day has become a bit of a habit, and truth be told, I wanted to check on you." He smiled at me with fatherly warmth and a cold sweat broke out on my neck.

"Thanks. I'm good and things are going better than I hoped. I can tell you some details if you like."

"That's great to hear, and no, no details necessary. If you need anything, let me know. I'll be around for the next hour, but then I have a board meeting."

"Of course," I agreed with a forced smile. *The board*. He walked out of my office, leaving the door open as he found it. I took several quick breaths before tears I didn't expect slipped over my cheeks. He was acting so normally. *Am I losing my mind? Had any of that even happened?*

I pulled up my shirt and inspected the bullet wound. Physical, grounding proof reminded me how real this all was. Gavin's poker face was so perfect. Did Mason have a shot at keeping him in line? I just didn't know, and the thought terrified me. I was so fucking scared.

I forgot all about Kiana until she appeared in the doorway. Thankfully, my shirt fell down a few moments before. "Claire, are you okay? Are you hurt?" Her eyes flicked to my hands on my stomach.

I grabbed a few tissues, trying to wipe away the tears. "Don't worry, I'm fine."

She moved to my side and reached out like she might put a hand on my shoulder, but she changed her mind and snagged me another tissue. "Did Gavin say something to upset you? He should kiss your ass for coming back early. We need you around here."

I laughed despite the fear still choking me. "No, nothing like that. I swear I'm okay." We talked for a couple of minutes about library business before she left again, but she threw me a worried glance over her shoulder on her way out.

At first, her leaving was a relief. Soon, the solitude and the foreboding atmosphere had me panicking. I took several deep breaths, trying to enjoy working with no one's scrutiny.

God, I wanted to call Mason, but how could I when he tried so hard to keep me from coming back so soon, and I made the choice against his advice? I didn't regret my decision, but fuck, I needed his support. My hands twitched toward my phone. *Distraction, distraction*, I searched the office, *literally fucking anything*.

My mind easily wandered to the places it obsessively dwelled these last few months: Charles Gains, Priscilla Gains and our resemblance, his unnamed victims. I grasped onto my obsession because said obsession originated from something outside of me. It brought me back to the library, forced me out of bed, and burned every part of me, but that pain was grounding. I could breathe again.

I was back at work for my career ambitions, but that could have waited. *This* could not wait. With my purpose in focus, I put myself together and did what I needed to. I pulled up a national news database and typed in the name of the online college "Tyler" and I worked for. One of the more recent articles talked about an admissions counselor who disappeared. When his coworkers reported him missing, they found nothing but a fake name and address—he had no paper trail.

The story was interesting enough but had garnered no legitimate attention. Someone with a fake name probably had a reason to disappear. I swallowed hard, so angry I could scream. *Why didn't you look harder? You could have found them.* The journalists responsible were scratching at a juicier story than they could've imagined.

I read every article written about the disappearance, all three of them. The information was the same in each one: a staff photo that "resembled him closely, but was not him", how everyone liked him and how surprised they were to find anything amiss, and finally meaningless speculation on who he may have been. The most absurd suggestion was a CIA operative.

I wanted to shake everyone in that office, especially Sandra. *I told you.* I imagined screaming in her face. *I fucking told you.*

I finished with those and moved on to a more general search, looking for anything odd concerning female brunette students. As one of the top online schools in the country, there were thousands of articles. Hundreds of the featured students were dead or missing, and most had nothing to do with Charles. I sighed at the thought of narrowing it down to the ones that did.

I included missing in my search parameters and started the tedious process of combing through them. Authorities had found most of the dead and missing. Which you wouldn't realize unless you opened the article and read the addendum. Hours slipped by without me making much progress.

Gavin must have left, but he didn't say goodbye to me, for which I was grateful. Emma came in at six to remind me she was locking up. I barely glanced at her as I wished her a good night, but I caught her nervously shifting from foot to foot in my peripheral vision.

Another few hours passed, and I was reasonably sure I had something. A pretty brunette named Erica smiled at me from her high school graduation picture. My stomach flipped uncomfortably at her happiness.

She was nineteen when she went missing, newly enrolled in correspondence school so she could still pursue her career as a model. She was younger and prettier, but we shared similar facial features. We both looked a lot like his mother.

I reached out, touching my fingers briefly to the screen. I tucked into the articles I found about her. She went missing about the time they fired me from the college, and guilt even more potent than I was accustomed to flooded me. I publicly embarrassed Charles in front of people he worked hard to convince he was someone else. Was this my fault? He told me he had planned to kill me that first night. If he succeeded, would his hunger have eased? Would Erica still be alive if not for me? *Oh fuck, was it her blood on my wall?* I was going to be sick.

Friends said she got ready with them and left for a date the last night she was seen, much like his plan for me. They dropped her at a bar, and several hours later, she sent a picture of his license plate to her sister. That was the last anyone heard from her. The plate was fake, and they never got a lead on the car.

A knock on the door interrupted my thoughts. Before I could respond, Mason pushed it open. He looked downright edible in his perfect black suit. He rarely wore black, favoring blues and grays, but damn if he wasn't a sight.

I was still angry with him for running out, lying, silencing my fake friends and whatever else.

He smiled at me. "Baby, what are you still doing here?"

"What are you doing here at all?" I tried to sound irritated by his presence, but thrilled and aroused were more accurate.

"I called Lawrence to check on you, but he told me you were still here, working away."

"Something like that."

"I have a couple of things for you."

"Oh."

He laughed at my attempt at nonchalance, knowing full well I loved surprises. He dipped out of the office, immediately re-emerging with a big old globe on its own stand. The thing was massive with gold filigree and heavy wooden legs.

I snorted at the sight. "What is that?"

"This is an antique globe, useless, antiquated, wrong as hell, but the old thing still matters. A smart and beautiful woman once told me, 'you don't need to be right to matter.'" My heart picked up its pace, and butterflies tried to fly straight out of my mouth.

"You remembered."

"How could I ever forget meeting the funniest, weirdest, most stunning person I've ever known?" He touched my cheek in an achingly soft gesture. "Speaking of, are you hungry?"

"I am, but how are the two connected?"

"You'll see," he said with that cocky smile that melted my heart and panties. "Come with me?" It sounded like a question, but the heat in his eyes told me I had no choice. He held out his arm, and I wrapped mine around his, happily snuggling up to him. All the anger over the orchestrated lies momentarily evaporated upon the contact. "So, why are you doing this?"

He led me through the darkened library and toward the exit. "You and I are... Out of sync."

"What do you mean?" I mumbled stupidly.

"We're missing each other as much as we want to be with one another. And even when we're near each other, we're not..."

"I get it," I agreed as I patted his arm. "I don't want to fight, but you realize most of our problems come from you keeping so much from me, don't you?"

"I do,"

I cocked my head toward him, so stunned I couldn't speak for a moment.

"But you intentionally misread my actions." Before we reached the front door, he pulled me to the side and into a stairwell. *The basement books*. He flipped on the light and held my hand as he took me down the stairs. "There isn't an inch of room in my heart or on my cock for anyone but you."

"Aren't you romantic?"

He smiled at my sarcasm. "Not normally, no, but I'm really fucking up if you worry for one minute that I'm cheating on you."

I paused on the step, pulling him to a stop below me. Instead of our usual height difference, my lips pressed to his forehead. He laid his head against my chest. "I don't think so, not really." I wrapped my arms around him, breathing in his warmth and comfort. "But it's hard to think straight when I don't know where you are and you're lying to me."

"I don't lie to you," he disagreed.

"You omit enough of the truth to turn them into lies, Mason, and you can't pretend otherwise."

"I'm not doing it maliciously."

"You don't trust me."

"I do trust you. I just love you so fucking much that I'd destroy the world and rebuild it if that would make the stupid place better for you. Hurting you is the last thing I want to do. You may not want to believe me, Claire, but I see you and you're struggling. I cannot add to your burden."

"I'm not—"

"Come on, I have something to show you." he interrupted me, and I didn't argue as he took my hand and led me the rest of the way. He was right about me struggling, and admitting to that burned. It surprised me to find the space warmly lit with electric candles. "I would never risk actual flames around the books," he told me with an earnest look on his face.

I burst into a fit of giggles, downright buoyant despite all the things left unsaid between the two of us. Someone had dusted, but it still smelled like old books and stale air, and I couldn't love it anymore. Between two shelves, an intimate table for two was set with thick sandwiches wrapped in tinfoil and a bottle of wine with glasses.

"Sit down and let me feed you; you haven't been eating enough."

"You don't feed me enough," I countered.

"I sent you lunch yesterday and I'm feeding you dinner tonight."

"So it was you! I thought it was Vick."

Anger rolled over his expression, and I couldn't make sense of it. He and Vick were close. "I take care of you, not Vick."

"You take care of me, no one else," I assured him as I led the way to the table, starving and wholly satisfied by Mason acting like a caveman over the thought of another man taking care of me.

I peeled back the foil and found an eggplant parmesan sub. "Mm, thank you." I picked it up and took a massive bite, groaning instantly as the flavors burst in my mouth. "DiNapoli?" I asked when I finally swallowed.

"Of course, baby. I know what you like."

117

He dug into his own sandwich but he watched me as I ate, making easy conversation about his day at work and asking questions about mine. I wrapped up the remaining half and leaned back with my hands crossed over my stomach. "That was amazing."

"I have something for you."

"What do you mean? You gave me a giant globe and an eggplant parm. What else could a girl want?"

He laughed, and my heart nearly ripped out of my chest. It had been so fucking long since I heard him laugh that I giggled in sheer shock and joy at the sound. He pulled a little box out of his jacket, and for a wild moment, I thought he was going to propose to me, except it wasn't a ring box.

I took the gift from him and ripped the lid off, stunned to find a little book nestled inside a bit of velvet. I picked up the treasure, admiring the way the light played with the stones. "It's not real, is it?"

"Of course it's real," he scoffed at the absurd idea.

"I love it," I went to put it around my neck.

"Open it; it's a locket." I did as he instructed and softly gasped, then laughed so hard I nearly cried. It was his cock, the same picture he sent me months ago, and on the opposite side, there was a note.

Ms. Hiring,
I'm yours.
-Doer of Jobs

"It's perfect." I sniffed as I closed it up and put it around my neck. "I love it."

Mason's hands were on me before I fastened the catch, instead of dropping the necklace, he caught it and helped me put it on. I didn't understand how he managed the delicate task with such wide fingers, and the distracting lust burning in his eyes.

He pulled me out of my seat and crushed his lips to mine. That mouth was too plush for his devastatingly handsome face. Nothing in life was fair when he had those eyes and cheeks paired with those achingly soft, sure lips. He tasted like wine-soaked sin. Heat exploded behind my vision and pooled in my panties as he hungrily grasped at me, kissing, biting, squeezing. One hand fisted in my hair while the other squeezed one of my ass cheeks with brutal force.

I whimpered into his open mouth. "That's right, baby. Whine for me."

He tugged my hair, tipping my head roughly. I obliged him, whining and gasping wildly into his mouth. He was punishing me for coming back here as much as he was trying to mend bridges and make up with me. Blind passion overtook my senses and I would have done anything he wanted at that moment.

"You know, I thought of fucking that mouth of yours the first day I met you here. I couldn't help thinking that smart, sexy mouth would benefit from sucking my cock."

"You should have." He smiled against my skin at the idea. "I would have loved it."

"Get on your knees," he ordered, with a flash of amusement in his eyes.

"No." I snapped. I wanted to, badly, but not like that.

"Naughty girl, were you thinking about what we did in my gym? How I chased you through the house and forced you to take everything I wanted to give you, every thick inch of me. There's no one here tonight, and I'd be all too happy to chase you."

That whine he seemed so fond of ripped out of my throat, and I nodded my head frantically.

"Are you feeling good?" I nodded. "Are you hurting?" I shook my head. "Are you lying to me?"

I wanted to tell him that *he* was the liar, but I wanted him to chase me down and fuck me more. I shook my head.

119

"Run, baby."

I did just that. My heart sped in my chest, banging against my ribs with excitement, not fear. Adrenaline rushed through me so intensely, that by the time I reached the stairs I was panting for breath. My feet banged on the metal, loud and obvious, but there was no point wasting precious time hiding my route when it was the only way out of the basement.

I had no plans, no thoughts outside of my single-minded excitement as I entered the main floor of the empty library. The only lighting was the glow of the emergency exits and the soft blue lights that intermittently blipped in the darkness. I took a deep breath, trying to come up with a plan. I wanted him to find me, of course, but what was the fun if I didn't make a concerted effort? Before anything brilliant could pop into my head, I heard his measured footsteps on the stairs and his smooth voice.

"It's almost like you want me to catch you, baby." I ran at full speed, fighting the urge to giggle and scream. This wasn't like the times I feared I was being followed through the library. In the deepest parts of myself, I knew I was safe. He would always keep me safe. The soul-deep release as I ran from him morphed into a shriek as his hands caught in my hair and crushed me to him. He turned my face toward his, kissing my open, gasping mouth in a frenzy of tongues and panted breath.

Both his hands tightened in my hair and with strength beyond what I dreamed of him having, he forced me to my knees in front of him. He released my hair, doing his best to free his overgrown erection. His button came loose with a pop, and his proud length bobbed deliciously in front of me. He rubbed the tip against my mouth, spreading his pre-cum over my lips. My tongue darted out to taste him, and he made a soft tutting noise.

"Did I hurt your pretty knees when I pushed you down?" the mocking tone made me want to hurt and fuck him equally, but the concern was genuine.

"No, but I'm going to hurt you if you don't—"

His green eyes flashed with pure heat, "If I don't what, Claire?"

My eyes were glued to the fascinating hand stroking the length of his erection. "You want this?" I licked my lips, staring hungrily. "Who am I to deny you anything?" His lips twisted in amusement. "Open,"

I obeyed him, opening wide and flattening my tongue for him. He grabbed the back of my neck and rammed his cock down my throat with brutal force. "Fuck," he hissed through his teeth.

I tried to perform for him, but he wouldn't let me. He pounded into me so hard that tears welled in my eyes and I choked. Only when my face turned hot and red did he pull out and allow me to breathe. Spit stretched between his achingly hard cock and my lips, almost as sloppy as the mess I had made of my panties.

"Fuck, lay down. I need to taste you." But instead of letting me go, he dragged me down to the floor by my hair, supporting my body weight with his strong arms. I expected him to descend on me, he looked so fucking hungry. "You remember your safe word?"

"Yes." I panted.

"Good," In a flash, he slid in between my thighs which were still clad in stockings. He snatched both of my wrists and swiftly connected them with a zip tie. The plastic stung as he tightened it down.

"You planned this," I accused.

"I dreamed of this," he countered.

He flipped me over, pushing me up on my forearms and knees, where he took his sweet time stripping me of my clothes. My blouse was bunched around my wrists, but I was utterly bare for him and that's what really mattered.

"Are you okay?"

"I'm not okay. I'm desperate. Please, Mase." I wiggled my ass at him doing my best to tempt him into hurrying up.

"You want it that bad, Claire?"

A savage mewling sound reverberated from the back of my throat, and I shook my ass harder, knowing that all the things he liked best were wiggling in front of his face.

"Are you trying to tempt me with this?" He slapped his large hand firmly against my ass cheek. I cried out at the impact like he was sucking on my clit.

"Yes, God, fuck me."

His hand came down on my ass once again, and while it stung I was certain he was taking it easy on me. "Not yet," he answered simply as he slid his fingers between my folds and played with my soft flesh in a way that drove me crazy and did *nothing* to get me there.

"Please, I need it so bad, please."

In a moment, his hands and mouth were on me, holding me down, running over me with tenacious, gripping fingers. He shoved his tongue unceremoniously between my labia and against my clit. "You want me to fuck you? Come in three minutes, baby. Do that for me and I'll fuck you in any way you like.

I writhed and grunted. The zip tie cutting into my wrists heightened the sensation. Being in a place that had proven dangerous turned me on, fucking liberated me. He hadn't even spread me out to focus on my clit. Mason consumed me, tasting whatever he could get his tongue on, and fuck if I wasn't going to orgasm in half the allotted time. "Mason, I'm going to cum."

"No, you're not," he grunted against my pussy.

"What, why? You told me to." I whimpered the words so pathetically that I would be humiliated if I wasn't so painfully aroused.

"I told you three minutes. You need to last, baby."

"Or what?" I challenged.

"I'll punish you." And just like that, I exploded around his fingers and over his tongue. "Baby, it's almost like you *want* me to punish you."

"Fuck, yes," I ground out through the last wringing clenches of my orgasm.

He laughed as he left me there and strolled over to one of the shelves. I couldn't see what he was doing, but I heard his footsteps on the tile as he rejoined me. He dropped to his knees behind me once again. "Claire, this is not a game. Are you feeling okay? Are you hurt, hurting, or uncomfortable?"

"God, Mason, you said you were going to punish me, not fucking *torture* me."

He laughed lightly, "This is going to sting."

Something hard and yes, stinging collided with my ass. I grunted an unrestrained sound of pain and pleasure. It came down on me once again. "I can't tell you how long I've wanted to spank this sweet ass with one of your books, Ms. Librarian. I'm so hard for you." The book landed against my ass once more with a loud smacking sound. Before my cry ended, he plunged his fingers inside me, prolonging the shout. He worked me in hard, desperate thrusts as he rained smacks over my tender skin.

"Fuck, you're going to squirt."

"What?"

"You're so fucking wet." He shoved his mouth against me, quickly working me to the edge.

Footsteps on the tile had Mason pausing. I was too close, and I genuinely did not give one fuck who it was. I ground my clit against his mouth crying, "Don't stop!" as if he would kill me if he did. He caught on to my desperation, perhaps as swept up as I was, and sucked hard.

I screamed in sweet agony as my orgasm tore through me with violent strength, wringing every drop of pleasure and cum from my body. Mason and I were both soaked, as was the library floor.

"Mason, we have a problem," Vick said the moment he was within earshot. I couldn't see Mason as he pulled away from me, but I saw Vick's outline in the darkened library and he faced away from us.

My cheeks burned bright red, and embarrassment coiled in my stomach. Much like when I didn't know Mason's real name, the embarrassment had me twisted up and aching in need. I wanted to cover myself, but with my hands tied and the position he propped me in, there was no chance.

"Is it serious?" he asked Vick, interrupting my thoughts.

"Very." My heart sunk at the realization my empty pussy was about to be left unfilled.

"I'll meet you in the car, Vick." He nodded and walked out. "I'm sorry, baby. I have to go."

"Are you fucking serious?"

He took the knife out of his pocket and cut the zip tie. "I will be home in no more than two hours. I *swear*. Lawrence is waiting outside for you. I love you."

He stood and kissed me on the lips before racing toward the front door and away from me, the same way I'd done to him the first time we met.

FIFTEEN

Mason

I followed Vick into the frigid night air, bristling from the wind's assault and the interruption to my evening with Claire. All of that planning to win back some of my lost ground with her had gone to shit. The hurt look in her eyes hung behind my lids, flashing each time I blinked. Her cum drenched my shirt, I left my jacket behind, and my cock refused to soften with the tantalizing scent of her everywhere.

"I should apologize," Vick's voice interrupted my running thoughts. He had made it to the car before I pulled my pants up, fleeing the scene like it was an explosion. "I didn't mean to *interrupt*," he continued. nearly choking on the word. I almost pitied him despite the angry animal inside of me that demanded some display of dominance as penance for seeing what was mine.

"Keep it to yourself." I shot him a death glare, and the words came out harsher than I intended. "I need a shirt." Claire would drop dead from embarrassment at the sight of Victor. I couldn't imagine forcing her to listen to his apology.

"There's one in the trunk." He dipped around to the back and pulled the shirt out before he climbed into the car to give me some space.

The idea of him seeing Claire screaming and writhing in pleasure, then bathing me in her juices, fucking enraged me. She wasn't for his eyes. But I was eternally grateful Vick found us and not James.

Vick would keep his mouth shut about what happened and genuinely regret walking in, James would have wound up getting the shit beaten out of him before the night ended. I could imagine his self-satisfied smirk and comments all too clearly.

I pulled my shirt off and changed in the frigid air, unconcerned by the people passing on the sidewalk. Part of me hoped to see Claire racing out of the library, chasing after me, but I knew her better than that. She was likely watching from the window, waiting until we were gone to have Lawrence take her home.

I buttoned the shirt up and climbed into the back of the car. "This better be good, Vick." I paused as I caught sight of Casey sitting in the bench seat perpendicular to the one I slid into. "Casey, what the fuck are you doing here?"

He made a slight coughing sound as he tried to speak, "Uh, I-"

"He has some intel, and said it's urgent," Vick answered for Casey. I looked the kid over, noticing the way he shook. Was it because of what he wanted to show us, or did he know I discovered his big fucking mouth?

"Is that so, Casey?"

"Yes, sir."

"Why should I trust you after what you did?"

His eyes snapped open with almost comic force. "I didn't do anything, sir," he spat the words out, but they caught on one another and jumbled together.

"Can you tell me why I ran into a person who knew why Victor, James, and myself were in the warehouse the night we met you?" Daniel was the person. While he claimed to guess my intentions, he was too nonchalant about it. He had a reason for knowing.

"Everyone knows, Mr. Sharp. I mean, come on, look at what you did!" He waved his arms, and his eyes widened in alarm. "You wanted to send a message, and you succeeded."

"Yes, but they wouldn't know why unless someone told them. You, James, and Vick are the only ones who were privy to my motivations that night. Who do you think blabbed?"

He swallowed repeatedly, trying to come up with an answer or figure out how to speak without pissing himself. "I did, but I swear to God I didn't mean to. It was an accident."

I pulled my gun out of my waistband and aimed at his chest. "That's quite the accident."

He held up his hands, his gesture pleading. "I just said you were looking for guys. You're recruiting, aren't you? I have friends and they don't like the way things are either. I thought I was helping."

"When I need your help, I'll ask."

He pressed his palms together. "Please, Mr. Sharp. This is going to be worth your while tonight. I swear I meant you no harm."

I lifted the gun up, pressing the barrel to his head. In the confined space, the mess would be unbelievable, and I wouldn't hear shit the rest of the night. I really didn't want to kill this kid. "Are you sure what you've found is worth your life?"

"Yes," he answered in a steady voice, a new level of assurance entering him. "But Sir, I need you to swear to me you won't do anything to harm them."

I tipped my head to the side, looking at him with fresh eyes. It was an incredibly bold ask considering the circumstances. I lowered the gun. "You care about the person you're bringing us to?"

"Please, sir." His gaze trained on the floor.

"Why was this something that needed to happen tonight? The interruption was incredibly unwelcome."

"I-it's going to be fucking cold tonight."

I wasn't sure what that had to do with anything, "I promise." Whoever this person was, they must mean a lot to him. I admired him for demanding someone else's safety with a gun to his head. I put it back in my waistband and settled into the seat. "Let's hope you're not playing games with me, Casey. I *only* promised safety for your friend."

He swallowed hard, but said nothing more as we moved through the darkened city and passed its limits. He occasionally told our driver where to turn. Phil was a nice enough guy and hadn't given me any cause to doubt him.

The length of the trip surprised me. The distance, as well as the lack of familiar surroundings, made me nervous about Casey's intentions, but he remained calm and still once I agreed not to hurt whoever this was. A kid leading me into a trap was bound to be more twitchy.

We pulled up outside a collection of storage units: rows upon rows of white boxes with red doors and rust spots. "Why are we here?" The small lights over each unit flashed above us as we moved through the rows on Casey's instruction.

"She's here." Who the fuck were we meeting in a storage unit?

He pointed out where to park and we covered each other's backs as we climbed out. He walked up to unit nineteen and knocked in a specific rhythm. A moment later, the small door on the side opened and revealed a teenage girl. Vick went ahead of me and scoped out the space before popping back out and waving me on.

I was sick to my stomach as I took in the surrounding room. The first thing that caught my attention was how fucking cold it was in here. They heated these units, but that meant they kept them above freezing for valuable items, not up to a temperate climate for a human being. The weather forecast predicted snow. Someone residing in this tin box probably wouldn't survive the night.

A dim light in the metal walls illuminated the space just enough to see. A tattered twin mattress lay on the floor with blankets strewn on top. Her only real possessions seemed to be a pile of old magazines, books, and a hot plate. The lack of a bucket comforted me slightly, but I wondered where she went to do her business, especially considering each time the door opened this place dropped below freezing.

I barely knew what to say as I took it all in. Casey interrupted the silence, "Mr. Sharp, this is Mila and she wants to help."

"Hello, Mila. Are you alright?" My eyes flicked to her. I spoke softly, having no interest in intimidating her. She wore a bulky old coat that was sized for a man, but I could see from her cheeks how slender she was underneath. Enough that I worried she was malnourished.

Her blue eyes were wide on her pale face. Was her chalky pallor a result of the temperature or a natural attribute? The faint blue cast on her lips made me nervous. *God damn it, Casey.*

She wasn't as dirty as I might have thought, given she had no running water, but she clearly wasn't cleaning herself or her clothing regularly enough. I had to work through the torrent of emotions plummeting through me. I knew people lived like this, and worse, but to stand here beside this girl and do nothing was not an option.

"How do you plan on helping me?" I asked her as I firmed up my plans to help *her*.

"I, uh, it's not actually *you* I want to help, sir."

Casey sent her a frantic glance, and her eyes darted to mine to check my reaction. "Who do you want to help then, Mila?" I gestured for her to continue.

"Girls like me." She ran her hand through her long dirty blonde hair. "I know a lot about the business that you're trying to stop." She looked around again, uncomfortable with so many people in her space. "I would offer you a place to sit, but..." Her cheeks turned a deep pink, and her fingers twisted in her hair.

"What business is that, Mila? And don't worry about us, we don't mind standing." I needed her to tell me expressly what she knew.

She sat down on her mattress, twisting the tattered blanket around her fingers. "The human trafficking. They abducted me in Slovenia when I was twelve. I was bought and sold a few times before I escaped." Her eyes flickered over to Casey, and I noticed a sparkle of adoration.

"You saved her?" *Impressive*.

"Yeah, when I was looking for my mom. They left her behind in a warehouse. They were packing the van and meant to come back for her. I took her first."

"And set me free," she corrected him with a smile.

"They believe she escaped. I've kept her safe."

"This doesn't seem like freedom." I looked around pointedly at Mila, "Or safety," as my hard gaze shifted to Casey.

"I know this doesn't look like much, but if you knew where I came from, you would realize how much better I have it now," her voice was soft but sure. "This is as free and safe as I have ever been, and that is because of Casey." I nodded my head, unable to make anything worse for her. To put it mildly, this incredibly strong girl was abducted and sold multiple times while I was ignoring the business and living my best life.

"Have you considered finding her a place to live that had running water, Casey?"

"Yeah, I'm saving up for a place for her. That's why I was working for Francis. Well, that and finding my mom." Casey sat down beside her on the bed and took her hand. She tensed subtly at the gesture, but he didn't appear to notice.

A sliver of suspicion laced through me. "Where do you live, Casey?" He didn't answer and he wouldn't look at me.

"Casey lives next door," Mila said.

I dropped my face into my hands. "You kids can't live in a fucking storage unit. You have no running water!"

"We've been here for two years," Mila argued. "Well, I have, but Casey has been here longer."

"I'm going to take you somewhere to get cleaned up, and then you can tell me everything you want to."

Casey's eyes darted back and forth between the two of us, landing on Vick like he might offer him an explanation for my decision. "I can't question cold and hungry kids." I spat at him as I turned and left the unit.

A few minutes later, they were both packed up in the car. I insisted that each of them take anything important to them.

"Where are we taking them, boss?" Vick asked as he gave Casey a dirty look for sitting so close to him.

"The gatehouse; I want to keep an eye on them."

"The gatehouse, sir?" Casey asked.

"Yeah. There's an apartment attached to James and Vick's place. The two of you can stay for tonight at least, and we can discuss what we need to." I had no intentions of sending them back to their cold metal boxes, but I didn't want either of them too comfortable just yet.

Mila wiped a hand against her eyes. "Thank you so much. I can't wait to take an actual shower."

Fuck, my heart. "You're welcome."

We pulled up outside the estate a little while later. "Woah, Mr. Sharp. This is where you live?" The awe in Casey's tone made my gut twist uncomfortably. I had always lived like this while my father's men abducted women. I enjoyed luxury while kids were raped or forced to live alone, cold, and hungry.

We dropped them all off at the gatehouse and I took a ride up to the main house with the instructions that they notify me as soon as they were ready to talk. Barely an hour and a half had gone by and that had to help. I didn't know what I was going to say to Claire, but if I told her about the state of the girl, she'd understand the urgency of the situation.

I sighed as I opened the door. I couldn't tell her about the girl, any of the girls, not yet. There was too much happening and she couldn't take the added stress. To my great surprise, I walked in to find Rochelle in the foyer. She should be off duty and in her wing by now.

"Hi, Rochelle."

"Hi, Mr. Sharp." She shifted from foot to foot.

"Is something wrong?"

"No, it's just that since I hadn't seen Ms. Green this evening, I assumed she was with you, and she doesn't seem to be." She styled her hair into an artful bun that was far too neat for this late hour.

"No, she's not. She never came home?"

Rochelle nodded. Dread unfurled in my stomach, and I picked up the phone to call Lawrence. "Is everything okay?"

"She just wants to drive for a while," he answered quietly.

"Is that him? Tell him to mind his own damn business!" her angry voice came from the backseat, but I swore I heard tears. God damn it. I was ruining everything.

"Thanks, Lawrence." I hung up the phone. "She's safe, Rochelle. Thanks for worrying about her."

"Okay, Mr. Sharp." She turned to go back to bed, but thought of something and turned around. "Mr. Sharp, I don't want to speak out of turn, but I am worried about her." There was a significance to the words that I understood all too well.

"Me too. Good night, Rochelle."

I walked up the stairs and went to our bedroom to take a shower and kill some time before Casey and Mila were ready. James sent me a text that Victor filled him in. He had looked into her and her story checked out. Milena Novak went missing when she was twelve. They assumed her dead, and there were no leads on her whereabouts. The picture attached was certainly the girl we'd met.

I took a shower and changed into a pair of slacks and a button-down shirt. The power suit usually worked well, but I wanted Mila a bit more comfortable. Another text came in from James: she was clean and ready to talk.

I walked down the drive alone, letting the wintry night air chase the panic and pain out of my lungs. The lights in the gatehouse were all on. I knocked as I entered, finding all four of them waiting for me in Vick's living room.

The warmly decorated space was comfortable but sparse. James and Vick weren't really "stuff" people and the lack of personal touch was as obvious as the heat blowing off the fireplace.

I sat in an armchair and smiled to myself as I realized they had set Mila up with a cup of tea and a sandwich—my guys were good people. "So, Mila, did Casey ask you to do this, or was this something you wanted?" I began.

"A bit of both. Casey told me I could trust you a couple of weeks ago, but I needed time to come around to the idea." She sipped her tea and shivered at the warmth.

"What would you like to tell me?"

"Well, I know a lot of the places they keep the girls, places they sell them too. I know a lot of grunts who push the girls around and rape them while they're awaiting sale. I know a lot of things, but the people I can point out for you probably know a lot more. Casey says your dad is the boss of all this, and that you want to stop him. Is that true?"

"It's very true. Vick and James here, too. Their mom had something similar happen to her. Though she worked on the street for years before they took her."

"Like Casey's mom?" her soft voice sounded so young just then.

We both looked at Casey for confirmation. I wouldn't presume to know that anything he said about his past was true, despite proving his name was Casey and had reported his mother missing a few years back. "Yeah, Mila. Just like what happened to my mom," he added with a hint of sadness.

"When they first brought me here, they put me on a boat. There were about thirty of us in a crate on a barge. It was awful. Three of the girls died before we reached the shore and the only thing we could do was pile them in the corner and try to breathe through the smell of shit and death.

"The first time they sold me, I didn't know where I was, but the room had cages and a rounded stage. People sat around bidding on me. Some of them were women, and I thought for a moment they might help me, but they didn't." She pulled a tissue out of a box on the side table and dabbed at her eyes.

"I was raped a lot the first year. The man who bought me was cruel and insatiable. I-I had a baby..." She drew in a ragged breath, gasping for air. "I don't know what happened to her. He took her just after she was born, and I never learned what he did with her. That's when he sold me because my pussy was loose and used up." My fists clenched at her words. Anger filled me, along with the desire to break and tear. She was barely even a teenager when this ordeal happened.

"They didn't bring me back to the same place. Maybe that's only for new girls. I don't really know. Another man came one day, slapped a collar around my neck, and told me I was his pet. He wasn't as bad as the first guy. At least he put me on birth control and never tried to get me pregnant. He died though. At least that's what I was told when they came to my cage and took me. I was waiting in a warehouse to be sold again, and that's when Casey found me."

Silence filled the air for a few minutes as we all processed her words. "If we took you to some of these places, would you recognize them?"

"Some definitely, but probably not all of them." She twisted a long wet lock of blonde hair between her fingers.

"That's perfectly okay, Mila. Anything you can remember will help us. We'll give you a day or two to relax, and then we'll get started. Does that sound okay?"

Her pale cheeks filled with pink. "Yes, I want them to pay for what they did to me and... my *daughter*..." her voice broke on the word.

"I will do my best," I swore. We talked for a few more minutes until I decided she needed rest before we could continue.

As I left the gatehouse, Casey followed me. "Thank you, Mr. Sharp. I cannot tell you what it means to me that you're helping her."

"You love her, huh, kid?"

"I do." The sincerity on his face was utterly believable.

"Then you want what's best for her?"

"I do."

"Watch yourself, Casey. There will not be a repeat of your lapse in judgment if you want to hang around long enough to see that girl living a real life."

"I swear it will never happen again."

"See to it." I turned and walked up the path back to the main house. By the time I got inside, Claire was asleep, curled up on the couch. She was making a statement that she didn't want to sleep beside me, but I didn't care. Scooping her into my arms, I laid her on the bed and climbed in beside her. She woke only long enough to sigh my name and tell me she loved me.

Sixteen

Claire

I made Lawrence drive me around for hours after Mason left me with the remnants of our date. Now, *that* was fun to clean up—my own cum off the library floor. I was tempted to go to a dozen different places to blow off some steam, clubs, casinos, or any random wild shit that would make me forget the reasons I was alone and embarrassed.

In the end, I traveled around the city on a personal pity party tour. There were a lot of historic sites; some of them were personal to my story while others weren't. I turned over angry thoughts and feelings of resentment for Mason, myself, and anyone stupid enough to stand in my path.

Eventually, I relented and went home, but I would not sleep next to him. It was a good thing the couch was absurdly comfortable.

A little disorientated, I woke to an empty bed that smelled of him, and with no memory of climbing in at all. He must have carried me. While my brain was angry as fuck at his pushy ways, my heart clenched at the knowledge that he insisted on sleeping beside me.

The shower was already running, so I went to one of the guest rooms to get ready, but before, I glimpsed him through the crack in the bathroom door as he stepped out of the shower. I was annoyed with myself for that as well. He was just too sexy not to look at when naked and wet.

I wanted to leave early that morning, so I rushed through my shower and got dressed as quickly as possible. There had to be some satisfaction to gain from being the one to leave Mason for once. He was already in the driveway, climbing into his black SUV before I made it down the stairs. The idea of besting him at anything was silly.

When he saw me walking toward the white SUV, he drove around to speak to me, and while he opened the window, he made no move to get out. "Good morning, baby. Have a good day at work." I realized his expectant expression meant he wanted me to kiss him.

I gave him a disbelieving look. He hadn't apologized nor explained what happened the night before, and he wanted to act like this was all normal. Him hauling me into bed beside him and snuggling me was not the same as making up. "You too."

Walking around to the right side of the car and ignoring any more attempts at communication, I leaned against the vehicle and waited for him to get out and talk to me or leave. After a few minutes, he chose the second option. I grumbled into my hands, unready to face James, who was already sitting in the car waiting for me.

The sound of two unfamiliar laughs filled the air. I looked up to find a pair of teenagers walking along the driveway down near the gatehouse. I couldn't make out their features from here, but it was certainly odd to find a couple of kids strolling the grounds. Everyone here, except for Rochelle, wore a power suit and a freaking earpiece.

"Hi!" I called down the slight hill and waved them over. I felt James watching me from the car as I pushed off the side and walked over to them, but I didn't care. He could come out and do something if he wanted to, otherwise, he could fuck off. I was far from over the revelation about him and Emma.

The two kids waved back and sped their pace up the hill, quickly meeting me about halfway. "Hi, who are you two?" I asked as soon as they were in earshot. The girl was stunningly beautiful, blonde and willowy, but she looked unhealthy: sallow skin, dull, flat hair, dark circles beneath her eyes as deep as bruises. The boy was cute, with dirty blonde hair and a surfer vibe. He was in better shape than her, but he also showed signs of neglect.

"I'm Casey and this is Mila. I work for Mr. Sharp," he answered with a smile like this was all perfectly normal.

"Are you staying here?" And why the *fuck* am I hearing about it from you?

"Well, last night we did, at least. Mr. Sharp left the situation kind of vague, but either way, we're awfully grateful."

"He helped you last night," I said the words with an assurance I didn't possess. Mason wouldn't tell me anything, but this kid clearly saw no issue in telling me things he assumed I already knew.

"We're so grateful," Mila told me with a genuine smile. Her soft accent made her words almost musical. "I can't even tell you the last time I took a long, hot shower." She sighed with satisfaction, and my chest defrosted a fraction.

"What are you two doing today?"

"Whatever Mr. Sharp says, but he said he wanted to give Mila some time to relax before she shows him the—"

"Casey, haven't you learned when to shut the fuck up?" James' angry voice came from about twenty feet away. I hadn't noticed him getting out of the car.

Casey turned bright red. "Oh fuck, I just promised him I'd keep my mouth shut. Fucking stupid!"

"Don't sweat it, Casey. You didn't tell me anything." I winked.

"Thank you. He's not all that forgiving." I wasn't sure that I agreed with Casey's assessment. Mason was forgiving, wasn't he? Or did I only believe that because I received his tenderness? No, I didn't believe that.

Smiling, I nodded my head. "I'll see you guys some other time. I have to get to work." They both offered some variation of nice to meet you as I turned around and headed back to the car.

Giving James a nasty look as we climbed into the horseless carriage, I settled as far from his as possible. He sat on the seat perpendicular to my own. God, these SUVs were ridiculous. Was I going to prom with a drug lord?

"He wanted to kiss you goodbye, but you avoided him."

"That's funny, James. I don't remember asking you."

One pitch black brow raised, "If I didn't know better, I would say you're pissed at me too, Claire. Here I thought we were friends."

"We *were* friends," I agreed as I buckled my seat belt.

"And what have I done that we're no longer friends?" he sounded so friendly and innocent. The whole act had me contemplating murder.

I shivered slightly, overcome with the intensity of the betrayal he helped propagate. I wanted a friend so naively, so desperately, I barely thought to be careful when I let Emma fill that role. Even after being shot, I let him become my friend with no great effort. "Nothing, I just don't like you."

"Nothing, okay." He pulled his phone out of his pocket. "Let me just call Vicky, and we'll swap for the day."

"Don't you fucking dare!" I nearly shouted, lunging forward to grab the phone from his hands in case I needed to. I'd already buckled my seat belt and it locked up on me.

He laughed at my efforts and shoved the phone away. "So, whatever I did to make you angry is less important than your embarrassment over what Vick saw."

139

"Please!" I threw up my hands, begging him to stop. "Oh, god." I dropped my head into my hands. "Which one of them told you?"

"Vicky, of course. Mason would never tell me that." He chuckled at my expense while I sat there beet red, angry and embarrassed. I groaned as I leaned back and laid my head against the glass.

"Come on, Claire. Why are you mad at me, buddy?" James had put on his irresistible charm, and if I were any less pissed, it would have worked on me.

"Emma," I sighed back,

He flinched, tensing so hard that his ears and shoulders nearly collided. "What about her?" The question was far from casual, loaded with all the pain and longing I heard between the two of them on the phone.

"There are a lot of little betrayals all centered on her. Maybe how you're stupidly in love with her? Or how you told her not to *tell* me about it or anything else she knows about this fucked up situation?" my voice casually raised in volume. "What about telling her to pretend to be my friend?"

"I didn't do that," he interjected, but I ignored him.

"Might I add that the situation everyone is supposed to hide from me is the same reason I'm sitting in the back of this tacky SUV with you, James?" I rubbed my thumb into my palm, trying to keep myself calm.

"Claire, as far as keeping things from you, that's Mason's business. I told her not to tell you anything because he's my boss. You're my buddy, but my loyalty to him comes first. If he says Claire can't know, Claire can't know."

"Fine, James. Just don't pretend you're my friend. Why aren't we leaving?" I was going to be late for work if Lawrence didn't start driving.

"You are my friend, and I swear I never told her to become your friend or fake a friendship with you. She *is* your friend.

Don't be mad that I'm in love with her. It's too late for Emma and me anyway."

"Only if you're actually as stupid as you act." I leaned forward and knocked on the partition. "Lawrence, please pull out. I'm running late."

"What's that supposed to mean?"

"All your little trio does is play games, James. Why don't you figure it out?"

He leaned back in his seat, and I felt him silently begging me to help him fix things with her. As angry as I was, my heart twinged. "I can't get involved, James. I can't even talk to her."

"I didn't ask."

"I know."

I tapped my foot hard on the floor, realizing not only were we not pulling away, but Lawrence never answered. Just as I was about to panic, Mason pulled the door open. "Get the fuck out, James."

James smiled to himself as he climbed out of the SUV. "Sure thing, boss."

"Where's Lawrence?" I asked, wondering what the fuck was going on.

"I called and told him to take the morning off. He'll pick you up later, and my driver will take you this morning."

"Oh yeah, he got out of the car while you were yelling at me." James chimed in.

"Fine, now go away, both of you."

Mason slid into the car next to me, pushing me over on the seat and pressing the heat of his body against my own. "Who would take you to work then?"

"I can drive." Not that I had in the last decade.

He smiled at me like I was *cute*. "I know, baby,"

It was intensely cold outside, and I was still chilly from my conversation with Casey and Mila. "Who are those kids you moved in?"

"You already met them, Claire, but that's not why I'm here." His green eyes were darker than normal.

"Why are you here?" The car moved, and my eyes shot nervously to him.

"My driver for the day," he assured me as the car pulled away and started the slow descent to the street. The ride took about half an hour in pleasant weather, but there was ice on the roads and we were going slowly.

Mason undid my buckle. "Hey, what the heck?" I protested.

His hands snaked around my waist, pulling me swiftly into his lap. I tried to pull away, but when his lips connected with the spot where my neck and shoulder meet, lightning singed through every inch of my body.

"I'm here to say I'm sorry," he murmured into my skin as he licked and sucked. His teeth caught my skin and his hand snaked around my throat, squeezing hard enough that a touch of lightheadedness came over me.

"You're sorry?" The words barely made a sound, and he released my neck long enough for me to take a breath. I tried to remember if I wanted to accept the apology, but I could scarcely think of anything except for his touch as I ground my hips into him; I had no control over the need rising inside of me.

"I'm very sorry, but that's only part of why I'm here. I needed to remind you what happens when you try to keep me away from what's mine."

"What happens?"

He palmed my breasts, rolling my nipples between his fingers through the sheer lace fabric. "I use your body against you."

"I could tell you to stop." I gasped the words as he increased the pressure on the sensitive peaks.

"And I would. Say it. Tell me to stop, Claire."

I whimpered in response.

"Tell me, baby. What's more satisfying? You keeping your sweet lips from me, or this?" His hands moved to the buttons on my blouse, undoing them, before sliding it off my body. He bit into my shoulder. The feeling was primal. Tantalizing shivers coursed through me, softening my thoughts as a ragged moan escaped.

Shaking, wet, and desperate, Mason slid his hand up my thigh and beneath my skirt, running his fingers along my pussy. His touch seared through the sheer fabric of my stockings. "She likes this better, but I want to hear what you have to say."

"This feels better," I gasped, forgetting why I should be angry.

"Do you want me to stop?" His teeth dragged along my ear lobe. I shook my head, increasing the pain of his bite.

"I'm sorry I left you last night." He pushed me forward, forcing me off the seat and my hands onto the floor. I gasped in shock, but he supported most of my weight as I fell. His hands slid over my back and ass, pulling my zipper down and over my hips as he went. The proficiency with which he removed each layer had my hips twitching. He bent forward to trace his tongue along my labia, carefully ignoring my clit.

I groaned and wiggled my hips in desperation. "Do you remember when you first came here, and I threatened to fuck you in front of my men? Right before you ran, and I chased you. Do you remember how excited it made you?"

"Yes." I wasn't sure I wanted to understand where he was going with this.

"Last night with Vick—"

"Don't say it," I begged as I pressed myself against his face.

"You came so hard, baby." He slid his tongue against my clit. I whimpered as his face dove deeper into me, kissing and sucking. He gripped my hips, lifting me until the tops of my thighs draped over his shoulders. I felt his breath as he laughed against my open pussy. Usually, I found these giant

143

luxurious vehicles ridiculous, but I suddenly found myself grateful for the space.

"Should I stop?" He trailed his tongue over my sensitive flesh with supreme confidence.

"Please, don't stop." The blood rushed to my head, and with him having choked me so recently, I was still lightheaded and slightly high.

"Then use your words, Claire. Tell me what happened last night."

"I came so hard!"

"When did you come so hard?" His mouth only left me as long as was absolutely necessary to speak.

"Don't make me say it," I begged, and his tongue slowed. I whimpered and bucked before I shouted, "I came so hard when Vick walked in on you going down on me!" For a moment, I forgot entirely about the driver.

I tensed and, like he so often did, he read my mind. "Yes, baby, he can hear you, but he won't look. I told him if he sees what's mine, I'll fucking kill him, but I wanted him to hear what I was going to do to you. I knew how hard it would make you come."

He pulled my thighs off his shoulders, sliding them around his waist and resting my knees on the seat. My pussy was in the perfect position for him. He took his cock out and lined himself up with my entrance. His fingers gently massaged my ass and for a moment, he seemed to relish the anticipation. Until he filled me with one swift thrust.

I shouted, but I was so wet he only met the resistance of my muscles tightening around him. "Your pussy is so fucking tight, baby, and your ass looks glorious above my cock." He was silent for a few moments as the car navigated the streets and the only sounds were the tires on the pavement, our ragged breaths, and flesh slapping.

"I will never get enough of you, Claire. Every time I have you, I want you even more. I'd do anything for you. I'd fuck you anywhere, any way you liked..."

"Fuck, Mase, just like that," I whimpered, beyond directly responding to any of the filthy things he said. He came off the seat, pounding into me with intensely deep, slow strokes. My clit touched the soft skin of his balls as he thrust the last inch and rocked his hips inside me. The pressure was just enough to drive me crazy.

"I'll do whatever makes you happy, Claire. Any man would kill to have you this way. I'm happy to show them what they're missing, but I'm the only one who gets to taste this pussy. This is the only cock your pussy will pump the cum out of."

I nodded my head, "What about you? Am I the only one who gets to pump the cum out of you? Does anyone get you besides me?" It was a question I often asked myself when he didn't come home at night and one he'd answered before, but somehow this wasn't about jealousy or fear anymore.

"It's all yours. I am all yours, baby." His words filled me with utter rightness. He reached around, pressing my clit in just the right way to make my body shake and my orgasm tear through me. He followed immediately after.

He pulled me off his lap and lifted my panties, skirt, and pantyhose for me to wriggle into.

"I need to go home and change now, and so do you," I said.

"No, baby. We're going to wear each other today."

Seventeen

Claire

M ason walked me to the door and kissed me deeply before leaving me practically shaking with my thighs still damp for the second day in a row. I rolled my eyes at myself for being such a pushover.

The black SUV pulled up, and the group of overgrown men played a game of musical chairs as they swapped vehicles. By the time they were done, Mason and his driver left in the black SUV, and Lawrence and James sat in the white one.

I unlocked the door and flipped on the lights. Emma was just behind me, and I said good morning to her briefly. I barely looked at her as we exchanged a few words about what I'd like done. I scurried away from her as quickly as possible.

Closing the door to my office felt like wrapping myself in a security blanket. At least here, I could pretend I controlled who had access to me. I sat down at my desk and started up the computer. I had a mountain of pressing work to get through, yet all I could think about was the impossible debt I owed to the victims of Charles Gains. Did all the other girls look like me, like his mom? His first victim, Rebecca, didn't. But Erica and I both did, and a twinge went through me. Would I ever know for sure if it was Erica's blood on my wall?

Probably not, just like I probably wouldn't find all the women he killed, but I believed Erica was one of them and if I could prove that, maybe the whole thing would unravel. I pulled up the news database and typed in her full name.

Numerous articles appeared. She was popular, involved in her community, and frequently featured when the football team and cheer squad made the papers. Stunning, with an innocent girl next door vibe, her long brown hair was beachy and bouncy. She looked more like Priscilla Gains than I did.

The deeper I dug, any remaining doubts disappeared. Erica was one of his victims. That realization came at the same time as another; no one had bothered me in a while, and quiet moments at the library made me nervous.

There were always little things volunteers needed to ask or tell me, and as much as Emma might want to avoid me, it wasn't really possible with her position and mine. I stepped out into the hallway, surprised by how quiet things were. From a cursory glance, the library was empty, but that didn't mean all the aisles were.

My heart pounded in my chest as I tried to keep my steps as quiet as my surroundings. Angry murmurs interrupted the silence, and I crept toward the conflict against my better judgment. I would be better off going back to my office and minding my business.

This place is cursed, my instincts screamed at me, or perhaps it was the anxiety making things up to scare me. The shooting irreparably damaged my fight-or-flight response and I couldn't decide which impulse to trust. Was I just as cursed as this building by choosing to stay here and learn its secrets?

"You can't keep coming here. Do you even care how hard you've made things on me?" Emma's angry voice demanded.

"You didn't have to tell her. In fact, you shouldn't have. Do you have any idea how much trouble you can get me into from trying to be a 'good friend'?" The quotation marks in his tone told me exactly what James thought about my relationship with Emma.

She let out an annoyed huff. "I don't care. She is my friend, and she needed to know. I feel so shitty she found out that way." The sadness in her voice made my heart ache. "I will not run and tell her everything, but I will *not* keep lying to her. I won't!"

"You have to."

She scoffed. "Why, James? Why the fuck should I do anything you or Mason or anyone else says? Are you threatening *me* now?" My skin prickled at the obvious threat in *her* voice. I smiled despite the ache in my stomach.

"No, shortcake. It's not a threat. Mason says she can't take it. She was stalked and shot. That piece of shit destroyed everything she owned. You didn't see what he did to her apartment. It was..." he took a deep breath, "it was fucked up. Mason thinks she's about to have a mental breakdown or something. He's scared shitless for the girl."

"And? What do you think?" she challenged.

He sighed like he was tired from having this argument repeatedly. "I think she's tougher than he thinks. She's struggling, but he's contributing to the situation more than he realizes."

"So, tell him to wise the fuck up."

"I tried!" he whisper yelled.

"She deserves more than lies from everyone who cares about her."

"The situation is not that simple. Giving Mason my heartfelt advice doesn't mean he'll take it. He's stubborn as hell."

"I'm not going to keep arguing with you, James. We're not even together. Why I'm having this conversation with you is beyond me."

"You know exactly why you're talking to me. I'm your person, shortcake, and being a bitch to me won't change that."

"Because you keep showing up where you're not wanted!" the irritation in her voice didn't make the words convincing.

"You love me as much as I love you, and I know how badly you want me here." She huffed. "Don't go blabbing everything to her just yet, sweetheart. Give me some time."

"To talk sense into, Mason?" If I wasn't so infuriated and hurt, I would have laughed at the comparatively docile tone of her voice. I imagined him stroking her cheek, and I didn't blame her for getting a little gooey when he spoke to her that way.

"I'll do my best."

"Better than your best. We both know how short that can fall." I couldn't hear anything else, and a moment later, James turned around and walked out.

I hid until they were both out of sight before I stepped out from the rack. I could barely breathe, torn apart by the conflicting emotions. Emma had lied and kept things from me, and I *was* angry about that. But I had very few people in my life who stuck up for me. The fact that she did meant she was worth forgiving.

But what made my heart sink and my stomach knot was how Mason spoke about me to others. How did he come to think so little of me, and what did that mean for our relationship?

Eighteen

Mason

I opened the partition fully as soon as I left Claire, silently daring my driver to say a word. His cheeks were bright red, and I'd bet his pants were too tight, but he was smart enough to keep his mouth shut. I meant it when I said I'd kill him if he paid too much attention when that divider closed.

I couldn't quite make sense of my emotions regarding the night before, and I was glad to be without Vick or James for once. The eventful end to our date proved to be another unneeded complication on an already long list. Claire was upset, and I was too. At least that's what I kept telling myself, but my dick getting hard each time I thought of it didn't support that claim.

The last thing I needed was another issue to sort through. Or a sexual awakening that involved other people. I wasn't the type of man to share. The idea of anyone other than me touching her made me half-feral, and my thoughts on those who looked at her weren't much better. Despite that, I couldn't deny how much it turned me on to see her like that and know it got her off.

I didn't understand the desires and emotions conflicting and aligning within me. But the protective urge to defend what was mine made me impossibly hard and tense like my body subconsciously prepared to fuck or fight with little concern for which. The fact that other men would never have what was mine—despite how much they wanted her—made me feel like a god. As long as I was the only one sinking my cock inside her, I didn't care if my hubris killed me. Then, there were moments I realized how fucking insane I sounded.

I wasn't trying to force forgiveness out of her when I claimed her in the car that morning. I just lost it. Kissing her meant something to me. Life was fleeting, fucking impermanent, and ready to end at any point. Living the type of life I was, dying wasn't an unreasonable expectation. The press of her lips meant I had something to hold on to, and I needed that. To connect with her, to remind her that despite everything happening, the two of us worked.

I walked into the club, shaking the thoughts out of my head. Focus, I told myself. The door pushed open easily beneath my hand even though it was the middle of the afternoon and they wouldn't be open for hours. As one who never overlooked simple favors, I appreciated the convenience.

A pretty blonde stood behind the bar polishing glasses. "We're closed," she sounded annoyed until she looked up and her eyes ran over me. "I'll make an exception, though, if you'd like a drink."

"No, thank you. I'm here to see Hector." I smiled and walked through the open space toward the hallway in the back. She didn't question me further, but her eyes stayed on me.

Hector had worked for my father since he was a kid. Dear old dad's financial backing made this club possible, but recently he stopped receiving wire transfers from David Sharp's offshore shell corporation. That lent some credibility to him appearing on both Gavin's and Francis' lists of defectors.

I smiled to myself as I passed the storage room I'd taken Claire to on our one-night clubbing. The entire night was a fucking disaster—the tip of the iceberg in a line of disasters, really—but that sex was too amazing to not harden at the memory.

I reached Hector's office and instead of remembering the toe curling sex with the girl I love, my mind drifted back to the time I almost bought this club myself.

Seven months earlier

A ripping sound cut through the air as I pulled the zipper up on my pants. "I'm not buying this." I gestured at the surrounding office, unimpressed.

"Are you serious?" Sarah huffed as she pulled up her panties and straightened out her skirt.

"Entirely."

"I thought we were celebrating!" Her hair was barely out of place, as she had been very clear that I was not allowed to not touch it. That was fine by me. I couldn't help imagining her as the rude little brunette from the library anyway, and her bleach blonde locks ruined the illusion.

I couldn't say the same for her blouse, which was completely wrinkled from me squeezing her tits as I pounded into her. They weren't her tits I imagined in my hands, but they'd done the job.

"If this was a celebration, then we've celebrated in every piece of property you've shown me." The first time she'd taken me out to some rundown shit hole she thought worthy of my investment, she bent over the bar and spread her bare pussy for me. Who was I to say no to such a gracious offer?

We fucked a few times, and while it was enjoyable enough to keep me focused at an exceptionally busy time at work, this wasn't anything special. Then, I'd met the girl in the library and my head hadn't been on straight since.

"Oh, come on, Mason. This place is perfect! It is exactly what you want." Nope. I wanted a brat with curly brown hair, pouty lips, and an ass I needed to take a bite out of.

I looked over at her and the room surrounding us. "No, I don't think it is."

"This is unbelievable." She threw her hands up in the air, letting them fall and slap against her thighs.

"This was okay." I corrected, signaling between us both. She made an angry noise as she stormed by, out of the office, and out the front door. I left it open behind me, knowing she had to lock the place back up and headed to my car. The scent of the leather relaxed me, as did the smooth power of the engine as I pulled away.

Sarah cared about the sale, not the sex. I wasn't trying to be a dick, but I was starting to think the idea of diversifying in this city was just asking for trouble. A short while later, I pulled into the parking garage beneath my office building and into my assigned parking spot.

Riding the elevator up to my floor, I walked into the office. Katie jumped up from her social media scrolling, looking nervous and pink as I passed. "You're taking advantage, Katie." I teased, genuinely not giving a shit if she slacked off a bit when I wasn't here. As long as she answered the phone and did her work, I expected her to be human.

The girl was as skittish as a mouse. "I'm kidding, Katie," I said, and I swore I heard her catch her breath.

I sat down at my desk and dug into my work. This was one of those weeks where everything was going at least partially wrong, but I would handle things. I was fucking excellent at what I did. The downside was my clients required more coddling than usual and dealing with these fucks was wearing my patience down to nothing.

Hours later, I looked up from my desk and noticed the door to my office open; Katie was long gone. I wasn't ready to head home. Sometimes, it was too much house for one guy, a housekeeper, and a seldom-needed driver. This office suited me more in most ways.

I needed a break, something to make me laugh. I pulled up a forum for casual encounters. Meeting up with someone wasn't my intention, but they were entertaining as hell and I enjoyed reading them. Who knew, I might find something exciting or unlock a new kink.

I perused a few of the listings, people shouting into the void, hoping to be heard. Humans were such base creatures. Dressed up with civilized things like pants and bureaucracy to pretend we're better than simple beings motivated by fear, sex, and hunger. Then I landed on the one that made my heart do a little flip like a girl in a movie, and my cock harden painfully.

I'm an attractive brunette, 26, lots of tits and ass, with a small waist. What I want is simple: I'm shy, single, and I need to get laid. I would go to a bar and pick someone up, but that's not my style. Seeking a man 25-40, fit, good-looking, and able to do the job right.

If I have to do this twice, I will die of embarrassment. You must chat online with me first and exchange pictures, just to prove to me you are who you say. I'm not trying to date you or see inside your soul. I want to make sure you're not a creep before I invite you over for some steamy, casual sex.

-Tired of Waiting

I laughed out loud, utterly charmed, and unable to explain why I was sure she was telling the truth about being beautiful. Some wishful thinking, most likely, mixed with the fact I was already harboring ridiculous feelings for a girl I'd never meet again. I imagined that girl from the library as I pulled my cock into my hand and typed my response.

I knocked on Hector's door as I cleared my mind.

"Come in,"

I eyed the room quickly as I opened the door. He was alone, which I hoped he would be, considering I came without backup.

James was with Claire, and Vick was tying up loose ends with Casey and Mila. There wasn't anyone else I trusted with my business.

From Hector's hand on his fly and the disappointment in his eyes, I easily deduced why no one else was around. I smirked at having caught him pulling his pants down, probably for the girl behind the bar. "Do you always take your pants off when you're alone in the office?" I clicked the door shut casually behind me.

"Who the fuck are you?" he barked as his hand twitched toward his gun.

I put my hands up, showing him I came in peace. I was taking a risk and leaving myself open, but that was my best option, seeing as I didn't want either of us dead.

"My name is Mason Sharp, and I'm here for a chat." The room was a pale gray, unlike the last time. He had a muted green desk and matching bookshelves. The effect was absurdly masculine and downright ugly.

"You can't be," he laughed, his bright white teeth gleamed unnaturally in the light hanging over his desk. I imagined a purple glow from the whitening process. He buzzed his dark hair and wore an eyebrow ring with a scar beside it like the original had been ripped out and re-pierced.

"Why's that?" I cocked my head to the side, sizing up his massive shape and the money he dumped into his clothes. He wore at least twenty grand in fabric and another eighty in watches and jewelry, but his calloused hands gave him away. He was new money, but he worked hard for what he had. It must suffocate him to know how close he was to losing everything.

"From the shit I've heard, Mason Sharp wouldn't dare. Daddy's Boy, towing the company line, killed the guy who fucked with his girl out of a jealous fit." He looked me up and down. "They say he's a bitch. Are you a bitch?"

"I don't give a fuck what anyone says. People talk a lot, Hector, but it rarely adds up to anything. Fists and blood are so much more concrete." I looked at my fists and flexed my knuckles. It had been years since I added to the scars, but they were pink and bright now, still healing from the last few months.

"Is that a threat?" Hector's eyes narrowed, and I chuckled at the truly confused look on his face.

"No, it's not, just a statement of fact. You don't strike me as the type that would be overly bothered by what people have to say."

"I suppose that depends on what they're saying and why they're saying it, but you don't know me well enough to assume that."

"Keeping my reputation questionable serves some people well. We all have a reputation, even you, but I didn't come here to discuss rumors. I have a proposition for you, and I think you would be wise to consider it."

"Fuck that!" he spat. "Get out of my office."

I understood his hesitance. He didn't know me and what he'd heard wasn't flattering. He was already on shaky ground, and taking a meeting with me would push him even further into question. "You're losing your business, Hector. You're not profitable, and your boss thinks that failure is because you're stealing from the bottom line—his bottom line. You're going to wind up dead, but I could help you."

"I don't need anyone's help, least of all yours. You can go." He waved toward the door like getting rid of me would be so simple.

"I've always liked this place. I thought about buying her myself earlier this year, but I backed out. Do you know why?"

"I couldn't give a fuck."

"It's because there isn't enough business here to make it profitable without a little extra. You're hemorrhaging money and your boss is not the most forgiving." I waved around the room. "This is all going to disappear along with you!"

"My boss is your daddy," he sneered.

"He's my daddy and yet, he's not my boss." I smiled at the displeased twist of his lips.

Hector stood. "Get the fuck out of my office." He puffed up his chest like he was ready to fight.

"Five hundred thousand dollars cash, injected into your business tomorrow."

"Excuse me?" He nearly stumbled as he pulled back in shock. "You don't have that kind of money."

I laughed outright then, "Saving your business is well inside my budget, I assure you."

"What do you want?"

"It's simple. I'll consider this an investment. I want my money back and I want a share of the profits once you turn them. But you'll never do that with a cover charge and the price of drinks alone. You need to expand."

"I'm not selling no fucking girls. I turned the other way a few times, but I'm not getting any deeper into that shit."

"That shit is not what I'm referring to. I have quite a lot of expertise to offer if you're interested in running a gambling ring, but I heard you had a soft spot for a good fight. There aren't any underground fights operating in the city right now. It's an entirely untapped market and a big one at that."

"I thought you didn't like crime, Mr. Lawyer."

"I *do* have a problem with some crimes. If people agree to gamble their money away or beat the shit out of each other, I don't see how that's anyone's business but theirs. But stolen girls aren't making those choices for themselves and they aren't keeping the money they make.

"I'm sold on the highlights. Let's hear the catch." He waved his hand in an impatient gesture.

"There's no catch. I give you a lot of money, help you save your business, help you save your life, and you give me your loyalty, and by extension, that of your men."

He glanced toward the door at the mention of his men, and I wondered who he was waiting for. It could be devastating for our tenuous peace if someone walked in and tipped the odds. "My men are your father's men. You should know that."

Hector was a solid liar, and dare I say I liked him, but I was well informed about his dealings. Among the paperwork Casey provided me was some rather damning evidence that Hector had a side project. "Ah, but that's not who I'm talking about."

His eyes widened briefly before he contained his reaction. "You don't know what you're talking about."

"I don't know that you've been sneaking soldiers into the country who hold no loyalties to David Sharp? I don't know that you've helped their children and wives get medical attention and housing for a priceless supply of unyielding loyalty? You're smart, Hector. Nothing makes someone want to follow you like taking care of their family."

"It's a convenient side effect, not why I did it. What would you want from them?" There was a hint of nervousness in his expression. I had definitely caught his interest, but I could see he cared for those people and was hesitant to sign them up for something that he didn't understand. I never felt more confident about my decision to seek him out than I did at that moment. Hector was no saint, but he was honorable, and that was enough for me.

"I need soldiers on the ground if I'm going to change the power structure in this city."

"Change the power structure? Jesus, you *are* a lawyer. Just love talking in circles. Why don't you say it straight, pretty boy?"

"I'm going to take control of this city, Hector, and there are two sides you can take. For other people, I understand sticking with David Sharp, but not for you. You're too smart to want to die and you're too proud to see your dream turn to dust when there's a chance to save it. This is not a gift. This is an investment."

He tapped a large finger against his lip, seeming to think so hard it was uncomfortable. "I'm sold on everything you're saying, but I don't know you. I don't trust you, I don't respect you, and I'm not doing business with someone I don't at least respect."

I nodded my head, unable to argue with that assertion, but I had an idea. "You value strength, bravery even."

"I do."

"How about a fight, then? No weapons, nothing fancy, just some old-fashioned bare-knuckle boxing."

His eyebrow kicked up in surprise. "So what? If you win, I work for you?" the scoff in his voice told me exactly what he thought of that.

"No, it's not about winning. It's about respect and meeting you on your own turf. You need to see what I'm made of, isn't that right? I'm giving you a lot, but I'm asking for a lot too."

He gave me a genuine smile, and I had him. "Fuck it, let's fight." He shrugged out of his suit jacket and undid the buttons on his cuffs as he stalked toward me with his fists raised. He smiled once more, before his fist connected with my jaw. I swung back, more than ready to show Hector just what type of investor I would be.

A while later, we were bloody and exhausted, but laughing and joking like old friends. "Let's do it, Sharp. Fuck your cunt of a father. It's time for a change."

"Show me the basement. I want to see where our fights will take place."

He clapped a big hand against my back. "Let's go."

Nineteen

Claire

After the conversation I overheard between Emma and James, I went back to my office to stew in my anger. Part of me legitimately wished to hunt Mason down and beat the shit out of him. The impulse surprised the hell out of me, given that I wasn't typically a violent person. Another part wanted to curl up in bed with him and convince the inflexible fuck I was okay.

That wouldn't work because, as James said, he was incredibly stubborn, and because... I wasn't entirely okay. My obsession with Erica Miller was taking more and more of my time. The nightmares haunting me were changing and coming more frequently.

There was so much mystery, enough that I might never sleep again. I couldn't stay focused on being angry with Mason when he was right about me. Not that I agreed with his actions. He was making things worse, but he did think he watched me die. I cannot imagine how I would have reacted in his shoes.

Despite everything, he still saw me in a way no one else did. Even in the face of his lies, he revealed my truths.

I wanted to forget the reasons Mason was worth forgiving. The anger was easier than dropping off into the abyss of our combined pain. That need to school my thoughts cleared my mind and eventually gave way to a plan. I would get justice for the victims of Charles Gains, *without* sending myself or the love of my life to prison.

If I collected enough compelling evidence and anonymously handed it over to the police, they might find some of their bodies and give the women proper burials. Erica Miller was the first girl I connected with on my quest for the truth, and the fact she originally lived only an hour's drive from Mason's house seemed utterly serendipitous for both myself and Charles.

Saturday morning I would slip away without a guard and see if anyone remembered Charles and Erica together. Police aren't supposed to decide who's guilty and work backward to prove it, but I was no cop and I didn't have any qualms about how I revealed who Charles really was.

I checked the map, and though the route was simple enough, I was grateful for the GPS. Finally, I printed a picture of Charles on the library printer reserved for flyers and such. I never bought ink, and a spiteful part of me didn't want to use Mason's fancy printers with their laser jets and ink economy. By the time I was done, it was about noon.

A small rap sounded on the door. "Come in."

Emma stood in the doorway with an extra pale cast on her skin. It was the first time I'd seen her for more than a second all day. After what I overheard, and after I recovered from the initial shock, I wanted to talk to her, but she avoided me. She scurried around the library, fussing over the simplest tasks like it was world book day, and the future of literature depended on her.

"I'm headed to lunch," she told me from the doorway.

"Where are you going?"

"I'm grabbing a sandwich at the place on the corner." She gestured over her shoulder, already taking a step to walk away.

"Would you like to come out with me?" I needed to clear the air. After hearing what she said earlier, I felt like an asshole for being so hard on her. This entire world of criminals was practically mythical to me last year. I couldn't expect Emma to miraculously understand how to navigate the situation better than I did.

Her eyes flashed in surprise, and she took a solid moment to think about my request. "Yeah, sure. Where did you want to go?" She tucked a strand of her strawberry hair behind her ear and glanced down.

I blurted out my first thought. "Uh, do you like Indian?"

"I do."

"I know a good place nearby. Did you bring your car today?"

"No, I rode my bike."

"It's not too far. We can ride together." I got up from my desk and gathered my things as I headed toward the door. "There is one little thing that should not be a problem. James is my *bodyguard* for the day." I rolled my eyes.

"Oh, okay. I mean, we're not eating with him, right?"

"Nope, I'm mad at him."

"You and me both, sister," she agreed as she grabbed my arm and led me out to the car.

The air rippled with the sexual tension between James and Emma as we rode to the restaurant. He stared at her, and she did her best to ignore him. That resulted in her glancing over every thirty seconds, give or take.

"Can you two kiss and make up already? For fuck's sake, this is painful." I blurted out when the tension got so thick I thought *I* might explode.

"You're supposed to be on my side, Claire." Emma hissed, her blue eyes widening in shock and anger.

"I *am* on your side, but I can't take this," I complained. "The two of you have some stuff to work out."

"There is absolutely nothing to work out between us." Emma scoffed, but her cheeks turned pink as she met James' gaze.

I made a disbelieving sound in the back of my throat, and James laughed throatily. "Shortcake, don't pretend you don't need me as bad as I need you. You can deny us all you want, but that doesn't change how we are together. Claire doesn't deserve the attitude when she's spot on."

"I don't need the flattery, James."

"Fuck this," Emma spat.

The car pulled up outside Sadar's restaurant. "We're here," I climbed out, relief flooding through me.

Before I could ask James to stay behind, Emma beat me to it. "You are *not* invited, James. Sit in the car and wait for us. You should be familiar with the concept."

"How many fucking times do I have to say I'm sorry about that?"

"Let's try zero more times," she quipped as she slammed the door. I wondered what James had done, but she was too annoyed for me to ask her about it now.

"Do you plan on giving him a break at any point?" I asked as we walked toward the restaurant.

"Where's the fun in that?" She winked at me.

"Being with the man you love?" I only just found out about their relationship, but the chemistry between them reminded me of what I felt with Mason.

She stepped ahead of me to open the door, deftly ignoring me. I followed close behind her, overtaken by the scents and colors.

The warm atmosphere and the heavy aroma of spices filled my senses. I closed my eyes to enjoy the complicated melody. Dim light gave everything a honey-tinged glow and, though the day was sunny, it felt intimate and secluded. Winter was a myth beneath the warmth of Sadar's restaurant.

Worn and crinkled faux leather wrapped the booths and intricate mosaics decorated the tables. Little candles flickered with tiny flames in their centers and I deeply regretted never accepting Sadar's invitation to come in person until now.

"Claire, is that you?" Sadar's friendly voice enveloped me and I glanced up, finding him running out from behind the counter. "What happened to you? I haven't seen you in so long. I was worried."

He wrapped his arms around me, and I hugged him back, relishing the comfort. Sadar never made things weird between us, and especially after the debacle with Charles Gains, a man that made me comfortable was a rarity.

"It's me." I laughed at the simple statement. Was it even true? "It's a long story though." I pushed back from him but gazed at his face. He really was a handsome man, safe and sweet in every way.

He patted my shoulder as he released me. "I heard about the mugging outside your building and after I didn't hear from you, I am ashamed to say I feared the worst."

"Well, you were right, except I'm not dead." I laughed nervously. The tension of the moment was too much for me to take and I waved toward Emma. "This is my friend Emma. Emma, this is Sadar."

"Hi, Sadar. Nice to meet you." Emma batted her eyelashes.

"It's very nice to meet you too," his voice came out a little softer than normal. Clearly, the blue-eyed minx beside me was his type. My eyes flicked to the door as James had just walked in.

I sighed as I realized Emma was trying to make James jealous. "Come on, Em. Let's sit down." I nudged her, interrupting whatever she was saying to Sadar.

"Of course, ladies. Wherever you like. Lunch is on me."

"Oh, that's unnecessary. I'm happy to pay." I said.

"No arguments. You can pay the next time you come in." He wrapped his arm around the back of my shoulder in a brotherly gesture. He led us to a table right by the counter, pulling out a chair for me, then one for Emma.

A trickle of guilt ran through me as Sadar looked at me with grateful eyes. I had no idea he thought of me, let alone worried about me. I should have stayed in touch. Were there any other people in my life who knew about the "mugging" and worried about me? *Definitely not my mom...*

Sadar and I weren't the best of friends, but he was a friend all the same and had always been kind to me. There was more to my life than I realized, and more people thought of me and wanted good things for me. I couldn't help but think about how that related to Mason. His motives were pure, even if his methods left me angry and hollow.

Sadar ran behind the counter as the phone rang, assuring the two of us he would be right back.

"So, what brought this on?" Emma began. She was uncomfortable, but that didn't prevent her from being straightforward.

"I overheard you and James fighting and what you said. I'm still mad about everything, but I care about our friendship, and I'm willing to forgive if you're willing to be more honest."

"Are you serious?" the disbelief in her tone didn't give me many clues about what she was thinking.

"I'm completely serious."

"So, we're here because you were spying on me. This whole thing began with you spying on me," she stifled a laugh.

"Well, I wasn't spying. You happen to be loud and fight with James at work a lot." At the mention of his name, her eyes flicked over to a table in the corner. Sure enough, he was chatting with Sadar and looking over a menu.

After taking two more orders, Sadar brought us a pair of creamy white drinks. "This is my lassi recipe. You will love it. There are so many things here you have never tried and should have. You were missing out." Sadar was in his element, and Emma and I giggled as he flew around like an ordered tornado, shmoozing customers, talking to the guys in the kitchen, and chatting with us.

"You never thought of dating him?" Emma asked me in one of the moments he ran off.

"I think I briefly considered fucking him, but no. Sadar is an amazing guy, and I love his food. It would be a real shame to not be able to come here after a messy breakup."

"True. He just seems like a catch."

"He's somebodies." I agreed.

"Maybe mine."

"I doubt it."

"And why is that? I'm nice and pretty. I deserve a guy like Sadar."

"Sadar deserves someone who loves him, and the man you love is sitting alone at that table in the corner while you feign interest in my friend."

Her cheeks turned hot pink. "James and I are done, Claire. I mean it, and you shouldn't go putting ideas into his head. He's persistent enough without your help."

"Well, I'm sorry. I thought I was picking up on something. Must have been my mistake."

"Exactly."

Sadar came back to our table and dropped off a few plates I didn't recognize. Emma and I dug in, relishing the delicious food. I ripped off a piece of bread puff and dipped it in chickpeas. "Mmm, why isn't this on your delivery menu, Sadar? It is so good."

"Because puri doesn't travel well." He smirked at me in satisfaction. "I told you to come in and eat. If I knew you had such a beautiful friend, I would have asked you to bring her in as well."

Emma giggled. "You should hire some help. I've been meaning to get better acquainted with you, but you're all over the place."

"I have two cooks in the kitchen, that's plenty of help, but maybe some other time I can cook for you and we can get to know each other better."

"I'm not opposed to the idea." Emma's voice was unnaturally low and falsely smokey. "What about a counter person? Wouldn't you like to take a break?"

"If I hire someone to do my job, what will I do?" His smile was flirtatious, and his brown cheeks looked darker than normal.

"Oh, I don't know. Run the business?" she told him as he pushed a bowl of biryani in front of us.

"Sadar, I can't eat anymore," I complained, unwilling to shove a single bite into my mouth.

"Try this. It's the last thing, I swear, and you can take the leftovers home. Your boyfriend will love them."

"How do you know I have a boyfriend, Sadar?"

"This is how I run my business, Claire. I know everything." He gave Emma and me a warm smile. "If you'd like to leave me your number, I would be happy to make good on my offer." Sadar smiled at Emma.

"She's not giving you her number." James' voice sent alarm bells ringing in my head.

"James, this is none of your business. Fuck off." Emma shot.

"Fuck that shit. You are my business, shortcake, and he doesn't need your fucking number."

"Hey, I'm not trying to get in the middle of anything. Your pal Sadar isn't into love triangles." He held up his hands in a placating gesture. I mouthed sorry to him, and he shook his head with a little smile on his face like he found James' antics mildly amusing.

"Are you two ready to go?" James' voice still had that threatening note in it despite Sadar's quick acquiescence. His eyes were on Emma and he looked pissed.

"Just a minute, James," I spoke in what I hoped was a soothing voice.

Emma rolled her eyes, and he walked away. "Is he ever going to give up?"

"Do you actually want him to?" I expected a quick answer, but she remained silent as she chewed her lip and packed up the food. I hugged Sadar goodbye when we left, and promised I would be back sooner next time.

The ride back to the library was filled with more thick sexual tension than the ride there. No one spoke a word, but I swore a match would have sent the whole car up in flames. By the time we climbed out of the car at the library, my panties were wet and I was willing to chase Mason down. If he wasn't off killing people and lying to me about it, perhaps he would come fuck me in my office. I fired off a text, hoping for the best.

TWENTY

Mason

I t was a long fucking day, and after the text I received from Claire, all I wanted to do was go home and give her the attention she wanted. My cock was hard and my heart hurt because that text was an olive branch and I'd rejected it.

I met up with Vick shortly after I spoke with Hector, and we headed into the dilapidated part of the city we both hated. The warehouse district was all lit up in reds and golds with the setting sun. I looked past the ramshackle buildings and toward the horizon, seeing the skyscrapers mixed in with squat historical buildings in the distance.

The bar was barely noticeable down a narrow alley and tucked into the back of one warehouse. A faintly glowing Budweiser sign from the eighties dimmed and flared as the neon failed in a long, narrow window. Otherwise, they blacked out the glass with paper and spray paint.

I pushed the door open, and Vick followed behind me. We walked toward an empty table in the back, avoiding eye contact with the multitude of people staring us down. The walls were a dark hunter green with splashes of stains.

Smoke hung heavy in the air. The reek of stale beer and sweat turned my stomach. A biting chemical scent stung my nose. Maybe PCP.

Vick settled into the seat beside me, sitting so still he was like a statue. A girl wiped a filthy rag across the table beside us, mopping up the spilled beer but leaving the surface still sticky. Vick was especially tense tonight with his eyes darting from person to person. This bar was a place he'd rather burn to the ground than have a drink at.

Music played from an ancient jukebox. A man and woman leaned against it, kissing and grinding like they were about to fuck. An older biker couple danced in the space between two tables they pushed apart. Their gang sat around them whooping and hollering as the man grabbed his partner's ass and dipped her. At least shit was going well for some people.

"You doing alright?" I asked Vick when I was certain he hadn't taken a breath in the last minute.

"Feels the same." His eyes zipped around the room. Vick and James spent a lot of time here as kids while their mom was looking for her next John. Vick's dad, her first pimp, was dead by the time Vick was two, from a heroin overdose.

By all accounts, James' father was a John, but there is a slim possibility the two of them share a father. Francis picked her up before Vick turned nine.

Dragging this shit up for Vick wracked me with guilt. I would have brought James instead. He was six by the time they stopped coming here and remembers a lot less, but Claire insisted she'd rather stay with James today. After what Vick walked in on, I didn't blame her for not wanting to spend quiet time with him.

People stared at Vick and me from the crowded bar. The tailored suits we wore were like a sign over our heads that we didn't belong. Whether we were law enforcement or syndicate enforcement was yet to be decided. Either way, the tense ripple in the air arrived with us.

A pretty, young girl with long brown hair played pool with a grungy-looking drunk in his fifties. Her curly hair and warm eyes reminded me of Claire. She could have been her little cousin. The girl looked to be fifteen or sixteen. Someone like her—young, vulnerable, and alone—in this kind of place, made my skin prickle.

"Mason..." Victor growled.

"I know." His mom was about that age when she met her first pimp, Vick's father. She dropped out of tenth grade to give birth to him.

The girl took the chalk, rubbed it on the end of her cue, and blew off the excess with overdone flirtation. The old man licked his lips as she bent over the table and attempted to break. It was a colossal failure. She made the perfect distressed pouty faces as she turned to him. "I don't know how I'll ever be able to afford to cover this," she gestured toward the money on the edge of the table.

"Oh, don't worry, sweetheart. I'm sure a pretty girl like you can convince me to take it in trade. Let's make it double or nothing. If you win, you get a thousand bucks and if *I* win, I get to test out that tight little teenage cunt of yours."

Her face scrunched up adorably, making her look even younger. "Well, I could use the money if I win, and if I lose, you'll be gentle with me, won't you, mister? I'm a virgin." I smiled to myself as I listened. She was laying it on thick, but the bastard fell for her act.

"Don't worry, pretty girl. Let's make it two grand. That sweet cherry is worth risking that much." His cock was hard in his pants and he openly adjusted himself, squeezing as he stared at the girl. He pulled more cash out of his pocket and put it on the side of the table.

"Do you want to break?" She fluttered her lashes at him.

"No, pretty girl. You do it."

He watched intently as she bent over the table, sizing up his winnings. She lined up her shot, hitting true. Several balls spun out and sunk into pockets.

"Stripes," she called lazily. She walked around the table, eyeing up the balls, "Ten, left corner pocket." She easily made the shot. "Twelve and fifteen, center right pocket." She lined up the shot, easily dropping both balls.

The drunk's mouth hung open as he tried to make sense of how quickly he'd lost out on the prospect of teenage pussy. "Fucking bitch!" he screamed. His face was a bright red mask of fury. "You think you can hustle me?"

The grimy bastard slapped the cue out of her hands and grabbed her around the collar. Vick vibrated with tension, watching the interaction even more closely than I did.

"Go get him before you burst a capillary." Vick wasted no time pushing out of his chair and meeting the guy head-on. Vick threw his fist into the side of his face without pause, knocking him onto the pool table. He dropped the girl as he fell, but she couldn't get her balance back and landed on her ass; she looked up at Vick with stunned eyes.

He reached down and helped her to her feet and the girl practically had hearts in her eyes as she looked at him. "You okay, kid?"

"I'm not a kid, but I'm fine. I could have handled him."

"How old are you, fifteen?"

"Seventeen," she huffed as if he offended her.

"You're a kid, so stop being a fucking idiot," she wanted to argue with him, but the drunk spat a mouthful of blood out on the table, interrupting their conversation.

"What the fuck?" the man garbled. Vick grabbed him by the collar with a vicious look in his eyes.

"Victor, we're here on business. Teach him a lesson. No need to tutor the fuck until graduation." The girl quickly grabbed her winnings off the table and headed for the door, not sparing a glance for the man who attacked her or the all-out assault

Vick was leveling against him. I stood, walking into her path and blocking her exit.

She sized me up, deciding what I wanted from her. I pulled some more cash out of my pocket and handed it to her. Even though she won two grand, that wouldn't last long. Especially if she had anyone she was taking care of. "Stay out of places like this. You're good enough to hustle upscale if you have the right outfit."

She flashed me a pretty smile. "Sorry, my pussy isn't for sale."

"Thank God for small favors, kid." Her face turned red as I clapped her on the shoulder and went back over to Vick. He was explicitly ignoring my instructions, pounding the guy into a bloody pulp.

"Vick, let's go." I slapped him on the back.

His fist paused midair as he got control of himself. "Disgusting fuck," he grunted at the heap of moaning, bruised flesh.

The filthy bouncer came over to us then. This wasn't the type of place you interrupted a fight straight off, but Vick had come exceptionally close to giving the guy some permanent brain damage.

"You two need to go." The guy puffed up his absurdly muscled chest.

"Leave it to you two to find trouble in the fifteen minutes I'm running late." A familiar voice spoke from behind us.

"Hey, Dan."

He rolled his eyes. "I have business with Mr. Dubois, Eric. Please escort the gentleman out." He nodded over his shoulder toward the guy Vick had just pummeled.

"When did he buy this place?" Vick muttered under his breath beside me.

"A few years ago. Though he hasn't changed it much." You'd think that with how he'd designed his office and buildings, he might do something with this place.

"Gentleman!" Dan exclaimed as he led us through a door and into an office that had recently been redone. "What the fuck are you doing here? Mason, if you want me dead so badly, kill me!"

"If I wanted you dead, you would be dead, Danny." I looked around the renovated office that clearly belonged to him. "Mr. Dubois?"

"You've been MIA a long time, Mason. Not everyone knows you, but the name Sharp would definitely let the cat out of the bag."

"Are you embarrassed to be seen with me, Dan? I thought things were coming along so well between us. I'm hurt."

He rolled his eyes and sighed as he slumped down into the desk chair. "What the fuck do you want?"

Sitting in the armchair across from him, I waved for Vick to take the seat beside me, but he shook his head. I appreciated his cautious nature. "I got Hector tonight."

"Really?" The barest hint of interest colored his tone. He pulled a cigarette out of his pocket and lit it.

My eyebrow lifted in question. "You smoke?"

"Only when I'm here." He took a drag, then waved the cigarette around the room.

"And how often are you here?"

"More often than I should."

I let him smoke some of his cigarette, and silence filled the room. Victor was tense as a drawn quiver while Dan more or less stared into space.

"I'm going to have a legitimate chance against my father." I interrupted his daydreaming.

His eyes flicked to mine, and I stared him down, waiting for him to reveal anything.

"Hector isn't enough." He shook his head, sighing heavily, smoke puffing out of his nose.

There were a lot of benefits that came with Hector that Daniel didn't seem to be aware of. That was a good thing. The fewer people who knew I had substantial forces at my disposal, the better. "Hector is far from all I have to use against him."

"What else do you have? Gavin Wolfe? One of your biggest mistakes. He updates your father on your comings and goings regularly. I can't believe how stupid you're being about that one."

That was exactly what I asked Gavin to do and as far as my twenty-four-seven surveillance said, he was doing it to the letter. I wasn't stupid enough to trust Gavin, but he and I both knew he was a dead man if my father discovered the boy he stole. I spoke softly, pretending to be affected by his words, "How do you figure?"

"That's the word going around."

"You're so full of shit. David's guys have been trying to keep news of me quiet outside of the rumors that I'm doing his bidding. He has too many discontented soldiers to let them know they have a better option. Where did you really hear it?"

"Gavin told me himself." Now, that came as a surprise because I was certain he didn't. Every inch of Gavin's life was wired, and he hadn't seen or spoken to Daniel once since Claire was shot. What the hell was Daniel playing at?

I nodded my head and exchanged a look with Vick. He knew as well as I did that conversation had not happened.

"I came here tonight because I hoped you'd thought about my offer and made the right decision, but I can see that's not the case." I stood to leave and Vick almost smiled; he wanted to escape so badly.

"What makes you think I haven't?"

"You're lying to me, Daniel. If you're lying to me about something so stupid, you haven't made the right decision."

He smiled, not a mocking one or any of the other fake expressions I'd seen, but one of victory. A sickening feeling settled in my stomach.

"Why are you so certain I didn't meet with him?" he asked.

I took a moment to think about how to answer. Playing stupid may have worked before, but now it was silly. "Because I know you didn't meet with him, Daniel."

"You're watching him." He concluded, that victorious smile still in place. "Every fucking move he makes, I bet! You'd have to, to be as sure as you just were."

"Alright, you got me. Why the fuck are you so pleased with yourself?"

"Before we met at the restaurant, I had a feeling you weren't half as crazy as people said you were. I was right, and I think you play into those rumors so your father and his loyalists will underestimate you. I respect that, Mason."

Vick and I both watched him closely. Vick's hand drifted slowly toward his gun, and Daniel caught the move. "Victor, no guns are necessary. I'm saying I think you have a chance, Mason, but Hector is not enough."

"Are you saying you're in?"

"I'm in."

Daniel poured us each a couple of fingers of whiskey and we drank to our new partnership. Shortly after, we headed back to the house where I found my girl, still ready for me despite her justified anger.

TWENTY-ONE

Claire

W hen I woke up on Saturday morning, I had to admit to myself that my plan was crazy. I hadn't driven since I was sixteen and first got my license. That didn't stop me from waking up before dawn, sneaking out of bed, and going into the garage to *borrow* a car.

Allowing Lawrence to drive me would have been easier and probably better for my nerves. But he would call Mason immediately once he realized what I was doing. At least this way, it might take some time for my absence to be noticed.

I thought about my driving lessons as I scanned the rows for whichever car would beep with the keys that I snagged off the kitchen counter. Mr. Rosero was a kind person, though he was a little weird. He trained pigeons, and while that earned him the nickname "the crazy bird man", it also gave him a lot of patience; his gentle guidance made all the difference.

I climbed into the black BMW sedan, buckled, pressed the button for the garage door and pulled out very slowly. My hands gripped the steering wheel too tightly while Mr.

Rosero's voice played in my head: *Brake before the turn* and *don't be scared; frightened drivers make mistakes.*

Something told me he wouldn't approve of my current choices.

The streets were slick with patches of invisible ice and snowdrifts blowing across the surface as I drove further into the country. I focused on staying within the lines and trying my best to drive at a reasonable speed. Only a few cars passed me on the opposite side, and thankfully, there was no one behind me. I did better than I thought I would, but I was terrified of the moment that would change.

My lack of confidence in my driving abilities aside, this was still a risky idea: take the picture of Charles Gains around to people, ask about Erica Miller, and discover something to pass along anonymously to the police. There was a reasonable chance I wouldn't find anything, and if someone reported my unusual questions, all of my explanations would arouse suspicion.

Erica was last seen in a black Mercedes sedan, whereas "Tyler" had picked me up in a silver Maserati. My gut told me that Charles used rentals to collect his victims, probably with a fake ID that looked close to resembling him. Just another way of keeping his identity secret. Erica sent her friends a text saying that he looked different from his picture, that he was way hotter.

My phone rested in the cup holder, speaking directions as I drove. The sun rose higher and kids came outside to play in their yards, building snowmen and making snow angels. White banks of puffy snow lined the road. It never snowed this much where we lived and I envied their childishness, their freedom.

I rolled into town a while later, not surprised that my driving nearly doubled the hour trip. At that moment, I wished I had a friend to lean on more than ever, though no one else would understand my need to do this.

I pulled up outside this town's library, which was situated inside of a colonial house. They'd done a massive renovation to suit the library's needs, putting in an enormous glass front and a wheelchair ramp. I stepped out of the car, slammed the door shut behind me, and clicked the fob. The parking lot was salted, but I still walked carefully. It would be my luck to fall and crack my head in a far-off small town with no one nearby to help me.

Pushing open the door, the aroma of books and tempura paint filled my senses. It smelled exactly like my elementary school library. Nostalgia hit me hard, twisted in my gut, and nearly brought tears to my eyes. The air was thick with dust. A giant sheet of roll paper covered in kids' paintings and handprints hung on the wall.

The walls were a soft yellow, and the bookshelves were a mix of metal and wood. The sweet building was so much more intimate than my library. For a crazy minute, I wondered if leaving the city and finding a little town like this might not be better for me.

"Good morning! Are you new to town?" a feminine voice interrupted the out-of-body experience. I glanced behind the desk to find a woman in her sixties with gray hair and a kind smile.

"Hi, I'm just passing through."

"Not many people pass through here, but this town has a lot of charm. If I can help with anything, let me know."

"Thank you." I said as I moved out of the way and into an aisle.

I navigated the rows until I found their local section that included the town's yearbooks and a handful of books published by authors connected to the town. News articles about their high school sports teams hung on the wall above a couple of chairs designated for this section.

I sat down and pulled a yearbook off the shelf, flipping mindlessly as I stared out the window and watched the day start up. I planned to visit all the businesses, which wouldn't be difficult now that they were opening. I walked up to the desk where the librarian was typing away behind an antique computer. "Hi, again."

"What can I help you with?"

"I've been doing some research into an unusual missing person case. It's a pet project, really. Do you... Did you know Erica Miller?" I met her eyes, trying to act calm when I was anything but.

"Erica isn't the missing person you're looking into, is she?" Her face crumpled in genuine distress and I wondered how well she knew her.

"No, she's not. Well, the situation is complicated. She has a lot of things in common with the person I am looking into."

"I'm sorry to hear that..." She gazed down at her hands. "Another young girl like her went missing?"

"Several, actually. I don't have proof that they're connected, but I think I would feel better if they were."

"I know what you mean. Hard enough to imagine one person capable of that, let alone several." I nodded my head. "What do the police make of the disappearances?"

"They're all different jurisdictions," I shrugged. That much was true. "No one has the authority or the time to make the connection I think I have. I will go to the police if I put everything together." *Anonymously*, I mentally corrected.

She thought for a moment, her lips pursed. "Well, yeah, I knew Erica really well. She and her family moved here when she was about five. Awful shame what happened to her. Her parents have never been the same." She cleared her throat, trying to dislodge the tears threatening to spill.

"Are you close with them?"

"No, not more than anyone else around town. We all see a lot of each other here and we're a close community."

"Sounds like a nice place to live," I mused over what that would be like. "Can I show you a picture and you tell me if you recognize the man?"

"I can do my best," she agreed.

I pulled the picture of Charles Gains out of my pocket and showed her. She wrinkled her nose, "I think I do, but from TV or a movie or something, not in real life." Nodding my head, I thanked her. I'd have to try elsewhere.

I said goodbye, leaving the borrowed car in their parking lot, and I walked across the street to a retro diner made of gleaming chrome. I moved extremely slowly, scared of falling on the sidewalk and having to explain to Mason exactly how I'd been injured and where.

He didn't approve of my vendetta against Charles and Priscilla Gains and a little voice in the back of my mind added that he would be furious when he found out what I did.

A bell chimed overhead as I opened the door and the scent of delicious diner food flooded me. If not for my true purpose here, the decor and ambiance would have thrilled me. People filled most of the tables, older couples and young families with children. The waitresses didn't wear little paper hats, which was a bummer, but as I sat down at the bar, they greeted me with "morning peaches", and that made up for the lack of paper headwear.

"Good morning," I answered. The woman was in her late forties, with blue eyes and graying blonde hair. I wondered if she and the librarian went to school together, and I was almost certain they did.

"Know what you're having?" She took a little pad out of her pocket.

"Can I have a cup of coffee, please, and a menu?"

"Sure thing." She pulled a mug out from under the counter and grabbed the pot off the machine behind her, filling it in one fluid motion. She placed cream and sugar on the counter along with a menu and walked off to help another customer. I flipped through the folder, not seeing anything but the glare against the plastic.

Did Erica come here a lot? This seemed to be the place to go for casual dining. I wasn't hungry, but I couldn't sit here without something. She strolled back around the counter with a smile. "Ready?"

"A waffle with bacon, please." I closed the menu and handed it back to her.

"You got it." I pulled my bag onto the counter and took out a notebook. Jotting down the notes from my conversation with the librarian only took a moment. A happy family. That's all I learned. I laid out some of my notes and clippings from news articles, trying to remember where some landmarks were.

The waitress, Melody, according to her name tag, placed a few packets of table syrup on the counter with a dish of butter packets.

She pulled up short at the sight of my papers. "Are you looking into the Erica Miller case?"

"Sort of," I answered casually. "Did you know her?"

"I did. Huh, you look a little like her, actually." She glanced over her shoulder, making sure no one was paying attention to her. "I saw the guy that killed her. Police didn't believe me, no one did, but I swear I saw him."

My heart stopped and then sped, racing straight out of my chest. I pulled out the picture of Charles Gains with shaking fingers. I didn't want his face on my phone or to hand over my belongings to each person I asked.

"Is this him?"

She took one look at the picture and narrowed her eyes before bursting into laughter. "The missing billionaire guy? I don't think so, honey." She paused, her head cocked to the side as she considered him another moment. "Now that you mention it, I guess the guy resembled him a little."

My cheeks burned. "Thanks for looking."

"You're welcome," she said with a sarcastic lilt to her voice. She walked away to take care of her other customers.

The stool beside me crinkled under someone's weight. My glance flicked instinctively over, and my mouth opened in shock as I realized Casey, the kid Mason moved in with James and Vick, was sitting beside me.

"Hey, Claire. What are you doing out here?" His dirty blonde hair flopped over his eyes. He wore an old leather jacket and jeans with rips all over them. My first instinct was that he liked the style, but as I took in the details, I realized these items were old; he wore what he had.

"I'm visiting," I spoke slowly, not sure what move to expect from him. "What are you doing here?"

"I saw you leave this morning, and Mr. Sharp likes you to take a driver and a guard. But you were alone and rather suspicious." He ran his hand through his hair and smirked.

He meant no harm, but the idea of being followed made me a little violent. People accepting Mason monitoring my every move, and even helping him in his task, was another deeply unsettling matter.

"I'm not actually worried about what Mr. Sharp likes, Casey. Thanks for checking in. You can go."

"I-I don't think I can, actually. If something were to happen to you and I could have prevented it..." His eyes flicked around, ensuring no one was paying attention to us, "he'd kill me. Really fucking slowly." All that confidence and bravado slipped from his face. "I would rather not die slowly."

"I'm not ready to leave." I set my jaw stubbornly and stared forward. He'd have to carry me out of here if he thought I was leaving without my waffle.

"I didn't call him *yet*, and I wasn't planning on making you leave. Following you like a creep wasn't fun for me either. I thought I should tell you I'm keeping an eye on you, and I'll take you home when you're ready. You don't feel confident behind the wheel, and I'm sure you don't want to drive back."

My cheeks got all hot again. "Oh really? And how do you know that?"

He turned bright red, and for a moment, I considered taking it easier on him. "I drove behind you the whole way, and you really didn't seem *overly confident*," he spoke the words carefully.

"I checked behind me the whole time. No one was driving behind me."

"I stayed a ways back."

"Jesus Christ," I muttered under my breath. Any hopes of continuing my day as planned evaporated. "I guess you're right. I'm not an *overly confident* driver." He let out the breath that he held as I laughed. "He's going to be mad that you didn't call him right away."

He paled. "I hope not, but if he is, I'll tell him the truth: there was no reason for me to think anything was wrong, even if I couldn't, in good conscience, let you go alone."

"Are you hungry?"

"Sure, let's eat." When the waitress returned with my waffle, he ordered a breakfast sandwich. The fluffy waffle and crisp bacon hit the spot, and the conversation with Casey was more comfortable than I imagined. He had a positive outlook on life, although life hadn't been too kind to him. It was effortless to talk to him and the time passed quickly. A few times he had to stop himself from saying too much, and I wondered desperately what he might have said if he continued.

Obviously, I didn't want him to know *why* I was out here, so after we finished, I told him I was ready to leave. I almost forgot that Mason was sure to be angry with me for taking a car without asking only to abandon it over an hour away in a town I probably shouldn't have visited.

When we pulled up, Mason was pacing the driveway in front of the main house. "You told him,"

"After you agreed to leave, not before. Plus, the car is still out there, and someone has to get it." Casey defended himself.

185

"Yeah," I sighed, understanding his point, but also terrified of dealing with the prowling man waiting for me. Casey stopped the car as Mason blocked our path. He was at my door in a flash, opening it.

His green eyes blazed like fire, and the muscle in his jaw ticked furiously. To my surprise, he unbuckled me and gently pulled me out of the car to wrap me in his arms and breathe in my hair.

"What were you thinking? The weather is shit and you hardly ever drive." His voice sounded so small, so lost. I barely recognized it as his.

"It wasn't a big deal, and I didn't need a babysitter."

"Why do you think you ride in that white Cadillac, Claire?" His warm breath filled my hair and heated my skin. The depth of feeling in his voice caught me off guard.

"What? Because you picked—"

"No, because the fucking thing is bulletproof, Claire. I don't want you in anything else. No one is ever going to hurt you again if you let me take care of you."

"I can take care of myself, Mason." I softened into his embrace, my tone not matching my words.

"Of course you can, but you should let me anyway." He lifted me by my thighs, wrapping them around his waist, and held my back as he carried me into the house.

"Are we going to talk about what's going on with you?" he asked as he laid me on the bed and cuddled up beside me.

"I'm doing some research. It's no big thing."

His eyebrow arched, "Into the girls that Charles killed?"

"Mm," I sighed softly.

"There is nothing you can do, baby. He's gone and his secrets went with him," he sounded sincere, but we both knew that wasn't entirely true. *We* could tell the authorities about our involvement.

I shook my head. "Not all of them. There are some left to be found."

He sighed into my hair, the exasperation clear. "Let this go. You're going to get yourself hurt."

"If you're so worried about me being hurt, then why are you hurting me?"

"What does that mean?"

"I notice every time you don't come home, Mase. Or when you come home covered in blood and won't even try to explain where you've been. People—including Emma—are being forced to lie and keep things from me. None of those things feel good. Not only does it hurt but it also makes me wonder how you can think so little of me."

"I don't think you're stupid," his hand trailed along my thigh.

"No, you think I'm falling apart and that hiding the truth somehow makes things better."

"I'm worried about you, and what you did today doesn't make me worry any less. You are suffering and the last thing in the world I want to do is add to your burden." A rogue tear escaped my eye as he spoke. "I'm sorry about Emma, but she knows a lot of things that no one should, not only you. She'd be smart to keep her fucking mouth shut."

"I want you to make room in your life for me."

"You *are* my life. I want to make the world a better place for you. You've been through enough. You *deserve* better."

"That's not up to you. The world is what the world is irrespective of whether you're doing what you're doing or not. The only thing you can decide is whether you tell me the truth about it."

He left me alone on the bed. "I've got some work to do." He muttered as he walked out of the room. The front door slamming came as no surprise. He was worried about me? Well, I was worried about him.

TWENTY-TWO

Mason

I was on the extreme edge of my patience, and unsure where to turn as I shot across the driveway and toward the garage. I couldn't go to James and Vick. They'd grown too close to Claire and while they would do nothing to risk my life, their allegiances were shifting to her.

They would probably tell me to get over it and apologize, and that wasn't the advice I wanted. Going anywhere alone wasn't an option with how fast things were escalating. As Lawrence was off for the evening, I pulled my black BMW out and drove down to the gatehouse.

Pressing a few buttons on the steering wheel, I called Casey and told him I needed him to work tonight. I hung up with him and immediately started another call.

"Dan, can you meet me?" I spoke the moment it connected, not giving him a chance to say hello.

I felt him bristling. "Is something wrong?" He didn't mean personally. He meant the tenuous business the two of us were arranging together.

"Yeah. Can you meet me?" I was full of shit, but I needed him to show up.

"I need a few hours. Text the burner." The line disconnected, and I grabbed my phone and typed out a text.

Stop being a fuck! Drinks at Isolde.

I sent the message as the passenger door opened and Casey stepped inside.

"What are we up to tonight, sir?"

"Just some business to attend to. I need someone to cover my back and you're up."

He was quiet for a moment, chewing on his lip, "Vick and James are both home."

"They are," I agreed, with no intention of explaining myself to him. We drove into the city. The sky was dark, though it was barely five o'clock. I glanced at my phone more often than I should, waiting for Dan to agree, Claire to reach out, even James or Vick to tell me I was being a prick and to get my ass back.

Casey noticed my distraction but wisely kept his mouth shut. I found free parking on the street, disgusted with the fortune that took. Couldn't lady luck smile on me when I needed her?

"Casey, tonight is going to be simple. Cover my back and do what I say. Okay?"

"Yes, sir."

I patted him on the shoulder before we both climbed out. The bar was small and comfortable, nestled between a bookshop and a café. Despite the history Dan and I had here, the sense of nostalgia was pleasant. This was the place we bid farewell to each other as friends before I left for school, the last time we spoke before I turned up at his favorite restaurant.

We walked up to the host, who seated us at a table in the corner. The waitress came by and I ordered a whiskey for myself and a soda for Casey. He gave me a disgruntled look as she left. "Sorry, kid, you're not twenty-one." The decision had nothing to do with his age. He was nineteen and his involvement with me and the syndicate was a lot worse for him than drinking. But I didn't know what his tolerance was like and I couldn't afford to risk our lives.

At least an hour passed as we waited. I had Casey order whatever he wanted. I suspected the kid was so thin because he didn't eat enough, and that set off some protective instinct that told me he was growing on me. The waitress offered us a check twice before Daniel and his guys walked in.

In the dim light, the two of them looked like twins, and the effect would have been comedic if it hadn't been so sinister. Daniel wasn't as massive, but he had a more threatening appearance in his own way.

The three of them approached the table in complete synchronization. "Why am I here, Mason?" Daniel asked with no attempt at pleasantries.

"We need to talk."

"About what? You're being cryptic." His fingers tapped against the back of the chair, but he made no move to sit.

"This is the place to say cryptic shit to one another, isn't it? That's what I remember anyway." I would never forget Dan's face as he refused my money to pay his tuition and told me he was choosing to stay with the syndicate.

"I'm leaving," Dan said.

"Let's go to the bar and leave the guards here. We need to speak privately."

"Isn't the real problem that your *guard* is too young to sit at the bar?"

I laughed, "That too."

"Fine, Mason. You two, wait here and monitor this one." They nodded and continued to stand beside the table. "Sit down; you stick out like a sore thumb."

We approached the bar and took two stools. I motioned to the bartender and ordered us each a drink. "So, the problem..."

"Yes. The one that interrupted my evening and dragged me out of bed."

"What was her name?" I asked. The bartender returned and set down our drinks.

He laughed softly, "Not sure."

"I needed a drinking, buddy."

"You can't be serious right now," he grit out.

"Sure am."

"I'm already under suspicion, and you're bringing me here to drink whiskey and bullshit?" his eyes flicked over to the table where Casey and the others watched us.

"Are you worried about those two?"

"Damn right I'm worried about them. Do you think that kid would stick by your side if you were definitively losing this fight against your father? They side with money and power. You, of all people, should know that." I nodded as I considered his words, but I didn't agree. After what Casey did for Claire and what he did for Mila, I trusted him.

I waved at the bartender, signaling that I'd like another. "Well, you could leave. I guess I'll drink with the kid instead."

"No need to be dramatic. I'll stay for a few minutes, but only if you agree that causing my untimely demise is a hindrance to you. I'm not willing to throw my life away on your vendetta."

"Vendetta," I mused. "I think we both know it's more than that."

"If you want your plans realized, you would be wise to be more careful. Including treating our meetings seriously because they have the potential to get me killed."

"You would be wise to assume that all of my moves are calculated."

The annoyed sigh told me he didn't, and I hoped that meant my father shared the same belief. "Why are we here, Mason?"

"My girlfriend."

His eyebrows raised in surprise for a moment. "I've heard a lot about her. Well, not so much about *her* but how valuable she is. They say she's beautiful." The warning settled like lead in my stomach.

I gritted my teeth. "Valuable how?"

"You're making waves, Mason. Fuck, you left waves behind weeks ago. Francis Santini is a fucking hurricane. Your father is playing the long game. He wants revenge for what you did."

"I expected he would. I didn't decide to act lightly." My father counted on Francis too much to let him live, and I had a promise to fulfill.

"He's planning to go after your girlfriend, Claire. Which is a fair enough reason to want to get together tonight, even if I think your methods make you an asshole."

"Go after her how?" Thoughts of his bullshit letter and his threat to send her to prison filled my mind, except I knew better than that. He wouldn't do anything so clean to her.

"He has a lot of ways, whatever he decides." I couldn't speak as I worked through the liquid fire spilling inside of me, but Dan continued, "What do you think you might get out of all of this, other than the two of you and everyone who helps you dead?"

"Him dead, for starters. Beyond that, I won't be discussing my plans." David Sharp wouldn't step within a mile of her.

"We're better off knowing as little about one another as possible," he agreed.

I winked at him. "That ship has sailed, old friend."

"A lot of shit happened to both of us before the age of eighteen. We shared a lot of burdens, but you would be stupid to assume I haven't changed in a decade." He took a small sip of the whiskey he hardly touched.

I had a strong buzz going and the stress and heartache from Claire bubbled inside of me. "Trust me, you condescending fucking prick, I am well aware how much someone can change in a much shorter span of time."

"Alright, Mason. If you didn't come here to talk about the vile shit your father plans to do to the woman you love, why are we here to talk about her?"

"You always gave me decent advice." I shrugged.

Casey and the twins stared at us so intently I wanted to clap my hands to see if they would blink. The noises of the restaurant and the distance hid the details of our conversation, but they paid attention like they heard every word.

"She's not been the same since she got shot." Giving words to the thoughts and fears I'd held for months now only worsened the tightness in my chest. I took a deep pull of my whiskey, hoping to burn through the sensation.

"Why do you expect her to be? That is some rough shit, Mason, and it didn't happen all that long ago."

"I don't know what I expect. She's always had heavy shit to deal with, but this is different. She's making choices she wouldn't have a few months ago. I'm afraid she's going to get herself hurt."

"You're afraid?" he laughed to himself, "Never thought I'd live to hear you admit something like that again."

"If something happened to her, I'd tear this entire city to shreds, and after what happened with Charles Gains, my temper where she is concerned is common knowledge."

He gave me a knowing look. No one who had anything to do with the syndicate missed that story.

"So, are you worried someone is going to kill her or she's going to kill herself? You picked someone you have a lot in common with, hm?"

My cheeks heated, fucking embarrassment and shame crushing me. I hated that this man helped me through those times. As for Claire, I believed her when she told me she was never suicidal.

Coming here was a mistake. I should have let James and Vick take her side and talk me down as they always did. This was not the same kid who convinced me I should keep on living when I truly thought I wanted to die. I was an idiot to hang onto something that wasn't there.

"Yeah, I guess so." I pulled out my wallet and went to slap some money on the counter.

"What the fuck? You go through all that to get me down here and you're just going to leave?" he sounded pissed, but I didn't care.

"I don't know what I was expecting, but I was wrong. This," I waved between the two of us, "this died right here in this bar a long time ago."

"Mason, sit down, and let's talk," his tone aimed to soothe. "The guys are staring, and if that twitchy-fingered kid shoots me, I'm going to be fucking pissed."

I thought about it a moment before I sat back down. "We don't have *that* in common. I don't think she's suicidal. She's desperate. I fear what she could do to herself unintentionally. I fear the lengths she's willing to go to make things right."

"What does she need to make right?"

"She thinks Charles Gains getting away with killing those women is her fault."

"Technically, it's yours." I didn't feel the need to dignify that with a response. "Survivors' guilt is one hell of a trip, man."

"So what do I do? How do I get through to her?" I asked him and the bottom of my glass with equally pathetic glances.

"Well, do you want me to answer that as someone who knows you well and would like to see you happy, or do you want me to kiss your ass and make you feel better?"

"The honest one." I sighed, knowing that meant I wouldn't like what he had to say.

"What are you doing to make the situation worse?"

"What are you talking about?"

"Mason," he gave me a hard look, "you're freaked. I've never seen you so fucking scared," he pointed in my general direction. "I remember how you used to act when things went off the rails and this is worse than that."

"I'm a little protective..."

"A little?"

"Okay, extremely."

"Does she appreciate that?"

"Honestly? I think she gets off on my protectiveness as much as it pisses her off." I was glad to leave it on something that was entirely true, if not irrelevant to the major problem.

"What else? There's obviously more."

I exhaled into the palms of my hands and waved for the bartender to bring me another drink. "I guess I've been disappearing a lot."

"You leave her unprotected?" a hint of shock laced his tone.

"Of course not. I assign several people to her at all times."

He nodded like what I said was more in line with his expectations. "What do you tell her when you 'disappear a lot'?"

"Usually? Nothing too specific. I want to avoid actively lying to her. I tell her she doesn't want to know where I've been. It's better if I don't tell her what's going on." I cringed at how my own words sounded out of context.

"Oof, that's something, man. You've got some serious shit you need to work out. I guess some things never change; you've always carried your shit heavy." He took a swig of his drink and made a face, "Seems to me like you and your girl have *that* in common. You don't get to manufacture reality for her. You're not God, Mason. Treat her as an equal partner or you need to let her go."

A startled, angry noise bubbled out of my throat and he grinned in response.

"Well, you won't let her go; I guess you should treat her as an equal partner."

"Fuck you, Daniel. Since when do you have all the answers?" The question was rhetorical. He had been giving me advice and helping me out of jams as long as I'd known him.

"Are you feeling better?"

"I'm feeling drunker." I countered, but I *was* feeling better.

"Well, now is as good a time as any to ruin your buzz and discuss business. At least if I end up with a bullet between my eyes because of this evening, I can pretend there was some justification."

"And?"

"I found the location and date of the next large shipment of girls. I don't know what you can do with the information, but you asked, and you received."

"When?"

"Wednesday,"

"Fuck man! Could you give me any *less* warning than that?"

"Maybe, maybe not. Just be grateful I'm telling you at all, considering I'm sure this is a test your father is expecting me to fail..." he picked up his drink and took a sip, "I'll be surprised if I make it home alive tonight."

"You're safe. You live in the city. He doesn't allow any bullets to fly in his utopia."

He narrowed his eyes at me. "Right, cause white vans don't drive off with people all the time."

"Don't get abducted."

"Don't be a prick. Oh, wait, too late."

Casey and I left Daniel and his twins a little while later. After dropping him at the gatehouse, I went home to face Claire. She sat on the edge of the bed, waiting for me.

"Where were you, Mase?" she asked in a supremely tired voice.

"I was out with a friend. Casey came with me in case I needed backup. I've known Daniel most of my life, though I only contacted him recently because he's tightly involved with the syndicate. We had drinks and talked for a while."

Her brown gaze met mine, and her mouth fell open with a little pop. "Oh, was it about, about business?" she stammered, trying to find the right way to refer to my criminal activities.

"Mostly personal."

Her eyes widened. "Did you have fun?"

I stripped out of my clothes and pulled on my pajamas. "Not exactly, but it was nice to catch up."

"Yeah, that is nice... Are you tired?"

"Exhausted," I answered as I climbed into bed beside her.

"Cuddle me?" she wiggled her butt against me.

"Your wish is my command, baby." I wrapped her in my arms, and we drifted off to sleep together. I wondered about how well she took the truth tonight, and if she would handle things that well if I were honest all the time.

TWENTY-THREE

Claire

Was this an escalation? Probably. Did I care? No.

On Monday morning, I asked Mason if Vick could accompany me for the day. The request surprised him, and he was suspicious, but I assuaged those doubts by telling him James was getting on my nerves. Which was true, but more importantly, the tension between Victor and me would keep him from asking me questions.

I climbed in the car with Lawrence and Victor, but instead of heading to the library, I gave him the address of a beautiful mansion in a *slightly* less prestigious part of town. Vick looked at me curiously, but every time I met his gaze, his cheeks turned pink.

Rebecca LaMontagne was Mason's high school girlfriend and Charles Gains' first victim. She starred in many of my nightmares, and though I never met her, I felt a deep connection with her. Talking to Rebecca's parents might be catastrophic, but it was one of the few options I had left, and I needed to do *something*.

Going alone seemed like a better idea than taking this crew, but after the stunt I pulled with Erica Miller, I thought it was best not to rock the boat with more auto theft. Besides, by the time my babysitters figured me out, *if* they did, I would be finished and on my way home before even Mason could stop me.

We pulled up outside the LaMontagne home and my heart sank when Vick turned to me with a pissed-off expression. "Claire, what the fuck are we doing here?"

"That's not your business, Vick."

"Whatever you're planning on doing, it's a mistake. The LaMontagnes do not need to talk to you today."

I opened the door and stepped out of the car, welcoming the freezing air as it cleared my senses. "It will be fine,"

"I'm calling Mason, and I'm telling him where you are."

"Call him. I'll be done by the time he gets here."

"I could stop you," he threatened.

A deadly chill rolled down my spine. "Victor, if you put your hands on me, you will live to regret that decision." He jerked back, genuine hurt flashing in his eyes, but I didn't stick around.

The mansion was beautiful, but not as grand as I would have imagined. They had money, but not like Mason or the Gains family. I walked up to the door, running over the script I'd practiced repeatedly.

Hello Mr. and Mrs. LaMontagne. Earlier this year, my stalker claimed he killed your daughter right before he shot me. He said his name was Tyler Hines, but later I learned his name was Charles Gains.

I don't have any evidence to give the police other than my word and with a six million dollar reward for information about him, they will be very unlikely to believe me. I thought you should know the truth anyway.

I knocked on the door, waiting before ringing the bell. Another minute later, a beautiful blonde woman in her late fifties opened the door. I was stunned into silence by the resemblance between her and her daughter.

"Hi, can I help you?" The cream sweater she wore was soft and elegant. The large pearls in her ears complimented the color of her hair beautifully. She was lovely.

"Hi, are you Mrs. LaMontagne?" my voice came out higher-pitched than normal and I had to clear my throat.

"I might be." She narrowed her eyes at me, probably wondering if I was going to serve her a subpoena. "My name is Claire, and I was hoping to talk to you for a minute about your daughter Rebecca."

I tried not to cry as I thought of Rebecca's face and the life Charles took from her. Standing in front of her mother was more difficult than I imagined it would be. Her gaze flicked behind me, checking who might be watching. Her eyes landed on the car and narrowed. "Well, I suppose you can come in for a moment."

She stepped back, holding the door open for me. The space was open and warm, with sage and coral walls and grand, sweeping ceilings. An ornate brassy lamp hung from the highest point of said ceiling. The stained glass panes were Moroccan in inspiration and incredible.

She led me into a small sitting room right off the front door. The room was just as interesting as the first, with cooler colors and panels of fine Chinese etchings.

"The only reason I agree to speak to people like you is that I want people to remember who my daughter was." I wondered what people she meant and how often she received them in this room so she could toss them out quickly.

"I'm not sure what you're talking about," I told her honestly. My speech didn't fit into the context of the conversation and the last thing I planned to do when I got here was wing it.

"You're a journalist, aren't you?" Her sapphire blue eyes moved up and down my business casual outfit. My purse was big enough for a notebook or laptop. "What do you want to know?"

"Uh," I stared dumbly at her for a long moment. This was not how I planned for this to go, but I didn't have a clue how to steer us back to the reason I came here. *I am not a journalist...* I repeated my speech quickly to myself, but I said, "What would you want people to remember about your daughter?"

Her slender brow arched in surprise. "You want me to tell you about her as a person?"

"Yes, I do," I agreed. I tried to talk to Mason about her once, and I was sad to learn that he remembered very little about her. Time had faded many of the details for him and the finer points of her personality remained a mystery. It felt wrong, almost voyeuristic, to have nightmares about her corpse and not even know what kind of music she liked.

"You can sit." She lowered herself onto a red silk couch, and I took the matching chair. "Becky was incredibly smart and pretty. She was kind too; the type of person I was proud to call my daughter. She had a temper, though, and she wasn't one to keep her mouth shut. She got into a lot of disagreements, and I often wondered if that had something to do with why she went missing."

"She sounds amazing," I commented through a haze of stunned disbelief over how incredibly wrong this plan had gone.

"She was," she sighed wistfully. "Top three in her class in high school, attended an extremely competitive school, Yale-bound before, well, whatever happened." She pulled a tissue out of the box on the coffee table and dabbed at her eyes. "Will you print that stuff?"

"I will." I didn't have a blog or anything, but I swore I would make one or do whatever to spread Mrs. LaMontagne's words about her daughter to the world, even a feature in the library newsletter. "You can tell me more about her. What kind of music did she like?"

She cleared her throat and tossed away the tissue, visibly hardening, as she spoke. "Why are you really here? I appreciate the song and dance, but you didn't come here just to learn what type of music my girl liked."

"No, you're right. I have another reason for coming." I was about to launch into my speech. To tell her everything I knew and fuck up both mine and Mason's lives.

"You noticed disappearances similar to hers?" she interrupted my admission. "Writing a story about teen girls who went missing? It's been about two years since the last of you came by and I thought this had ended. What do you want to ask so I can go on with my day?"

"I, uh, I'm not..." *fucking spit it out, Claire.*

Mrs. LaMontagne grew angrier by the moment. "Ask your questions and go, please. I need to move on with my life. This is hard to keep going through even after all this time." I *thought* she deserved honesty, and yet, as I looked into her tired, gaunt eyes, the truth felt like a burden she didn't deserve.

"My questions?" My eyes flicked around the room, noticing the pictures of Rebecca in different stages of life, with her family, winning awards and competitions. Mrs. LaMontagne was determined to remind the people who came here asking questions about who her daughter was.

"Please, get on with it," she waved her hands and leaned into the red cushioned couch.

Calling on a reserve of courage I didn't realize I possessed, I asked the questions I needed to decide what to tell her. "Do you presume your daughter to be dead?"

She flinched. "The police do."

"And you? What do you think?"

"For a long time, no I did not, but now..." She took a deep breath to continue, "too much time has passed," she sniffled softly as a few stray tears fell.

"I'm so sorry for your loss."

"Everyone is, aren't they? Everyone tells me how sorry they are, and I wish I could pretend it means something. But it doesn't, it means nothing! I'm nothing without her. So, ask your question, and let me get on with my day."

My chest tightened, and my eyes pricked with tears. "If your daughter's killer was dead, would you care who he was in life?"

Her blue eyes matched Rebecca's perfectly, and when they flicked up to meet mine, they were full of pain. "What kind of question is that?" Her brow crumpled hard, revealing lines I was sure she paid well to hide.

"One I want you to answer honestly." I hated myself for coming here today, but I might as well forge ahead. "If I told you someone murdered him, would you care who he was?" I let the question sit between us, let her consider how she might think or feel about this. Despite being a coward and hoping desperately she didn't want to know, I would honor her wishes and tell her if she did.

She was deathly silent for a long while. "No, I wouldn't. I like to think of my daughter how she lived, not how she died, and if justice is already served, there is no reason to dwell on that—" she dragged in a ragged breath, "whatever they were." She cleared her throat. "Do you believe her killer is dead?"

"I have my suspicions, ma'am. Full disclosure, the police do not agree with my theory. I think it has merit, and it's a good story." She gave me a withering stare. "Journalism is a cutthroat business," I said as an excuse for why I came and asked such probing questions.

"Get the fuck out." Her words stung, but what did I expect?

I did as she said. The walk out was mercifully short, and I was grateful for the room. The door slammed behind me, and something I didn't even know was mine, broke inside of me.

Vick stared me down as I climbed back into the car, feeling more lost and alone than I ever had. He waited a moment before speaking, likely deciding if I was about to cry.

"I told you that was a fucking awful idea," he sighed heavily. "You want to go home?"

"Yeah." I agreed blankly. *What were you thinking?* I demanded of myself as the car pulled away, noisily turning up the stones on the driveway.

TWENTY-FOUR

Claire

S pending the day in bed was the obvious choice after the misadventure at the LaMontagne estate. Vick and James switched back immediately after having caught on to why I asked for Vick. Mason was disappointed in me, and I couldn't blame him. I was too, but he didn't say much more than that, and we went to sleep in each other's arms.

Tuesday morning went normally. Emma had the day off for an appointment, and Kiana and I had a pleasant morning together. All the odds and ends for my winter holiday event were coming together nicely and despite the general mayhem my life had fallen into, I was looking forward to the excitement and the happy kids.

Sean, one of the original volunteers who was standoffish to me, got involved in the planning and warmed up to me a bit. I didn't think he would ever like me, but getting rid of any tension in my life had to help.

At lunchtime, I left the library. My feet quickly ate up the pavement as I approached my awaiting carriage: the armored

SUV. My gloved hand rapped a little too hard against the window. James rolled it down and gave me an amused smile. "Do you need something, Claire?"

Since our lunch with Emma, and the things I'd said about her giving him another chance, he'd been incredibly chipper with me. Mason and Vick were both pissed about my series of ridiculous events, but not James. He thought we were the best of friends, although I was still pissed at him.

"I'm going to the coffee shop a few blocks over. You don't need to follow me, but would you or Lawrence like something?" I didn't want to offer, but I felt guilty they spent so many boring days waiting around on me. If I said nothing, they were likely to drive down the road at ten miles an hour to keep pace with me. At least Emma could distract James, but Lawrence had no such weakness.

"It's cold. You don't want a ride?"

"Nope, you wait here," I said like I was doing him a favor.

"I don't mind," he smiled cheekily. "Sitting in a car all day can be awfully boring. I'll walk you over." He slapped the partition, and I sighed in defeat. I wondered for a moment if they always kept it closed during the day when they were together or if they had a particular need for privacy I stumbled into. "Lawrence, would you like anything?"

"Lunch and coffee," he responded simply.

James climbed out of the car and onto the sidewalk beside me. His gaze trailed over the library. "She's not here today," I interrupted his pining.

"I know," the joking tone was missing from his voice. I started walking silently, having decided conversation with James usually led to some sort of disagreement, and ended with me annoyed. Best to focus on the burn in my lungs as I dragged in the freezing air or the way my boots crunched against the salt on the ground.

"I've never seen you come here before," James commented as we approached the door. There was something odd in his tone, and I looked over to catch him smiling secretively. I thought about pressing him, but decided I didn't care.

My eyes darted behind the counter, expecting Leyla, but instead, I found a man I'd never met. Disappointment filled me, and the intensity surprised me.

It took me a moment to place why I wanted to see her so badly. She saw Tyler following me. She tried to warn me and feared for me. That level of concern was unexpected from a stranger. Her effort to keep me safe meant something to me.

I ignored the feeling and ordered a sausage roll and a latte for myself, just like every other time. I looked at James. "Make that three."

The man handed over our food and continued to make our coffees. I sat down at a table while James waited for him to finish, and once the drinks were done, he sat next to me.

"You waited for me?" he teased.

"Years of ingrained manners," I said, but I wished I had just eaten the damn sausage roll.

He laughed, "You're going to forgive me soon."

"Keep dreaming." Emma was easy to forgive after hearing the way she defended me to James, and her insistence that she wouldn't lie to me any longer. With James, I had no such assurance. He would keep lying to me as long as his *boss* commanded it of him. I didn't know why that hurt me so badly, maybe because he'd been a friend through such a difficult time.

He opened the paper and peered at his food dubiously. "Is this any good?"

"Bite it and find out," I answered as I took a huge bite of my own. *Fucking magical.*

James did as I suggested and groaned outright. "Fuck, these are amazing. I need like six of these."

I laughed, thinking he was joking, but he polished the pastry off in another couple of bites and went back to the counter to get more. He came back to the table with two full shopping bags and an impish grin on his face.

"James, what the fuck is this?"

"All of them. I bought them all."

I rolled my eyes and went back to ignoring him. I should have taken a longer lunch and spent more time enjoying my food and my coffee, but being babysat was chafing on me. Quickly finishing, I rose from my chair to leave the café.

Before I could take more than a step, I came face to face with someone I recognized. It took me a moment to place the older woman as someone who'd worked in the admissions office, and a further moment to remember her penchant for drama, lies, and bullying.

Another breath later, "Barbara, hi," popped out of my mouth.

"Claire? I haven't seen you in a long time. Are you *well*?" The condescension in her tone made me grit my teeth. I guess after my outburst in the office where I rightfully told them all to go to hell, it was easy to assume I was crazy. Better than facing the fact that you and everyone you work with are awful people.

"I'm fantastic, thanks." I should have left it there. This woman deserved none of my time, and yet I explained, "I'm the librarian at the City Library, over on second."

"Oh, how nice for *you*." Her fake smile was unconvincing, considering how well practiced it was. Her mouth twisted around the word 'you', like for anyone else, this wouldn't be a big deal but was impressive given my issues.

My blood simmered as I thought of all the bullshit I'd suffered from her and the people at that office. To add injury to the insult, their golden boy shot me.

"The position is highly coveted," I answered with a confident smile, hiding all traces of my displeasure except for a slight catch in my throat.

"Oh, I'm sure it is, dear," she nodded her head, and I saw something malicious flash in her eyes.

"Well, I ought to go," I spoke before she could, turning to run.

I barely took a step when she said, "Have you heard from Tyler?"

The question stunned me and stopped me in place. "No, why would I?" I answered after a beat too long.

Her eyes narrowed. "Well, the two of you did date for a bit, and you were obsessed with him. It makes sense for you to *run* into him."

Did this bitch actually suggest I was stalking *him?* Had that piece of shit actually told people I was stalking *him?* The injustice of it swelled like a balloon in my throat. I opened my mouth and closed it again, using all of my mental fortitudes to push the obstruction aside and answer her.

"That's not precisely what happened. Either way, I haven't heard from him or anyone from the office since I quit."

She eyed me dubiously, and whatever she found pleased her. Her thin lips curled into a smile. "So, you don't know?" She leaned in with an excited look on her face.

"I have no idea what you mean, so I definitely don't know."

"Well, a couple of months after you were let go, he stopped coming into work. It was the strangest thing. He never called. He disappeared and when we tried to report him missing, the police said he didn't exist. His home address, his number, everything was fake," she paused for dramatic effect and to check if I was sufficiently interested.

"What? How crazy! That can't be right, can it?" I hoped the line sounded convincing. The truth, *he's dead, he's dead, he's fucking dead,* wouldn't help at this moment, despite how much I might like to watch this odious bitch cry.

"We all said the same, but it was true. Even the picture in the staff directory wasn't him. Looked a heck of a lot like him. Many people think the worst of him, but the police aren't worried and neither am I. I think he was a secret agent or something."

"What do you mean, think the worst of him?" *Oh, god.*

"Well, it's silly."

I waited, barely able to take a breath. "What is?"

"You know Charles Gains, the fellow who went missing, the billionaire?"

The banging of my heart was reckless and dangerous like an unbalanced load of laundry slamming on the side of the machine. *Bang, bang, bang,*

"Of course, his family is all over the news." A sheen of sweat broke out over my lower back and I thanked God she couldn't hear the way my heart raced.

She looked back and forth, checking if anyone was listening. She raised her voice, hoping to catch the attention of people sitting at nearby tables. "Some women at the office think they're the same. They believe Tyler actually was Charles Gains."

She paused for dramatic effect again, "I will admit they look alike, but if the police aren't buying into it, neither am I." I gasped, and she smiled victoriously. My world slowed to a stop. Everything chipped apart slowly and fell into nothingness. As I always feared, I was nothing.

I knew I should say something, and I was terrified of what my face said for me, yet I couldn't move, let alone speak. The police knew that Tyler and Charles were the same person; they simply didn't care. They let this go entirely. I was going to be sick all over Barbara's shoes.

"No, I don't think so either."

"You really didn't know he was missing, did you?" her voice filled with candy-sweet sympathy. "He didn't feel the same way as you, darling, but I'm sorry for your pain," she patted me on the shoulder, and I was too numb to do anything. "You take care of yourself and the books, okay?" I nodded my head like the world's biggest idiot, and she walked away.

"Claire, are you okay?" James asked as he stepped up beside me.

"No." My body shook, and my blood pounded in my ears. I heard my heartbeat, and felt it in my throat.

"Do you want to leave?"

"Yes."

He waited a moment for me to move, but when I didn't, he grabbed my arm and pulled me along beside him. I leaned into him, grateful there was someone to hold me up when I had nothing left to stand on.

He helped me to the street and onto a bench, where he called Lawrence. A couple of minutes later, the car pulled up and we climbed inside.

"Back to the library, please, Lawrence." James handed him his coffee and one of the many sausage rolls.

"No, take me home, please. Call Emma and ask her if she can come in for the afternoon and help Kiana close up." Somewhere deep in the broken pieces, part of me felt guilty for disrupting Emma two days in a row.

"Okay, Claire." James scrutinized my expression as he dialed the number. Lawrence pulled away. Heated murmurs filled the space as James and Emma argued, but I couldn't focus on the specific words. He put the phone back into his pocket. "She wasn't happy I was the one to call her, but she's headed in now and she hopes you're alright."

"Tell her I'm fine, please," I murmured as I rested my head and closed my eyes.

"Are you?"

I shuddered. "No, but tell her I am anyway."

"Okay," We sat in silence for a few moments. "Should I call Mason?"

"Don't bother him." Though I told him not to, I was sure he would.

The drive to the mansion passed in an infinite loop of anger and pain. Justice for those women had become my obsession. So much of me hinged on them. Yet, one of the biggest connections and oddities about the case lay in front of the police and they didn't care.

I don't know when the rage inside me bubbled over into tears. Only when James handed me a couple of tissues did I notice them pouring torrentially down my cheeks. I'd been storing up the storm of the century's worth of pain, and it was only now cracking free.

I gasped for breath, and James hovered, not sure of what he could do. "Claire, are you okay?"

"I am not in physical danger. Stop fucking asking me if I am okay."

He stayed silent the rest of the ride and by the time we arrived home, my tears had dried. I wasn't relieved as I normally would be after a good cry. Spilled tears would leave me headache ridden and exhausted, but refreshed to some extent.

Not this time. This time I was angrier, more incensed than I had been only moments before. This thing inside me was expanding, getting hungrier and more desperate. I didn't think I could keep fighting.

Each indignity, each injustice, was a weight around my neck, drowning me. I was down to the last vestiges of my stamina, and weakness crept along every inch of me.

I stomped out of the car and up to the house, beyond leaving a word of thanks with Lawrence for him waiting on me all day as I usually did. I couldn't tell James not to worry. The look on his face only made my situation more real. We both knew he should be worried.

I ran up the stairs, not sparing a word for Rochelle, who greeted me as I opened the door. When she realized I was crying, her face crumpled in sympathy. I threw the door to our bedroom open and climbed into the bed fully dressed and with my fucking shoes on.

I lay there as my heart galloped. My heartbeat pounded in my head and behind my eyes. That rhythm was the only thing

I could focus on for a long time. Eventually, noise filtered into my consciousness.

"Please, my son is a good man. We deserve to know what's happened to him, and if he's dead, we deserve to bury him." A miserable choked sob and a cacophony of sniffles made my headache worse. I'd left the TV on this morning. The news, my obsession, the worst part of my day.

I thought I was broken, every piece of me destroyed. Maybe I was because what happened to me at that moment was more than destruction. It was rebirth too.

Everything inside me screamed fight or flight. The urge made no sense as there was no imminent danger, no threat stood in front of me. Fuck, the danger was *dead*! Hardly in the position to do anything to me. But I was surer than I'd ever been: I was an animal and the only way out of this fucking suffering was action.

TWENTY-FIVE

Claire

I couldn't sleep that night. The few times my eyes fell closed, they popped open immediately and my chest filled with panic. I reared back, ready to punch Mason in the face when he climbed into bed beside me.

I let him wrap me in his arms, and while his hold eased the emptiness, the sense of foreboding never left. The threat of something awful lurked nearby, scratching at the walls. The intensity of the pressure made it cosmic and utterly insurmountable.

I wasn't crazy. The crushing disappointment pummeling me was based on a situation I'd created. All I wanted was for the police to connect Charles Gains and "Tyler Hines". I built that revelation up in my mind as if that one thing could fix the entire problem. Like fixing me was just a matter of finding the right piece...

But the authorities turned over the most pressing stone, and it still led to nothing. They had made the necessary connection to discover the truth; how could they not see it? Was it possible they simply didn't care?

The aroma of expensive cologne mixed with Mason's natural scent surrounded me; his sheets always smelled faintly like him and clean. The combination was fantastic and mind-altering. His deep, even breaths set the perfect tempo for me to count the passing time by, and although this was one of the worst nights of my life, having Mason beside me made it okay.

I should have talked to Mason and told him about what I learned. I didn't even try, because of the impending doom. When morning came, I climbed out of bed with the loose threads of a forming plan.

As soon as it was a reasonable hour, I texted Emma and asked her to cover for me again. Mason and I ate a quiet breakfast together where he intently observed me as he devoured the sherried mushroom omelet Rochelle made him. "Do you want to talk?"

"Talk about what?" The innocent act never worked with him before, but what was the harm when I had so few options?

"You don't seem like yourself this morning," he spoke with unnatural softness like I was an injured animal.

"Whereas you seem exactly like yourself."

He ignored the sarcasm, "James called me yesterday."

"And what did he say?" I poked at my eggs, attempting to disturb them enough to make them look eaten. I didn't need to give him any more ammunition, but my raw stomach ached too badly to eat.

"Claire, I would much rather you tell me." He popped a potato in his mouth and his lips closed around the tip of the fork. A dull pang of lust heated my skin.

"I would like to know what James is reporting about me." I put down the orange juice I was considering rather than drinking.

"He didn't have much to report. He didn't recognize the woman you spoke to, and he overheard only a little of your conversation. You were really upset about whatever she said to you and he was worried about you."

"You all talk too much and follow me too fucking intently. At what point do *I* have a say in what happens in *my* life?"

"You always have a say, but I need to keep you safe. Victor and James keep you safe. Lawrence keeps you safe. I am not holding you here as a prisoner. I am protecting you the best way I can."

"If that were true, he wouldn't report anything to you. He would keep me safe and keep my confidences. But that's not his job, is it Mason?"

He said nothing, and the muscle in his jaw ticked as he chewed and drank his coffee. His eyes bored into mine, trying to convey something I was unwilling to understand. I tried not to stare back.

His appearance shouldn't affect me, but it did. His green eyes pulled like the gravity of a massive planet, and I was nothing but a helpless satellite. My lack of self-control with him was a well-established and accepted weakness.

My mouth watered at the sight of him angry, in his suit, eating his breakfast as if the world should bow at his feet. *I* wanted to bow at his feet. I needed to pull his cock out of his pants and suck him until he spilled. Fuck the eggs.

The emotions inside of me were so intense, and at odds with one another, I had to be losing my mind. I got up and walked around to him, pushing his chest roughly, until he scooted his chair out from under the table. I leaned forward, trailing my lips along the edge of his jaw and gently biting the soft skin at the corner of his mouth.

"What are you doing, Claire?" the anger stayed in his voice, tangled up with intense heat. It flowed through us both, binding us in an earth-shattering current of need.

I bit his full lip before I kissed him hard. "Stop talking."

He chuckled, amused by the change in dynamic. I dropped to my knees, touching his ready cock through his slacks. I opened the zipper, pulling him out and into my mouth nearly in the same movement. He tasted clean and delicious. I couldn't wait to hear him grunt and curse as I sucked his orgasm out of him.

"Baby," he moaned as he pushed his hand through my hair. "Why are you doing this?"

I popped off him long enough to mutter, "Because I want to suck your fucking cock!" And shoved it back in.

"*Fuck*, that's so good," he groaned, and the sound set my heated blood aflame. I bobbed my head against him, sucking him back into my throat. "Stop, Claire."

I did as he asked, but my chest flipped painfully at the threatened rejection. "Why?"

"I can see how wrecked you are, and we need to talk. This is fucking amazing, baby, but I want your pretty mouth to talk to me, not suck my soul out."

"But *I* want to suck your soul out, and *you* want me to." I leaned forward and licked the head of his cock. He shuddered, and the hard length twitched toward me.

He grabbed me by my face, both hands resting tenderly against my cheeks. "Talk to me."

Burning, stinging rejection. "I don't want to fucking talk," I bit out as I got off my knees and stomped out of the kitchen. I understood he wanted to be supportive, but him stopping me from sucking his dick *was* my problem.

Every bad feeling that faded into background noise while he was in my mouth came back in full force, multiplied even. The loose plan I formed throughout the night suddenly seemed like a much better idea.

I waited until Mason, James, and Vick were leaving. I kissed him goodbye to ensure he wouldn't double back. He pulled me tight against his body, his hand twisted in my hair and the other caught around my waist. "I'm going to be gone for the day, but I won't be home too late."

"Where are you going?"

"Work, nothing pretty. I'll tell you what I can when I get home. I promise."

"Okay."

"If you need to go anywhere, let Lawrence take you." I didn't agree, because I didn't want to lie to him. He sighed, "I didn't stop you because I didn't want it. Baby, I need you to talk to me."

"I don't want to talk. I wanted to watch you come and to forget for a few minutes."

Guilt flashed in his eyes. He pressed his lips to the hollow beneath my ear and his teeth grazed my neck. "I'll make you forget anything you want when I'm finished."

"You missed your chance, Mason." In a silent response to my challenge, he bit down hard and then kissed me once before he left.

I waited long enough for him to arrive in the city and when I was certain no one was paying attention to me, I snuck out to the garage. Six cars stood in a row, all of which used to have the keys hanging inside the house. I let out an exasperated sigh. Not that big of a deal.

The enormous garage could feasibly fit another four cars. Toolboxes and a workbench lined the industrial metal walls. The overhead lights shined almost too brightly. Opening random drawers and things, I found the keys in an old coffee can. They kept the garage in fucking pristine condition. No trash or debris littered the space, so their hiding spot stuck out like a sore thumb.

I poked around some more until I found the gas cans. A critical part of my plan, but one I was least excited about. I shook them, disappointed to find them empty. Stopping at the gas station meant valuable time. Time that Mason would use to stop me.

I put them in the back of the car and climbed into the front. I hit the control for the door and took a steadying breath before I pulled out and down the driveway. Casey stood near the side of the gatehouse with a concerned expression on his face. *Fuck,* I didn't have any time at all.

I tore out, heading down the road, passed the closest gas station in favor of one a bit out of the way. By now, I'd bet good money Mason already knew I left, but at least he wouldn't know why I did.

I assumed he had a tracker in the car, but he was probably in the city and it would take him a while to get back to this area. I didn't think he would send anyone after me. The knowledge he would always be the one to come for me made a separate thrill shimmy down my spine.

I pulled up outside the station, thanking divine providence this plan came to me in the winter, and my oversized hood shielded my face from the cameras. I filled the gas cans, doing my best not to spill any on me or the ground while still hurrying.

That part of the plan utterly failed, and by the time I hung up the nozzle, I reeked of gas. I placed the cans in the trunk and headed down the road again. It didn't matter if I was covered; the smell was everywhere.

The location of the Gains estate burned itself into my mind. Charles had been the focus of my attention for months now, and I saw the sprawling manor often enough on TV to recognize it easily.

I lacked the unease behind the wheel I had the day I visited Erica Miller's town. The rage had morphed into a single-minded determination that removed the pressure from operating the vehicle and turned it toward realizing my goal.

I arrived at the estate, noticing the guarded gate. The idea of getting close to the house by simply driving in wouldn't work on a normal day, especially not when I stunk like gas and had a slightly frenzied look to me.

Driving around the block, I searched for places to park along the street that would get me closer to the house. No law prevented me from parking beside the giant gates. The only way through was over, and I mentally calculated how I could haul myself and the gas cans over with a tenuously healed bullet wound and lack of upper body strength.

Stepping out of the car, I took stock of my surroundings. The freezing air nipped my cheeks as I looked over the neighborhood decorated for Christmas. Through the bars, I saw a reindeer and sleigh lit up in the Gains estate. The Grinch stole Christmas when everyone was asleep. What did it make me if I burned it in the middle of the day?

I dragged the cans out of the car and lined them up beside the gate. Burning down the entire palatial mansion would take a lot more than two cans of gas. But if I could burn down one of her larger buildings, that would satisfy my need to destroy.

Why should Priscilla Gains, the monster who started this mess, sit on the news and cry for her missing murderous son with no retribution? Why did she get to live in an elaborate mansion when her wicked spawn, who she abused until he fucking snapped, killed women? *Pedophile,* I wanted to cut the word into every surface she owned.

Because of her, Charles took those girls from their families. Then he stole my safety, my security. He left me nothing but my life, and at that moment I didn't care about me. A sob threatened to break free at the guilty feeling the thought brought on.

I'm sure any of his victims would rather be alive, but I had no gratitude for that gift. I was the epitome of wrong and awful things thrived inside me. My mother and the father I never met both understood how broken and worthless I was. I would never be enough for anyone, least of all myself.

I grabbed onto the gate, and finding a decent foothold, I climbed a few feet into the air. The wound ached, and I realized I should count myself lucky *if* I could haul one can over; I definitely would not be getting two. I reached down and picked it up, shifting my footing to keep my balance. "Ugh," I tried to be quiet, but the moan of pain escaped anyway.

I paused in the act of lugging it over the fence, suddenly sensing I was no longer alone. I glanced back over my shoulder, and of course, *he* was there.

TWENTY-SIX

Claire

"**A**re you fucking *crazy?* What are you doing here, Claire?" Mason growled as he barreled toward me. An angry shade of red flooded his cheeks, and I could have sworn steam blew out of his nose. He wore a handsome peacoat that fit him beautifully, and that beauty stunned the thoughts out of my head. When he reached out and yanked me off the fence, I yelped.

I landed against him with a huff. The gas can in my hands fell and sloshed against the ground, splashing us both. "What are you doing?" I grit out as I scrambled against him, trying to get my feet planted.

"Stopping you from getting arrested, and whatever other shit you were planning to do that you would no doubt regret!" he spoke in nearly a hiss, and while I had seen him angry before, this was by far the angriest he had ever been with me.

"She deserves this. She fucking deserves so much worse. All of this shit is her fault! They're all dead because of her and she gets to cry on the news and the world pities her. Where is the fucking justice?!" I thrashed against him, digging my heels into the snow, getting myself muddy as hell but not escaping Mason. He held me tighter. My head pounded with the effort of the struggle, the adrenaline from coming here, and the plans I formed. Or maybe it was the gas soaking us. My eyes, nose, and throat burned with each breath.

Mason's arms found better purchase, and he swung me off the ground and squeezed me against his chest. My love for him was the only reason I didn't kick the fuck out of his balls. He stared into my eyes like he needed to convey the most serious message.

"Charles killed those women, Claire. Not Priscilla. She is a fucked up bitch and I wouldn't give a shit if she dropped dead, but I just pulled up on you dragging a gas can over a fucking fence to burn her house down. This isn't justice either. This is you with a death wish! Fumes are rolling off you. You were more likely to light yourself on fire than the fucking house!"

"I do not have a death wish. I'm *lucky* to be alive." My cheeks burned with the lie. Hadn't I just been thinking the very thing he accused me of? "All I want is to be able to look in the goddamn mirror!" That much was true. "I can't face myself, not knowing how many women died, how badly they suffered, and their families *still* don't know where they are! I can't take this, and everything is her fault."

I shoved against his chest, surprising him enough to drop me. I dug my feet in and tried to run with every intention of climbing back over the fence, dragging the gas with me, and lighting her mansion on fire. Maybe I was crazy because her security would surely stop me before I succeeded. Crazy, desperate, miserable, and alone like I had never been, despite the man I loved being by my side.

That's why I thrashed against his hold when he got his arms around me again. "Fuck you! Put me down!"

Lights flicked on from the gatehouse and some last vestige of self-preservation kicked in as I let him toss me over his

223

shoulder and haul me into the car. The door slammed shut behind us, and a moment later, Vick was driving. James sat in the passenger seat. "Who's going to take the car back if the three of you are all watching me?"

"Casey," James said.

Vick pulled away at an incredible speed.

"I'm not going to jump out of the car, Mason. Let me go." I thrashed against him once more, fueled by the watching men and the feral thing inside of me refusing to be caged again. He loosened his hold and I moved as far from him as I could in the ridiculously large, opulent vehicle.

"What the fuck were you thinking?" he growled at me—actually growled—and I laughed in his face.

"What I was thinking is none of your goddamned business. You're not around. You lie to me about everything. What the fuck do I matter to you?" James' eyes flicked over my face in the rearview mirror and there was pity. "And you, James, fuck you too!"

The pity only deepened and my disgust at the thought of being touched was the only thing keeping me from flinging myself at him and scratching his fucking eyes out.

I stared out the window, ignoring them as much as it was possible given the small space, but I felt the two brothers silently communicating with each other.

"So, Claire, were you going to burn the place down?" James asked.

"At least some of it," I quipped back, unable to give another fuck about what anyone thought. "I didn't bring much gas."

"What the actual *fuck* were you thinking?!" Mason twisted toward me, grabbing me by the neck and pulling me into him. He squeezed hard enough a soft, pained noise escaped me, but it sounded more like a pathetic mewl. I stared at him in shock as his raging eyes consumed me. I hated my soaked pussy as surely as I wanted to hate him.

I didn't answer him, pushing my lips tightly together. His firm hands around my neck shook, jostling me and making my head throb. "What the fuck are you trying to accomplish, Claire?" He loosened his hold enough that I could breathe. "Are you an arsonist now?"

One hand moved from my neck to my hair, fisting in it until I squealed. He held each centimeter of my attention in his brutal grip. "You are going to stop this *bullshit.* If you want something burned down, you *ask me!*" he yelled in my face, and I jumped in surprise, but I didn't fear him. He was beside himself, angry and scared, but he would never hurt me.

"I will burn every inch of that estate. I will burn this city to the fucking ground if you want, but if I ever catch you dragging your ass over a fence with a gas can again, I can't be held accountable for my actions." Everything about him hardened and became more angular. Frenzied determination replaced every hint of the softness and caring he normally regarded me with.

"I'm fucking shaking." I quipped. The hand in my hair jerked hard, revealing my throat to him.

"I will never hurt you, Claire, but I swear to God if I ever see you do something this stupid again, I will use your body against you," his lips skated over my pulse point as he continued, "I'll break you down until you're nothing but a sobbing mess, and I'll be the only one who can put you back together." His teeth bit into my bottom lip. I squealed in pain. Heat exploded through me, both at his threat and his punishing bite.

"You don't fucking *own* me." I tried to push him away, shoving angrily against his chest. I wrinkled his collar pretty thoroughly but achieved no distance.

"That is where you're wrong,"

Outrage, single-minded fury. How dare he? Who was he to tell me he owned me? "We're over, Mason. I mean it, we're done." The tension snapped into place like a rubber band breaking, and then intense electric energy hung in the air, waiting for somewhere to go. The fine hairs on my arm stood on end in response.

The car went deathly silent. James, who had been stoically avoiding looking at us, stared in the reflection of the rearview mirror like he was hoping to prevent an explosion. Even Vick's impassive expression was replaced by one of shock. My gaze flicked to Mason, and I couldn't take the intensity of his stare. His eyes trailed along my face, burning me.

"I need a little time to find a place to live," I continued, hoping that by treating this as if it were a done deal, he would be agreeable, "but I'm sure we can avoid each other until I do." This was the first time I even considered leaving him, and my heart screamed this was wrong, but what other choice remained?

He let go of my throat and my hair and leaned back into the seat. The distance between us ached with such intensity, it surprised me. With everything else fighting for dominance and battering my insides, how could I contain this pain too? I couldn't risk a look at his face. I didn't want to see his expression.

Our relationship was a mistake from the beginning, and somewhere inside I knew that. I fell for him too fast and much too hard. He made me feel things I never dreamed existed, and no man should hold that much power over me. I believed I would be better off never having experienced a person who was like magic and lightning in my veins.

He lit me up so brightly that I was less than dimmed in his absence; I was fucking snuffed out. And how could I carry on that way? The world was shitty and hard. Was I supposed to spend my life desperately, achingly, devoted to a man who would leave me in the end? Whether it was through choice or death, Mason would leave me eventually.

Loving someone the way I loved him was dangerous. No person should be able to decimate you entirely. I thought I learned that lesson young. The disappointment of my parents' love was part of me, but somehow this was more crushing. I never knew love like his or pain this deep.

I forgave his lies, no matter how much they tore me up. He killed people, but I cared little beyond the existential crisis it caused *me*. I only truly cared that he lied to me. I didn't know where I started and he began anymore.

He ripped me off a fence, slapped a gas can out of my hands, pulled me around by my hair and throat, and I loved it. It pissed me off and infuriated me, but it turned me on and filled me with a satisfaction I scarcely understood. *He was trying to protect you,* a small voice whispered in the back of my mind. *He's the only person who has ever tried to protect you.*

Before my tender thoughts could soften me and pull me back from the edge, every horrible aching feeling I had in the last few months, and even before, pushed to the surface, oozing their way out like my body was trying to rid their infection.

The spots our bodies touched moments before stung. My lips buzzed from where he grazed and sunk his teeth. My pussy ached in hollow, desperate need. That bitch needed to keep out of the decision-making because if it were up to her, I would spread my legs for him right here in front of James and Vick.

My nerves told me to talk, fill the space, and make sure he knew this was it. I really was ending things, but I kept my mouth shut; mobster lawyer ex-boyfriends were definitely the type that anything you say *can* and *will* be used against you.

The car ride was achingly quiet, painfully silent. My clit pulsed and my blood pounded. The dramatics of my fight instinct fizzled out. Flight came next, and I needed to escape him. Even if I were crazy enough to jump out of a moving vehicle, I wasn't physically fit or skilled enough to roll my way out of the impact and avoid the subsequent injuries.

His eyes burned along my skin, though I refused to look at him. He didn't touch me again, and said nothing. When the car finally pulled to a stop, I threw the door open and stormed out. I didn't know where I was headed, but I wasn't going inside that house.

TWENTY-SEVEN

Claire

I stomped across the snow, over the grounds, and toward a guest house, though that's not necessarily where I was headed. Before I crossed half the distance, he grabbed me around the waist and hauled me up and over his shoulder.

"Put me down!" I screamed at the top of my lungs, relishing in the release of letting my frustrations out.

"No. With the way you're acting, you'll go commit arson and freeze to death in the snow," he gritted out, so angry his self-control hung on by a thread.

"It's none of your business. We are *done!*" I flailed against him, not caring that my wound and soul ached.

His hand gripped my ass hard, his fingers delving between my cheeks and squeezing until I whimpered. "We're going inside," he enunciated each word slowly and somehow the quiet tone of his voice made the words cut deeper.

I wanted to fight, but it was useless. So, I let the fuck drag me into the house. When we got to his bedroom, I started thrashing again. If he had just put me down, I could've headed for any of the other million bedrooms. He lifted a heavy hand and brought it down hard against my ass cheek.

"This is your room too, whether you believe it or not, and you're staying in it." I didn't know how the man read my mind so easily. His knowing me so well disconcerted me and prickled across my skin like his touch. Was it love or fear? And why did I think he would be the death of me?

"This is where you sleep," he told me. The gravelly texture cut deep into my bones, not needing any volume to drive his words home.

He opened the door and shoved it out of his way before stomping to the en suite bathroom. He walked us both, fully dressed, into the shower and flipped on the spray.

"What the fuck!?" I shouted as the cold water poured over my face.

"You're flammable, Claire." He put me down and stripped out of his clothes, quickly and angrily scrubbing at his skin. "Seriously, wash up if you don't want me to do it for you." Part of me wanted him to, but I undressed and carefully washed my body. He didn't speak nor look at me through the entire process; the dual shower heads made interacting with one another unnecessary.

Washing the gas off my skin was a relief, but the smell wasn't likely to fade anytime soon. The chemical headache mixed with the smell of Mason's soap was messing with my head. The anger was still there, but it calmed beneath the water. He finished up first, and when I stepped out, he silently handed me a robe. He watched me wordlessly as I wrapped myself in it and then left the bathroom with a determined expression. I followed him out, curiosity getting the better of me.

"What are you doing?" I asked stupidly as I found him bent over the fireplace.

"You want a fire so fucking bad? Here's a fire," he snapped at me. I looked at him in disbelief. Could he really be the same funny, sarcastic man I fell in love with? He had to be. He had the same sense of humor, but now it was turned against me. I stared at him, saying nothing. My face, however, said a lot.

"Sit down. You must be exhausted and hurting." A bit of his normal tone returned, and instead of welcoming the reprieve from his anger, mine burst into flames.

"Stop telling me what to do!" I demanded, and while it was stupid to argue because I was profoundly tired and beyond sore, I couldn't stop myself.

The flames quickly licked over the logs, and the crackling sound was intensely comforting. The fight died out of me as my body slowly calmed. My anger all but evaporated, but our relationship was still over. It had to be if I was going to have any chance of understanding all of this.

I was about to open my mouth and tell him exactly that when he said, "No."

"No?" I repeated.

"I see your face, and no, you are not leaving me," he clarified his point as his eyes ran over my shaking legs.

"That's not your decision to make," my words came out breathless, and despite the conviction I still held, I softened to him.

"It's not yours either," he approached me as he spoke.

"Then whose is it if it's not ours?" The sadness in my voice rang as did the exhaustion and the sense that I could not keep going this way.

"Fate, destiny?" he offered. So close now, I thought I could smell him. The gas on us was overwhelming, even after the shower, and I wondered if I imagined it just to complete the comfort of his nearness. My head was buzzing from the chemical and the ache behind my eyes bloomed into something fierce.

"You're not serious." He couldn't be. A man like him couldn't believe in destiny. A bunch of small things all fell into place. Of course, he believed in fate. It explained so many of his actions.

"You're damn right I'm serious." He grabbed my face and pulled me to him. He kissed me hard, claiming me, tasting me, punishing me. His lips were soft and lush, but they moved against my own with a desperation that tasted like every good and aching thing in existence. "We're inevitable."

"I want to believe that." He tore his lips from mine and took a step back, leaving me bereft and alone.

"Tell me to leave," he spoke so clearly and yet I couldn't understand what he meant by that.

"What?"

"You want this to be over? You think you have the power to end this? Tell me to leave, Claire." I stared at him blankly, my mouth hanging open like a fish. "I have always respected you and always given you a choice, whether you believe that or not. Do you want to leave me? Tell me right now."

I couldn't speak, I couldn't think. I knew in my bones he was speaking the utter truth. All I had to do was tell him to go and mean it, and he would. He would probably gift me this house if I wanted.

"What about my apartment? I didn't have a choice there."

"No, Claire, you didn't, but neither did I. Your landlord threatened to evict you if you didn't leave willingly after everything that happened. I didn't think you needed to deal with that on top of everything else."

"So you..."

"Paid the piece of shit whatever he demanded to fix the place and moved you into my home, where you belong."

I stared into the fire, trying to work through what he was saying. "So you weren't being an over-the-top possessive asshole?"

"I was, just not for the reasons you seem to think."

"I'm not sure what to think, but I don't want you to leave."

"I have to warn you, baby," his hand slid languidly down my cheek, "If you don't get rid of me, you're going to need to take your punishment. You were a very bad girl tonight, and that cannot go unpunished. You could have died, wound up in prison, been burned so badly the rest of your life—" I held up my hands to stop him. I thought over my options for a few more moments, but we both knew I would take whatever it was. I was furious, half-crazed with fear, guilt, and grief, but I was stupid where he was concerned, and his nearness was enough to soften the rest of my resolve.

As I stared at him, the hard anger and sexual tension morphed into something incredibly raw.

"Don't you see I'm trying my best? That I'm doing everything I can to protect you?" he crooned the words into the space between my ear and neck. The sentiment and his breath on my skin left me senseless. "You don't belong mixed up in this shit, but I love you too much to let you go like I should.

"I loved you too fucking much to walk away, when I should have, months ago before you were in danger. Don't you get it, Claire? You are the only thing that shines in all this darkness. *You* are the shiny prize that those who want to hurt me are salivating to get. Your pretty face,"

One hand tightened in my hair as the other traced roughly along my cheek and chin, pinching my bottom lip before thrusting his thumb inside, "This mouth," he continued, pulling his thumb free and dragging my spit down the column of my throat. He slid the sides of my robe apart fondling my bare breasts, "these tits," I moaned as he pinched the hardened peaks.

"This perfect pussy," he growled as he unceremoniously slid his fingers between my wet thighs and found me bare. Plunging them inside of me in a swift motion, his other hand trailed the cleft of my ass, "this virgin hole. Don't you understand you are everything to me? They would take you just to hurt me, baby, but once they had you..." he tutted at me, "you are too fucking sweet not to defile."

I was a panting mess. As he pumped his fingers into me, the look in his eyes was wild; he was a man possessed, incensed by the thought of someone else taking what was his, of me choosing to leave him.

He slid his fingers out of me, making me gasp at the emptiness. Dropping to his knees in front of me, he pulled the sash off the robe, dropping it to the ground and exposing me to his gaze. I shifted nervously, and before I could regain my footing, he ran his tongue along the seam of my pussy.

I dragged in a ragged, frantic breath. He sucked my clit into his mouth with strong, sure strokes of his tongue. My knees weakened and nearly buckled as he forced an intense wave of pleasure upon me. "I worship this pussy, but do you know how satisfying it would be to defile?" I moaned gutturally, desperate for anything he wanted to do to me.

"You like that? The idea of someone taking you from me and ruining your sweet body, fucking this tight wet hole while you beg them not to?" there was an edge to his voice that would have scared me if I didn't know that he would protect me with his life.

"No," I whimpered back.

"Then why are you sopping wet? Why are you moaning like that?" I couldn't deny the evidence dripping down his chin.

"I want *you* to ruin me. No one else, only you." I whispered, no longer remembering the reasons why we should go our separate ways.

"Do you want to leave me, Claire?" he breathed against the soft skin of my clit.

"Never," I vowed, and pleasing him made my body hum.

"That's right, baby." He sucked my clit, applying too much pressure, then bit the sensitive flesh. I screamed at the top of my lungs, tears slipping down my cheeks. It hurt and forced me toward my orgasm. He softened the attack with the flat of his tongue, lapping away the pain he caused. It quickly faded, soothed by the luscious sweep of him savoring me. At that moment, I would have done anything to come.

His teeth clamped down again, and I shouted through my tears as his fingers stroked my g-spot. The orgasm building within me was wild, out of control, and it scared the fuck out of me. When it crested, my cum gushed over him and down his bare chest.

It was more than my cum; it was every aching and agonizing bit of me rushing out in an unparalleled moment of release. I was certain I would never experience something quite like that again.

Licking up my juices, he hummed a masculine sound as he relished the taste of me. Happily taking my burdens as his own.

"Holy shit, Mason."

"Too intense?" He looked up at me through his dark blonde lashes.

"Yes," I barely kept myself standing.

He gave me a wicked smile, "You are nowhere near having learned your lesson yet. We have a long night ahead of us. Now, go bend over the end of the bed."

I obeyed him, leaning my body over the edge and spreading my legs in a tempting display of flesh.

"Does that position hurt your stomach?" he asked from across the room. He fiddled in his closet, and I couldn't see what he was up to from here. "I want to make sure you're okay after all your *escapades.*"

A nervous thrill went through me. I knew how fucking angry he was, and whatever he planned, he would not take it easy on me, but God, I needed it.

"No," I answered honestly. My wound had been feeling a lot better lately. Between my pathetic sleuthing and arson attempt, I expected more pain, but I was okay.

"Good," he leaned over me, pressing his front to my back, putting weight on me but not all of it, "What about this?"

"No,"

"Good, I only want to cause you pain you enjoy. That's the only reason I have *ever* lied to you or hid the truth. It's the difference between me and the hungry fucking animals waiting to tear you to shreds. That's why I keep things from you, Claire."

I whimpered again, and this time it wasn't lust, but fear. "That's right baby, you should be afraid, but only of me. I'll protect you from all of them, but I'm going to enjoy breaking you." He gave my ass a smack, followed by a firm bite, and I cried out in shock, pain, and pleasure. His hands on me and his teeth digging into my skin had my already soaked pussy desperately twitching and begging for all of him.

He stood directly behind me, no longer leaning against me. He spread my ass cheeks in a dirty, possessive move.

"You know, I've wanted to fuck this ass for months, and I would have by now if I weren't taking it easy on you, waiting for you to heal. You would already know how good it feels to come while I'm buried deep in your tight ass, how wrong and perfect you'd feel being filled by me in every hole."

I knew he was right. I would love it; I was his perfect, pretty, little slut, just like I always was when he pushed my boundaries. But I was not ready for that yet. "No, Mason, please don't," I choked out.

"Have I stretched your ass, Claire? Have I made you wear plugs and worked you up to taking a dick here?" he thrust his thumb against the entrance, proving a point with the small pinch of pain.

"No,"

"No is right, and I would never try to shove my cock inside of you without properly preparing you. It would tear you apart, hurt you, make you cry, and bleed. I would never, but the people who want to hurt you would fuck this ass dry and use your own blood as lube." As he spoke, he dripped a cool substance over my asshole, and as he rubbed it in, I realized he was applying the lube he promised me his enemies wouldn't bother with.

He pressed a finger against my tight ring of muscles, massaging before pushing past my resistance, sinking into me. "Relax, baby, this is just my pinky, and I'm going to make you feel so good before I make you sob your heart out."

I took a deep breath, and remembering how much I enjoyed everything he had ever done to me, my body loosened.

"Good girl," his praise opened me up to him and his finger slipped more easily into my ass.

He pumped into me a few times before trading his pinky for a larger finger and another until he speared his thick middle finger deep inside my ass. He lined his cock up with my entrance and slid home inside my pussy. I was so wet, that he met no resistance as he plunged all the way in.

"Fuck, you're so tight. You like being that full, baby?"

"Oh, God, Mason, fuck,"

"What is it? Do you want to come again? Don't worry." His free hand found my clit and rolled it between his thumb and forefinger until an orgasm hit me with the force of a freight train and I was screaming and convulsing around him.

"Oh, God, Mason, fuck." I called out again. It wasn't original, but I was liquified and behaving like a skipping CD. A loud buzzing drew my attention. I shouted some nonsense as he placed the vibrating wand against my clit on the highest setting. The sensation was so intense it was painful.

I sobbed into the bed. "Mason, please, I can't take it," I begged, knowing my cries were useless. He told me he was going to ruin me, break me into little pieces, and punish me for all the stupid shit I pulled.

That was exactly what he planned to do. He moved the wand in time with his finger deep in my ass and his cock in my pussy. "I can't, this is too much!" my throat ached as I screamed.

He pushed a second finger into my ass, stretching me nearly to the point of breaking. With a blinding light, I came again.

Screaming so loud my voice broke, dipping into and out of silence as I wailed. My head disconnected from my shoulders.

I cried and convulsed, pathetically mewling and begging him for a reprieve. He didn't let up, clicking the wand on what was actually the highest setting.

The increased sensation reminded me of burning. How could the unbearable fire ache so fucking badly and still have my body twitching along toward another release? My limbs spasmed hard, rattling my teeth. I was barely conscious of my cum spurting out of me like a broken fountain.

"Do you want me to ruin you, baby? Just remember, I'll always put you back together. It's you and me, Claire. Do you get that?"

"No, I can't." I sobbed, tears streaming down my face. "Please, Mason, I can't."

"Safeword or you're going to come again," he grunted as his cock slammed into my pussy and my ass twitched desperately around his fingers. Before I could think about it long enough to decide, I flew over the edge into the most intense orgasm I had ever experienced. It fucking hurt, my God it was agony. Soul crushing, devastating, life-altering.

"The end!" I cried, tears pouring pathetically down my cheeks. As soon as the words were out of my mouth, he stopped all movement, pulling the wand away from me as I continued to twitch around his digits and cock inside of me.

"No more orgasms, baby," he comforted me before leaning back like he was going to pull out of me.

"I need your cum, but no more orgasms, please."

He leaned over me, kissing my salty, tear-soaked lips. "Don't worry, baby, your pussy is choking my cock so tightly, trying to milk me of my cum, it won't take long."

He used both his hands to hold and stroke my ass as he pumped into me. Tears continued to slide down my cheeks and my eyes fell closed. After all the times he made me come and the intense vibrations of the toy, his cock inside me was soothing, only building a dull pressure that wouldn't explode without some serious effort.

He grunted a supremely sexy male sound as he painted my insides with thick ribbons of his cum. I laughed out loud, fucking deranged between the orgasms and the tears. He laid his forehead against my back and let his cock twitch inside of me for a minute.

He pulled out of me and dragged us both up onto the bed. He left me naked and dripping his cum, but wrapped his arms around me and laid my head against his chest.

"I love you more than my own life. I would be nothing without you." The fire in his voice made it impossible to doubt, yet he filled my soul with doubts. Sometimes I thought their weight might crush me.

"That's not true. You would be fine." I told him, not sure where my beliefs began and my doubts ended.

"You cannot do things that will take you away from me," he continued, not caring to argue with me when he already told me so clearly how he felt.

"Mason..."

"Promise me," his demand was low and harsh.

"I promise, Mason, but I'm already ruined. Does it even really matter?"

"You are far from ruined, beautiful girl."

TWENTY-EIGHT

Mason

After I finished with Claire, I tucked her into bed and slid in behind her. I held her until she was snoring, which took only a moment. With everything she put herself through, and the way I wore her out after, she would be asleep for a long time.

I stayed beside her for a while for my benefit, memorizing every detail of her face. How her golden skin wrapped around her high, rounded cheekbones, the perfect m-shape of her top lip, and the light freckles dusted over her nose and cheeks. Exactly how her curves dipped, swelled, and held onto the diffused glow of the dimmed lights.

I could have lost her in so many ways, and the fact I was partially responsible chewed away at my insides. I regretted lying to her, along with the way I acted when I found her. When Casey called and told me she had taken off, I went a little crazy. But what the fuck was *I* supposed to do when *she* was the one who kept putting herself in danger?

After the stunt with poor Katherine LaMontagne, I didn't understand or trust Claire's intentions. With tensions ramping up between my father's men and mine, *this* would be the time for someone to strike, and she was out alone with no one to protect her and plans that guaranteed trouble.

The thought of her hurt and broken made me deranged. I couldn't live through that again. We canceled our meeting with Hector and followed the tracking device into the high-end neighborhood. I didn't make the connection at first until I saw the mansion that Priscilla Gains so often stood in front of on the news.

Claire pulled up along the side of the estate, and I watched her for a few minutes, trying to figure out—

She had fucking gas cans. All rational thoughts left my brain. The rest of the memories played through my mind, and I oscillated between shame and helpless rage. Finally settling on some combination of the two that sickened me.

I had to compose myself. Tonight was the night Dan said the girls were being brought in. Gavin typically performed an important role in these transactions, but they had given him minimal details. That *was* unusual, but I couldn't say whether my father had lost faith in him or something more nefarious was at play.

I took my phone out of my pocket and dialed his contact as I slid out of bed and walked into my closet to pick out a suit for the night.

"Sharp," Gavin's voice came through the phone.

I paced the rows of designer suits, searching for something dark and comfortable. "Gavin, what do you know about tonight?" I didn't bother with any pretenses or civility as I picked out a wool Ralph Lauren number that would keep me warm. I also didn't mind ruining it with blood splatter, unlike the Stefano Ricci I wore on my first date with Claire. Of course, I hoped our mission wouldn't come to bloodshed, but these things so often did.

"Not much. I was told to contact my buyers about a rush auction in a few days. Other than that, *nothing*." He believed my father's suspicions about him were getting more serious, and while that was true, I was still unconvinced that was the issue tonight.

"Don't worry, Gavin. You're not dying just yet." A cruel smile curled my lips. I eagerly awaited the day I could kill him myself, effectively relieving my father of that pleasure. Gavin was a sick pedo who helped my father make moves against my girl, and few things would give me more joy than to cut him into pieces, soon.

"As if you could prevent it," he scoffed.

I made a noncommittal noise. Like Dan, he didn't know about Hector's soldiers. "What are your instincts about what's going down tonight? The details I have are shaky." The last thing I would ever tell Gavin was—well, anything—but most definitely not that Dan was my source.

"There are only a few places these exchanges happen. They're not bringing them to even the top three usual locations. They're taking extra precautions." He paused for a moment and cleared his throat. "I'm not in the habit of doing more than asked where anyone is concerned—especially you—but I'll warn you to be careful. They may not be expecting *you*, but they are expecting *someone* to cause problems," his voice lowered, assuming that he was the eventuality they planned for.

"Thanks for the tip," my tone lacked all snark for once. I was too busy seriously considering what he had just said. After I hung up the phone, I got dressed, kissed Claire's sleeping face, and locked her in the room. The door unlocks from inside, meaning she could leave, of course, but it gave her one extra level of protection should she choose to remain inside.

I moved through the darkened house on silent feet, finding Lawrence in his office. Like Rochelle, he lived on-site, though he maintained a separate residence for his days off.

"We're headed out, Lawrence," I told him from the doorway.

He turned away from the security footage he was reviewing and nodded his head solemnly. "You'll be careful," he stated.

"And you'll keep her safe."

"With my life," he promised. Lawrence was ex-military, and his extensive training was why I hired him years ago when I first came home from school. I tried to live as normally as possible, but I always knew I would need someone with a gun to cover my back.

"Thank you," I told him as I left the office. I passed by our bedroom one last time. Tonight might be a trap, as Gavin suggested, and if not, we wouldn't be rescuing these girls without resistance.

I loved Claire so much. Leaving her behind, not knowing for certain if I would see her again, was almost unbearable. *I will come home to her.* I told myself as I left the house, ripping my heart in half and leaving the best parts of me with her.

Closing the front door, I turned to face the small army I amassed. I did not need to speak; the plan was already discussed and cemented.

I nodded at my guys who waited at the head of the driveway, "Let's move." Victor, James, Casey, and I climbed into one of my fully decked-out black SUVs.

"You shouldn't come with us," Victor told Casey what all of us had been telling him for days.

"You're not ready for this," James agreed.

"You guys know why I have to. What if my mom's in there?" His sandy blonde hair hung in his eyes as he stared at his feet. Casey still resembled a kid with hints of precious innocence and optimism.

"Your mom is not in there. These are international girls being brought in. They're probably all under eighteen. Little European girls, much like Mila. That's what these top-shelf scumbags want. The people that bought our moms are a much

243

different clientele," Victor continued, attempting to crush that hope. The truth was harsh, but Casey needed to hear it.

"There is a *chance*," he argued, his face reddening, "and even if not, I want to help those girls just like I wanted to help Mila."

"And what did Mila say about your mom?" Vick asked.

"That she won't be in there..."

Despite my early misgivings about Casey, I had grown fond of the kid. What he did for Mila, and the selfless way he tried to protect her, earned my respect. Besides that, I liked him. I wanted to tell him he *couldn't* come, but I wouldn't force him to stay back because he had a baby face. He was a man, even if only barely, and I understood the sense of duty that compelled him.

"Enough arguing," some grumbles followed, but everyone fell silent. "We all need to focus."

A while later, we pulled off the road a mile back from the pier. Security guards patrolled the perimeter, but other than them, the lot stood completely empty. Still, arriving on foot would arouse less suspicion and hopefully reduce the need for bloodshed.

The musty brackish water of the bay wafted on the air, slightly salty, with a hint of fishy stagnation. I crept along the bank's edge, wondering how the wind came off the bay at such frigid temperatures. The water was quiet here, but the ocean roared out in the distance.

Daniel called me earlier in the day to update me that the girls were coming in container TTNU 106775 22G1 and the rough location of the crate in the yard. He wouldn't be amongst our crew tonight; he'd been clear he was not risking his life further than he had to for me. Dan insisted I tell him nothing of our plans.

His refusal to take the leap should insult me, but I couldn't blame him for not wanting to die. I also didn't want to die, and Gavin's words about being careful rang in my head despite what I liked to believe about Dan's intel and intentions.

James and Vick hung back a few steps from me, letting me lead the way while covering my back. Most of our men moved in silence between the containers, sticking to the shadows to avoid being seen on camera.

Cranes swept into the sky, fixed in place while waiting for the next ship to arrive and unload. Odd-looking trucks and vehicles for moving the crates provided prime locations for someone to observe or shoot from.

The stacks of metal spread incredibly far, and a lot of the numbers were simply hard to read. Without a master list for the yard, finding the specific crates was tedious. In the dim light from the lampposts, it looked like an abandoned city. I wondered if more girls were hidden here, more stolen people waiting to meet fates worse than death.

By the time we found the one we searched for, a creeping suspicion raced up and down my spine. Something didn't feel right beyond Gavin's warning and my own misgivings. It was too easy. I hadn't even seen a guard. "Keep your eyes open. Something is wrong." I spoke into the headset that allowed me to address all the men.

"I feel it too, boss," James agreed.

The shipping container Daniel identified sat stacked on top of two others. It would be quite the climb without one of the massive industrial forklifts or cranes.

"Should we call up and see if anyone answers?" Vick asked.

"I don't want to risk exposing our position if we're being watched. *Which* I am nearly certain we are. Someone needs to climb up and listen. We don't do anything too aggressive before we're sure." Eyes prickled against my skin, and that natural warning of danger sunk in as adrenaline coursed through me.

"Not it," James whispered.

I flicked my gaze toward him. "You can go, James. *Do* be careful."

"I called not it," he complained.

"Nose goes," Vick shot back with his finger pressed to his nose.

"Honestly, Victor. I expect this shit from him."

He smiled at me briefly, "I can do—"

Casey stepped up behind us in the shadows. "Let me do it. I'm a good climber, definitely better than James, and Vick is too heavy. He's done for if he falls."

"No," I said plainly, and the tops of his ears turned red.

"Come on, boss. Let me do this. Seriously, I am a damn good climber, and I will not fall. If any of these other guys do it, they're going to draw unnecessary attention. I'm the smart choice."

I thought about it for another minute before I nodded my head. "Be careful. Do nothing but confirm people are inside. Seriously, Casey. Confirm and return."

"You got it." He stepped forward and grabbed onto the shipping container, grappling with the smooth side as he steadily climbed up. I couldn't deny he did it with skill and balance James and Vick both lacked.

It took him a few minutes to climb to the third level, but when he did, he dropped back down almost immediately. He caught himself twice along the way down, but still landed hard on the pavement.

"They're crying, boss. The girls are crying in there, right now! We have to get them out!" He stood up at an odd angle, trying to hide that he hurt himself as he fell. The utter desperation replaced all traces of joking bravado.

"We will, Casey, but we need time to decide how; someone may be watching us. We need to go slow and do this right." I put my hand on his shoulder, holding him in place as he twitched to escape.

His blue eyes flashed up to mine. "No! I'm not waiting. I'm getting them out." He twisted out of my grip, bending my wrist back and taking me by surprise.

He ran at the container and scaled the side, leveraging himself against one side of the door while he yanked down a metal slide. "Casey, don't!" I yelled, aware that I was confirming our position. *Something is wrong.* My heart beat too hard, too quick.

The sounds of cries filled the freezing air, but they sounded hollow, tinny, *recorded*. He glanced back at me and our eyes met for the briefest moment.

Blinding flashing light exploded from within the container, and a vibration that seemed to rumble up through the ground from the bowels of the earth shook the pier. The sound of the blast deadened my hearing. Metal shot like shrapnel through the air with the force of the explosion. Some cut my shoulder and my face. I fell to the ground, as did the other men near the container. Those on the furthest outskirts remained standing.

My side ached relentlessly, and I was sure I had broken ribs. I searched beside me, and through the smoke, found Vick. The blood dripping from his mouth wasn't a positive sign, but he was already trying to stand.

To my left, James sat on the pavement, working up to standing. A moment of potent relief hit me. They both lived, but Casey... I worked through whatever concussive bullshit was going on in my head until I stood on my feet.

Choking smoke thickened the air along with the scent of explosives. It was so fucking cold. The night air swept the smoke away but did nothing to soothe the burns along my skin.

I looked around, finding fewer dead than I feared. I was grateful that most were only injured, but Casey...

My eyes searched the ground. If he lived, he wouldn't be standing. "Find Casey!" I shouted to Vick and James, though I wasn't sure they heard me. I kept looking and after a few minutes, I found what had to be Casey. His burns were so extensive I barely recognized him.

I knelt beside him, checking for a pulse, and found nothing.

My phone vibrated. My love for and worry about Claire were the only things strong enough to grab my attention, but it wasn't her. It was *Daniel*.

Something's wrong. Whatever you're planning, don't.

A soul-deep ache sunk from my chest to my stomach. Did he set me up?

Men groaned around me, pushing to their feet. The ringing in my ears wouldn't let up, but I could hear through it. "What should we do, boss?" Victor asked, and I was only sure because I watched his mouth as he spoke.

"Get everyone medical attention. The fact they haven't started shooting is a good sign they're not planning to, but keep an open eye and cover each other's backs."

"Yes, sir," he answered, slipping into the formality he and James first used when I welcomed them back. It took me weeks to convince them to stop, but the best I got from them was "boss".

"I need help. His body is pretty bad, but we need to get him out of here." I told James, and he nodded. Tears rolled down his cheeks, and while my eyes burned, no tears fell. I hated my father so much at that moment—I thought the feeling alone would consume me. But guilt followed swiftly, crushing me and grinding me into dust. *Why did I agree to bring him here?*

A man I didn't recognize appeared beside me, and we worked together to lift Casey's burned body into one of the SUV's the least injured men retrieved. We loaded the rest of the dead and injured before we climbed into our vehicles and left the pier behind.

Casey's burned face would haunt me for the rest of my life. Not because it was even close to the most gruesome thing I had ever seen, but because I could have actively changed what happened to that decent kid.

Claire came to mind, and I wondered if I should have let her go when she tried to leave me earlier. *Look at the life you lead*, I told myself, hating that I inched my way back into this world, and hating that I inched my way out when people still needed me.

I didn't know what was right and wrong anymore. All I knew was that I wanted nothing more than to lay my head in the lap of the woman I loved and confess my sins. As soon as I finished dealing with this mayhem, that was exactly what I intended to do.

TWENTY-NINE

Claire

Mason disappeared during the night and didn't come back. Normally, I would be angry and suspicious, but this time felt different. James and Vick were also gone, and he always left at least one of them with me. The intuition that something was terribly wrong pressed down on me like a clear shift in barometric pressure.

I called Mason's phone, but he didn't answer, and neither did James nor Vick. At six, he texted from an unknown number, assuring me he was okay. But he never responded to the text I sent back. I got ready for work and let Lawrence drive me simply for something to distract me from my worries and my recent failures.

When we pulled up, Kiana waited for me on the sidewalk. "Good morning, Claire!" Her black hair was piled high on her head in a mass of curls. She painted her lips a bright red that complimented her brown skin beautifully.

Despite being pleased to see her, I needed all of my concentration to behave and interact normally with my worries. "Good morning, Kiana. You look really pretty today."

Her eyes popped in surprise and a grin spread across her face. "Thank you!"

I unlocked the door with shaking hands, hoping she didn't notice how my body buzzed with tension. "Are you excited about the kid's holiday party this weekend?"

Fuck! I forgot. "Yeah, super excited. It crept up quick, huh?"

"Oh my God, yes. This month has flown by. I don't think I'm ready for a new year."

"You and me both," I agreed, a bit too seriously, and her brown eyes widened in concern. "Well, I have a ton of work to get through. If you need anything, you know where to find me."

"Okay, Claire. Thanks."

My steps echoing in the hall filled me with dread. What happened to Mason last night, and why wasn't he answering me? I pulled out my phone and called him. Still no answer. The four walls of my office did nothing to ease the dread creeping along my skin. I tried my best to focus, working sluggishly through the simplest tasks. After spending two hours accomplishing nothing, I walked around the library searching for some purpose.

Despite my anxiety, I was clearer-headed and more myself than I had been in a while. I spent a lot of time thinking the night before, and I left all thoughts of *"arson"* and revenge against Priscilla Gains behind me. I gave up on the idea that I could bring justice to the situation when I wouldn't tell anyone the truth of it. Finally, the reality of my PTSD set in. That's what my doctor said he suspected when he referred me to the psychologist I never called.

I walked down the aisle where the teens liked to have sex and stood on the spot where Emma fought with James, wondering what the fuck I was doing. Not just here, walking around

251

like an imbecile, but in my life. What good had I planned to do by spending my time trying to solve a crime from the shadows without facing the consequences of my complicity?

I was being selfish, and I understood that now. If I *truly* wanted the justice I claimed I did, turning myself and the love of my life in would accomplish my ambition. But I didn't do that, and I wasn't willing to. I couldn't keep pretending that my efforts or my desires somehow improved the situation. I had been the target of a villain and I had become a bit of one myself.

Mason was a good man, despite the many bad things he did. I believed that wholeheartedly, but there were many people who rightfully saw him as a villain. If I wanted to move on in my life, I needed to stop all of this. Letting go of those things sounded next to impossible, but I had to try. I may not have been perfect, but I believed I deserved more than what I was giving myself.

That didn't make me good, but I wasn't evil either. I had been stalked, shot, and pulled back from the brink of death. The methods I used to survive belonged to me, and if I planned to live a long life, I couldn't continue this way.

I drifted toward the door to the basement. Not the dusty place I met Mason, but the secret one I heard Gavin talking to David Sharp in the day Charles shot me. A long time passed since this mysterious room kept me up at night. How could it when other pressing matters overloaded my system? But I had that feeling I sometimes did, when things were coming full circle. An urge to return to old places, and solve older, presumably simpler problems. I turned the doorknob and was unsurprised to find it locked.

I wouldn't be giving up so easily this time. Running away never helped, and neither rage nor pain fueled this decision. This one thing I *could* control, and I didn't give a fuck about the consequences. I would find out what they hid down there. And if Gavin fired me, so be it.

The library was deserted. Kiana busied herself at circulation and Emma was due in after lunch. I weighed the possibility that this would make me miss the kid's holiday party, and decided whether or not I worked here, I would still show up—Gavin never came to those types of things. Christmas was only six days away, and this was my present to myself.

I assumed there may be an alarm system. If so, I would run away and feign innocence. If there were cameras, that wouldn't work, and Gavin would definitely fire me.

I searched on my phone for how to break down a door and finally settled on the method that involved breaking off the doorknob with a mallet. There was one we kept for when we occasionally needed to assemble things. I walked back to my office, smiling at Kiana and the volunteers as I went.

Thankfully, none of them paid any attention to my weapon as I returned to the door. I was far enough away that if they heard anything, it wouldn't cause alarm. Unless an actual alarm went off.

I brought the mallet down on the doorknob far too lightly; it glanced off, and I nearly tripped as it swung into the floor. The next attempt proved better. The effort took me a while, and I sweated profusely, but no alarm sounded as I beat the shit out of the doorknob. With a satisfying metallic clang, the knob broke off and hit the ground. I tried the extremely heavy door, and after some serious pushing and another couple whacks with the mallet, I got in.

I walked onto the darkened landing, feeling along the wall for a switch. My fingers tripped over the plastic, and the lights kicked on. Confusion flooded my mind as I took in the elegant space and then my heart sank. The room was enormous, but not so large as the entire basement. There must be additional rooms. That didn't surprise me nearly as much as the opulence. Gleaming wood surfaces, crystal chandeliers, comfortable chairs, couches, and benches.

While all of that shocked me, the cages built into the wall had me holding my breath as I descended the stairs. The two of them were open and empty, with cream-colored walls and short black carpeting. The cells didn't have even a bathroom or a bucket, so they couldn't be designed for a long-term stay. Who did they cage here and why? The possibilities filled me with a soul-deep dread.

A low stage sat in the middle of the room, a theater in the round set up. A lectern placed in the middle shined under a spotlight as if academia simply flourished in its natural setting. Resting on top lay a gavel. What the fuck was this place?

Rows of ornate and cushioned wooden chairs surrounded the stage. Soft lights glowed from the floor, and if it weren't for the fucking cages, it would have felt like a lecture hall in a museum or a high-end hotel. What the fuck was really happening here, and did Mason know?

My eyes found a door off the side that must lead to the rest of the basement. If these cages stood here in the relatively open room, I could only imagine what horrors lurked in private. I walked to the door in the corner which was unlocked. My heart sped as I pushed it back, half expecting to find someone waiting to grab me. Instead, there lay a similarly ornate hallway lined with doors and a damp smell. I closed the door, on the terrifying hallway. I'd had more than enough close calls lately without adding this to my list.

Whatever satisfaction I thought I would gain from this was a fantasy, and the horror of the situation set in. Did they put people in those cages? Did they sell them on that stage? I needed to get out of here before someone found me and I wound up for sale. My feet pounded as I ran.

I didn't want to alert anyone to my being here, but I couldn't control myself enough to quiet or slow my steps. I nearly fell on the metal before I reached the top of the stairs and barreled through the door and into the hallway. My stomach ached, and I clenched my arms tightly around myself.

I ran back to my office, ignoring Kiana and the volunteers as they tried to talk to me. I called Emma and asked her to come in a few hours early. She heard the distress in my voice, but I had no words for what I'd seen. Before she even arrived, I snuck out and had Lawrence drive me home.

THIRTY

Mason

I, along with my and Hector's men, took the rest of the night to clean up and take care of our injured and dead. Hector came to help, and though he did it for his soldiers and not me, it filled me with profound respect for him.

There were no words for the heaviness weighing down my heart as Vick, James, and I pulled up the driveway. Casey and the other dead all waited at the morgue to have fake causes of death assigned to them. Blood and soot caked the three of us and we stunk like smoke and explosives. My ribs ached terribly along with the burns on the side of my face and hands. I made a mental note to get checked out when things settled.

"What should we tell Mila?" James asked once the car stopped. None of us moved.

"Nothing. Let me shower and I'll be down to talk to her. I owe Casey that, at the very least." I dropped my face into my hands as I spoke, trying to scrub away the shame and sadness.

"I can't face her." James shook his head emphatically. "If we go down there, she's going to be all over us."

"Neither can I." Victor agreed.

"Come inside or make yourself scarce, but you will not tell her. This is my responsibility."

They both looked at one another for a moment. "We'll come in, boss. Better for her not to see any of us like this." Vick said.

"Definitely. Borrow whatever you need from my closet." I opened the door and stepped out into the achingly cold December afternoon.

The three of us went inside and broke off to our respective bathrooms. In my own, I found Claire's wet towel and realized she had gone to work. I assumed after recent events she would have taken the day off, but that assumption meant I was desperately *off* my game.

My instincts kicked in and the reality of last night being a setup hit me. The very person I went through all these lengths to protect was currently *not* in a secure location. With a resounding "Fuck", I accessed the library cameras through my phone.

In what felt like forever, my screen lit up, showing me a moving picture of Claire walking out of her office with something in her hands. Some relief washed over me, but last night still remained unsolved. I dialed Lawrence and filled him in on the details, putting him on high alert and telling him to get Claire home the moment she went for lunch.

With reasonable precautions in place, I showered and dressed so I could talk to Mila before Claire came home.

Vick and James wore my borrowed clothes, and Rochelle handed us sandwiches as we walked out the door. I mustered up as much courage as I could as we walked down to the gatehouse. I was thankful for the chance to breathe and get my bearings, even if my ribs ached each time I inhaled. Also, for the fact that James and Vick were still here to walk beside me. I had not taken a real breath all night, but I forced myself to do so now.

A white curtain flicked back in a window, and I saw a flash of Mila's face before she disappeared.

"Fucking hell," James muttered.

She appeared outside the front door in an oversized t-shirt and a pair of leggings. "Hey, guys! Have you seen Casey? He didn't come back last night."

I walked up to her and gestured toward the door behind her. "Mila, let's go inside, okay?"

Her brow furrowed in confusion and she solidified her footing, determined not to move. "What do you mean? Why do we need to go inside?" Her expression quickly morphed into anger. Her normally mild accent thickened with her concern.

"It's cold, you're underdressed. Let's just go inside and talk," I reached toward her to put my hand on her shoulder and lead her inside, but she stepped back, avoiding my touch.

"No! No, I am *not* going inside!" She stomped her foot in an obstinate gesture, her eyes glassing over.

"Mila, please, it's cold." She opened her mouth to argue some more but, I took her hand and pulled her back into the gatehouse. She resisted lightly but didn't actually try to escape. Having to push her around this way would have annoyed the fuck out of me if I didn't know why she wanted to avoid this so badly.

"Sit down, Mila,"

"I'll stand." She ran her thin hands through her long blonde hair repeatedly. "Please, tell me what the fuck is going on. You're scaring me."

"Mila, please,"

"Mr. Sharp, I cannot sit when I'm pretty sure you're about to..." she sucked in a ragged breath, unable to continue. Tears welled in her eyes and spilled over. "Where is he, Mr. Sharp?" she choked out. "Where is he?"

"Last night we were—"

"I don't give a fuck! Tell me where he is!" she shouted at the top of her lungs. Her chest heaved, and her hands balled into fists. Her mascara dripped down her cheeks and the agony on her face broke me before I even spoke the words.

"Casey is dead, Mila. I am so very sorry." I wanted to tell her the whole story. She deserved to know what a hero he was. His kindness and desire to help were the reason he died, but she wasn't ready to hear anything. The sound coming out of her reminded me of a wounded animal. Her tears increased in intensity, pouring down her face as she sobbed hopelessly. She pressed her fists against her eyes and let out an agonized wail. I tried to place a hand on her shoulder, but she shook me off.

She screamed again, a wordless cry, and cocked back her fist to hit me. She punched me in the chest and with the injury to my ribs, it fucking hurt, but I didn't stop her. Two more hits before she collapsed against me and laid her head on my shoulder. I held her and let her cry.

A long time passed in silence. I didn't understand why I stayed like this. I had no experience comforting anyone, but I knew Casey wouldn't want me to leave her alone.

"He just told me he loved me," her soft, broken voice interrupted the silence. "He said he loved me since the first time he saw me. He didn't want to make things uncomfortable for me. Or make me feel like he was another person trying to buy me. He had loved me all that time. We wasted our chance, and now he's—" her sobs cut off her words.

After another ten minutes, I was sure this would not stop soon. I picked her up and carried her to her apartment. I lay her down in her bed, got her a cup of water, and closed the door behind me. My chest ached heavily. I could barely put one foot in front of the other. That girl would never want for another thing in her life. *That* was my promise to Casey.

Though I showered, I still stunk of smoke and explosives. The stain this night left on my soul would never come clean.

AURELIA KNIGHT

My father would pay for what happened last night; and if he knew, so would Daniel.

THIRTY-ONE

Claire

Lawrence repeatedly asked me what was wrong as we drove back, which was completely out of character for his normally stoic nature; my face must have looked worse than I thought. Though I never did it before, I closed the partition to consider the heinous shit that had been happening right under my feet in private. Did Mason know?

Is this what he thinks I can't handle? I wanted to vomit, and there was no way I could have hid that. For once, I was thankful for the ridiculous stretch SUV and all of its amenities.

We pulled into the driveway, passing no one, but by the time we arrived at the top, Mason was walking up from the gatehouse. The sight of him was enough to make my stomach drop out of my body. He was hurt and favoring his side. Cuts marred his face. A lot of them. "He's burned," I gasped to myself.

"What happened?" I jumped out of the car and bounded toward him.

He didn't hear me. The words were barely more than a whisper. My feet tore up the distance between the two of us. He watched me with a blank expression, and the fear for him only grew deeper. I wrapped my arms around his neck and pressed my lips to his.

The move caught him off guard, and for a moment, he was still under my assault. With the swipe of my tongue, his brain kicked in and he was kissing me back with nearly painful intensity.

Nothing but us existed, not even the freezing air biting at my exposed waist as his hands pushed up my shirt to touch my bare skin. His fingers were like ice, but they left fire in their wake as they skated across my skin. I shivered hard, unable to decide whether to blame the cold or the lightning zipping between us.

I pulled back from him with all the strength I could muster, but he followed me, catching my bottom lip in his teeth. He bit down and I squealed. "Are you okay?" I spoke with my lip trapped between his teeth, marring the words in a barely recognizable jumble of syllables.

He almost laughed as he released me. His hands stayed on me. "Come to bed with me. Let me taste every inch of your skin and fuck you so thoroughly you'll feel me for days."

God, I wanted to, I really did. Part of me was desperate to forget everything I'd seen, everything standing in front of me now, and let him do exactly that, but I couldn't. "We need to talk before we go to bed."

He opened his mouth to argue, but a horrible sobbing sound came from the gatehouse. Had it just started or was I noticing now that some reason had returned to me?

"Mila," Mason answered my unspoken question. My heart dropped once again to think of what caused her that much pain.

"Is she... Is she okay?" That was stupid.

"No. Casey—"

"No," I told him stubbornly. I didn't want to hear what was sure to follow. Casey was barely more than a kid, and a sweet one at that.

"Casey is dead," he said the words so simply, with no inflection or discomfort. If I hadn't seen his expression, I would have easily believed he didn't care. But pain ripped across his face, and that usually cultivated mask was nowhere to be found.

A tear slid down my cheek. Casey was a really sweet kid, and this world did horrible things to good people.

"I think it's past the time I deserved the truth," I answered simply, rubbing the tears from my eyes and assuming a businesslike persona that would hopefully keep me on target and out of his bed. "Let's go inside."

He nodded, and we walked up to the main house at my pace. Mason stayed beside me even though I was moving especially slowly. So many problems fought for dominance in my mind, but the two winning the battle were the cages in the basement and the sound of Mila's heart-sick cries.

Mason opened the door and held it for me, closing it softly behind us. Rochelle was milling around near the kitchen, but she took one peek at the two of us and scurried off.

He headed for the stairs. "No. In here." I told him as I continued down the hall, past the kitchen where Rochelle likely hid in the pantry, and to the breakfast nook he designed after his mother's.

I sat down at the table, and he took the seat across from me. This was the only part of this house where I felt truly comfortable. He stared at me like I was expecting him to do something that might kill him.

I was determined to let him speak first, but the more I glared at him, his face, his hands, and the way he held his side, the more I took pity on him. "Did you know about the library? Did you know what's going on?"

He met my gaze with the fake calm I knew so well. "There's consistently something happening through the library. It is a center of the community and one of the syndicate's major hubs. There has always been involvement between the library's board and the syndicate."

I took a steadying breath. Why did he have to be a lawyer? He was too good under pressure. "Did you know they are selling people?" The desperation in my voice was palpable. "There are cages and a stage, Mason. Are they sex slaves? Are they trafficking people through the fucking library?"

"The human trafficking is something I have *known* about and abhorred nearly all of my life," his voice thickened, contorting with the surprising depth of his emotion. "Not necessarily about the basement. I'm going to have to investigate what you found. But I've had my suspicions about what may have been happening at the library for a long time. They have not used the cages and stage in the basement since I came to my agreement with Gavin. *That* I am at least sure of."

"Mason, come on."

"What do you want from me, Claire? I'm being honest. I'm telling you the truth. Ask any question and I will answer honestly."

"That assurance is not enough, and this is all too little too late! How could you let me find out like this?" Tears rolled pathetically down my cheeks. *This* was happening under my nose this whole time because he thought I couldn't handle it. "You should have told me."

"I know," he agreed sadly, and for a moment, he was silent. His eyes lifted and he leveled me with an appraising look, as if to say maybe he had underestimated me after all. "How did you find out, Claire? I'm sure no one gave you the key, and I hardly think someone described the room to you." His perfect eyebrow arched at me and my temper flared.

"I broke the fucking door in! Is that a problem?" I ran my hands through my hair, smoothing out the wild curls that betrayed the strenuous effort.

He shook his head. "This is exactly why I have been keeping things from you! I was trying to protect you. You are not acting like yourself. Why would you break the door down after everything else?" His hands fisted on top of the table.

I ignored his question. "And you *are* acting like yourself? This is who you want to be? This all feels right to you?" I shouted my questions at him. "What happened last night, Mase? Why is Casey dead?"

"I'm still not entirely sure."

My eyes widened, and for a moment, I felt as crazy as he thought I was. "Start talking, Mason."

"My old friend, the one I told you I had caught up with, he gave me the location of some girls being brought into the country. I've heard of other trade-offs and sales. I didn't have enough manpower to do anything about it before, but this time I could've stopped it. Only it was a trap... one I'm not sure who set."

"Manpower?" I gaped. "How much manpower convinced you to make that bold of a move?"

"About seventy."

My mouth dropped open in astonishment. *Fuck*, I didn't know about a lot. "Tell me what happened from the beginning."

"Last night," he began.

"No, Mason. All of it." He did as I asked, filling me in on every detail of what happened leading up to him killing Charles Gains and everything thereafter. It took me a few minutes of silent shock to process the details.

"Why, Mason? Why did you keep all of this from me?" Tears rolled down my cheeks as I considered all the unnecessary ways we both suffered.

"Because I didn't think you could take it. You haven't been the same since that piece of shit shot you, and I couldn't bear to put anything else on you that might make things harder." The unbearable sadness in his eyes broke my heart.

"I'm not the same, but how could I be? Mason, you've been treating me like a child. How can I feel safe and loved when you're engineering which parts of yourself you share with me and which parts of the truth you tell me? I have never loved anyone as much as I love you. I have *never* been more alone than when I wait for you to come home without a *clue* of where you've been.

"I would have handled this. I *proved* to you I *could* handle this by sticking by you, but you lied to me and repeatedly stomped on my trust in you. There is no pretending that this shit with Charles and the girls he killed, and getting shot hasn't fucked me up. It has, but I am *here* doing my best. Where are *you,* Mason? You lying to me *is* making everything worse."

He stood from the chair and walked around the table to stand in front of me. He grabbed my face in his big hands, and I tried to slap them away, but the effort was halfhearted.

"I am *so* fucking sorry, Claire." The words were a solemn vow, and I wanted so badly to let them wash everything away. His soft green eyes appeared unusually electric in contrast with the unshed tears surrounding them.

"James tried to tell you, even he wanted you to tell me the truth." I gazed up at him through tear-filled lashes, feeling profoundly small and insecure.

"Victor too. They were both right. I should have trusted you to handle the shit I have had to deal with, but you should have trusted me with your shit too. You have *never* opened up to me about how you're feeling or what you need. All of this daredevil, punishment-seeking bullshit, all of it needs to stop." I nodded my head, unable to argue with that summary. "If you want to be punished, I'm all too happy to oblige you, but the avenues you've pursued are much too drastic."

"You've let me wallow in this shit for months, obsessed about these dead girls when *living* women are being sold into slavery under my feet. *Literally!* I could have helped them. I could have helped *you*. All this wasted time, effort, and pain."

"I've made a lot of wrong decisions, Claire. I am trying my best to take my father out of the equation, to make things safe for you again, but my plans are taking time. There is nothing we can do right now, but I haven't forgotten those girls either."

"What do you mean by right now? Do you have a reason to think we might be able to do more in the future?"

"I trust you, Claire. Do you trust me?"

"I think I *can*, with a little time and a lot of honesty," I answered, wondering what the fuck he was talking about.

"I have to tell you the truth."

"Okay..." I thought that was what we were already doing.

"When I kill my father, someone has to take over his position. There is no one I trust not to abuse that power. I intend to assume that position for myself, dismantle all sex trafficking in our city, and establish victimless crime like gambling and voluntary fight rings to make up for the drop in income. You would be with a criminal. I will continue to kill people when I have to, and there will always be some level of danger. Is that something you can live with?"

"You've thought a lot about this." I stammered out, not sure how to answer him. I had thought about these things, but not as deeply as I wished I had at that point.

He nodded his head solemnly. I broke eye contact and swallowed hard, seriously considering what he was asking me. After everything I lived through recently, I honestly believed that the definition of the right thing meant the greatest good to the most people. I trusted Mason to be a better man than his father, even if there would always be a criminal element.

Another part of me didn't give a fuck what the right thing was anymore. This particular part just wanted the power and the ability to instill fear and protect herself from anyone stupid enough to move against her. Her man at her side and her city at her feet, but I silenced her. I wanted *safety* for as many people as possible.

Mason regarded me seriously before pulling a ring box out of his pocket and dropping to one knee in front of me. He opened the black velvet box, revealing a gorgeous platinum engagement ring with a jaw-dropping pear-shaped diamond surrounded by emeralds. "I've had this for months. It's a little different, but the moment I laid eyes on it, I knew it was yours."

"Uh, I was not expecting this."

He half smirked at me, "I love you more than my own life. Marry me." There was no question, and for a brief moment, that annoyed me. This man had made so many fucking decisions for me. That response quickly faded to the butterflies laying siege to my entire system, not just my stomach.

"Yes," I told him simply, choking on my emotion. He slid my ring onto my finger.

"I am going to marry you as soon as I can give you the wedding you deserve. You're mine, forever."

"Forever," I agreed.

THIRTY-TWO

Daniel

M y hair smelled like smoke despite having showered twice before arriving at the airport. David Sharp expected me in one of the private planes, and the two of us had a lot to discuss.

My guards stood behind me, as quiet and obnoxious as ever. At least these two kept their mouths shut, unlike the last two I'd put a bullet in. David's plane sat parked in the middle of the tarmac, with the steps down and waiting for me. I took a deep breath as I climbed the stairs and made my way toward the man who had been like a father and a mentor to me.

David was an exceptionally hard man, probably a wicked one, but he'd done a lot for me. He was the reason for the life I had now. The reason I had enough money and power to make this meeting necessary.

White leather seats and warm polished cherry wood lined the plane. David sat on a couch near his private bar, sipping a drink. He read something on his phone, but he glanced up as I approached him.

"Dan, it's good to see you." He spoke in a voice so similar to his son's that it was eerie. Their faces were more similar than I'd remembered as well. It was a bit of a shock the first time I saw Mason again at the restaurant.

"You too, David. How was Beijing?" David had been expanding his sex trafficking business from eastern Europe into Asia.

"Beijing worked out very well. I got myself a new pet, a movie star. Well, she used to be anyway. Now she's a whore," he laughed at his own joke, and I smiled back. "You want a look at her?"

"Sure, let's see the little bitch you let ride out of her cage."

"If they're well trained, there is no need to cage them." *Agree to disagree on that one.*

He smiled like he guessed exactly what I was thinking. "Ju, come."

A stunningly beautiful woman walked around the partition and came to kneel at his feet. Her long black hair hung in a silken sheet around her thin frame. Perfect dusky pink nipples, perky little tits. Her ass was a touch smaller than I liked, but looked plenty tight. Her cheeks were broad and high, her lips full. An image of all the ways I could make the pretty bitch cry filled my head and hardened my cock.

David reached out a hand and stroked the top of her head. "Good pet," he cooed, and she smiled demurely. David always had a pet, a sex slave, but I never understood how he could be so gentle with them. If they behaved, he didn't beat them at all. I *enjoyed* beating them.

"I haven't needed to correct Ju once, yet." The green eyes that matched his son's ran over her with the adoration one might have for a prize-winning show pony.

"I could correct her if you like." I offered in a joking tone.

"You can have her when I'm done."

I grinned to myself as her small smile dropped. Had she imagined she might have a good life with the kind billionaire that bought and sold whores like cattle?

"Oh, Ju, I'm going to have so much fun with you." Her throat worked through a swallow, goose bumps pebbled her skin. "Does she speak English?"

"She does, though I don't care so much about that." I did because I liked to hear them beg.

David sighed tiredly. "We need to talk, Daniel. Unfortunately, it's not all whores and catching up."

"Things didn't go as planned but—"

"You tried to murder my son," he cut me off.

I plastered on one of my perfectly crafted expressions: confusion. "I didn't. He had amassed more men than I realized, and I wanted to take some of them out."

"You may disagree with my methods and my motives, but you will not make another move against Mason. He is my son and I still plan to leave him my empire. It may take some time, but he will come around."

"And how do you plan to make him come around?" I bit back, acid burning the back of my throat.

"I have plans for his little girlfriend. That will be highly motivating for him." David smiled, no doubt imagining Claire at his feet beside Ju.

He was right. Mason would do anything for her. She was like a shiny toy. I wanted to break her solely to keep her away from the friend who had more. He always fucking had everything, but what would he do when he had nothing? When I took, broke and threw away the one thing he wanted more than anything else.

"If it was just the explosion, I might let things go, but there is more."

"What more is there?" I cocked my head to the side.

"Your relationship with Delano Agrest, for example."

"That was just a story to get in with Mason," I answered, perhaps a beat too quickly. I knew it when suspicion flashed in his eyes.

"If it was just a story, you were awfully thorough in fabricating evidence, evidence Mason never saw."

"I spoke to him briefly," I admitted, not wanting to reveal my hand yet, but an outright lie would do just that.

"I know what he offered you." David tapped a long finger against his chin, another mannerism he shared with his son.

Shock lanced through me. I wasn't sure how he would have discovered that Agrest offered to help me take his empire out from under him. That knowledge just pushed up my timeline. "If that's true, then you're stupid to mention it."

"I'm hoping you'll make the right choice, Daniel. You understand what can happen to those who make the mistake of doing business with him. Be careful about the snakes you choose to associate with."

"What is the right choice, David? Do as you command, help you bring Mason into the fold and answer to him one day?" He stared me down for a moment and then nodded at me like it was so obvious it didn't warrant words. "Maybe I want more," I told him.

"You have more than you ever should have." He gestured to the surrounding plane. "Do you think you really belong in places like this, Daniel? You may be incredibly smart, and gifted too, but you're trash. I picked you up out of the gutter. I gave you the scholarship that brought you to Rutherford and into my son's life. You should be grateful for whatever scraps I give you, and I have given you choice cuts. Your greed will be your end, Daniel."

He turned to the men seated off to the side, pretending not to be there but listening closely to every word. In a moment, five guards stood around him. "Please escort Daniel off the plane and make proper arrangements, the kind befitting traitors."

None of the men moved. Instead, they watched me. I planned this for a long time before acting and I prepared each of them to side with the victor: me.

I pulled out my gun and aimed. "No, David. My greed will be *your* end."

With that, I shot him in the head. It happened so quickly that he barely had a moment to register the words I spoke, and half a moment to shift his expression to one of surprise. His eyes were dead and staring before they made their way to fear.

Ju was coated in blood. Her creamy skin looked even more delicious beneath the carnage. "Come, Ju. He's done with you, and I have work to do."

I reached out a hand to her, and she took it, standing on shaking legs. Tears streamed down her cheeks, and I smiled.

"What should we do with him, boss?" One of the men I flipped last year asked.

"Hide the body and keep this quiet. As far as anyone knows, David Sharp is alive, and he's out for blood."

Also By

The Illicit Library Collection Book 3 is coming in December 2022 preorder now!
https://www.amazon.com/gp/product/B0B5M5MPRL

ABOUT AUTHOR

Aurelia Knight is a hot mess, doing her best to keep it together most days. Words are the greatest love of her life second only to her husband and sons. If she's not typing away, getting lost in her own world, she's reading and slipping away into the worlds of other writers. A caffeine addict who believes sleep is secondary to the endless promise of "just one more chapter".

Follow Aurelia!

Join Aurelia's mailing list for updates, book recommendations, and a free novelette coming soon!

Website:

https://www.
Aureliaknight.com

Facebook:

https://www.facebook.com/aureliaknightauthor

Instagram:

https://www.instagram.com/aureliaknightauthor/

Tik Tok:

https://www.tiktok.com/@aureliaknightauthor

Made in the USA
Middletown, DE
04 June 2023

32054594R00170